■ □ ■ □ ■

FIRE ON WATER

Writings from an Unbound Europe

■ □ ■ □ ■

ARNOŠT LUSTIG

FIRE ON WATER

PORGESS
AND *THE ABYSS*

NORTHWESTERN UNIVERSITY PRESS

EVANSTON, ILLINOIS

Northwestern University Press
www.nupress.northwestern.edu

Printed in the United States of America

10 9 8 7 6 5 4 3 2 1

ISBN 0-8101-2219-7 (cloth)
ISBN 0-8101-2220-0 (paper)

Library of Congress Cataloging-in-Publication data are available from the
Library of Congress.

♾ The paper used in this publication meets the minimum requirements of the American
National Standard for Information Sciences—Permanence of Paper for Printed Library
Materials, ANSI Z39.48-1992.

Porgess was translated from the Czech by Roman Kostovski.
The Abyss was translated from the Czech by Deborah Durham-Vichr.

■ □ ■ □ ■

CONTENTS

■ □ ■ □ ■

PORGESS

To disturb the peace of the dead is the same as killing a man. According to Jewish laws the body of a man still has a living soul, though it is already dead. It remains with him even when his bones and skull turn to dust. The earth in which he is buried belongs to him till the end of time. To disturb the peace of the dead is a crime. To steal the soil, which surrounds his grave, is unforgivable.

Talmudic Academy, Brussels

■ □ ■ □ ■

AND SO IN SPIRIT I WAS BACK IN ITALY, ON A FRIDAY AFTERNOON, October 6, 1950. I was not too far from Rome's Palace of Justice in Lungotever, across Ponte Umberto, along the Vatican side of the Tiber. The building had a chariot on its rooftop with a rider steering four horses. Two workers, secured by leather straps attached to scaffolding, were cleaning the horses with sand. The building was caving in along both wings, though only a few thousandths of a millimeter. It would have been funny, as my friend Tanga once thought, when we were in the Great Fortress of Theresienstadt in September of 1944, if hell were at the center of earth and the palace were to fall all the way through. The workers on the roof were shouting at one another, and the wind carried their words away.

Down below in the bar on via Calamatta, a popular song was playing with lyrics suggesting that a man should look upon a woman the way he looks upon himself—and that a woman should do the same. And then they played another song, which compared a quarrelsome woman to a day full of rain—from morning until evening. What is it that women envy about men? And what do they no longer envy after their first sacrifice of love? What do men envy about women? The ability to give birth?

An old man wearing a *L'Unità* cap was sitting on a white marble stairway. His palms were spread out toward the sky, as if he were trying to catch the rain. I tossed him a lira ten note. Was I being pretentious by doing this? The beggar looked as if he were down to his last breath. Tiny drops of rain were bouncing off the tip of his nose into his mouth. I didn't know whether I wished to pity him more or whether I wanted to gauge my immediate well-being by comparing it to the misfortunes of this old Italian comrade. (The old-timers from the journal *We Shall Return!*—the first ones who, after the war, took over the quarters and printing shop on Panská Street 8, where the *Prag Tablat* was once located and where *Der Neu Tag* was during the war—they turned everything inside out.)

I was in Italy because I survived. Between September and October of 1944, someone else, instead of me, went up the chimney in Auschwitz-Birkenau. This process of selection would happen time and time again, without me truly deserving it, the entire time I was there. Then it would happen again, when I was elsewhere, because the Germans had exploited their death factories to full capacity, both day and night—today, every day, week after week, month after month, and year after year. It is even said that one time Heinrich Himmler, the former chicken farmer, came to view the work of the Einsatzgruppen in Poland. Along the graveyards, in the wheat fields, and in the forests, he watched the Einsatzgruppen slaughter men, women, children, the elderly, the sick, and the helpless. They slaughtered them one by one, stripping them naked and then shooting them up close with a revolver, machine gun, or rifle, so their victims would fall into the pits they had dug themselves. As Himmler grew sick, someone quickly had to bring him a chair. Apparently, he said that there had to be another way. He wanted to achieve the same thing, to continue the murdering, but rather, let's just say, in a pair of white gloves. He saw too many drunk and demoralized SS men. And so they matured to murder by gas. This Himmler would no longer have to see. He only had to listen to the reports. Hitler, too, never crossed a gate to the camps. He shunned it as much as he avoided signing orders. (It was in Wannsee, on the outskirts of Berlin, January 20, 1942, when fifteen heads of the Nazi regime, in ninety minutes, agreed around a long conference table to the "necessary cooperation of all military and police forces for the final solution of the 'Jewish Question,'" and then already standing up to depart to their offices, they told one another jokes from the *Stürmer,* drank coffee and French cognac, and smiled satisfied smiles, like some members of a city council.)

The Germans would verify absolutely everything: even the most insignificant of administrative offices was not left untouched. Everything had to be directed toward victory for the Reich. It was obvious, as Erwin Adler once put it, that "one and one was two." Was I allowed, according to Bobby Lenta Mahler, from Belgická Street 24, to say B if I had already said A?

Someone painted on the Palace of Justice, with a brush dipped in tar, the words "Every crime against humanity begins with inequality." While the other side of the building revealed another statement: "One cannot demand freedom for an individual and a strong government for others. Chaos and freedom is better than the justice and order of a tyrant." Next to it was yet another: "We know what's going on!" The letters seemed as if they had little bristles of hair growing out of them. "Let Mussolini's body rot peacefully in his grave. If we dig him out it will bring out the stench.—Enrico Caruso, Napoli."

I was glad to be among the living, even though I wasn't exactly proud of it. I blamed myself, a bit, for reasons that are more powerful than myself. As if we, not Rottenführer Jochen Reiger or Hauptsturmführer Manfred Rudnick, handpicked ourselves to go up the chimney during the selections. I would laugh to myself when the old-timers from the Whale, the editing room for the journal *We Shall Return!* would say over and over again that every beginning was difficult. When a forest was being cut down, one had to expect some splinters. I was holding on to an opportunity. Nothing could be compared to the camps. I was willing to render my best to those old men and to the Whale. Above the bar on via Calamatta there was a sign: THIS IS THE PLACE FOR LIARS, HUNTERS, AND FISHERMEN. HERE YOU BELONG. HERE YOU ARE KIN.

I was still learning, with the exception of one particular area, that after my experience in the camps, I no longer needed much education. I was going over a few photographs in my mind. Photographs that would present a moment, what led to it, and what followed afterward. Some of the photos were signed by Henri Cartier-Bresson, my namesake (Dessau 1945)—one depicting survivors from the camps discovering a woman who was a snitch for the Gestapo who tried to blend in among the refugees. A photo from Robert Capa, from August 1944, depicting people in Chartes as they ridicule the French mother who had an infant with a German soldier. Her head was shaved. A Japanese officer with his arms raised, holding a sword above the head of an Australian pilot shot down in battle. (American, Australian, and British pilots apparently handed out this photograph among themselves to remind them of what would happen to them if they survived a crash.) The pilot in the photograph was still alive; he was originally kneeling, but in that moment, he had landed on his heels, blindfolded with his arms tied to his body. The last sound he would ever hear was the whistle of the wind being cut by a sword—all in a matter of a second. How long could a second like this exist in a photograph? Until the paper turns yellow and withers away?

After the rain, the air was fresh. It was a pleasure to breathe. From somewhere, I smelled the scent of oranges. I no longer wanted to think about what sort of line of selected prisoners it would be. To see the faces of those who replaced me or paid for my life with theirs—their expressions, eyes, and wrinkles. The things they could have accomplished in life, in their own professions, or even in mine. Adler subsequently read me the statistics out loud. Do Jews have more influence than they deserved, even after the war? Should Nazism be condemned? Who was to blame? All Germans? All Italians? All Japanese? Don't we already know that when guilt as well as innocence poses for clarity, with all their complexity, no one can ever draw a definite shape of their face, name, or address in a single stroke of a brush? Should we continue to write and speak about this? Shouldn't we, just once and for all, cross everything out with a thick black line? Existence is a weight alloyed from the metals of humiliation. As if I didn't know that. Adler would make up quotes from the Bible and noticed that no one (besides experts) would dispute him. If all this is impossible to confess to anyone, because it is inexplicable, could it be inexplicable to one's own address as well? What drives a man to insanity? Was there only the word in the beginning? Will it be also at the end? "Go to hell!" Adler would say. He didn't have to shout. I would have heard him if he whispered. I would have heard him if he was completely silent. It wasn't a matter of distance. It was primed by the music from the bar on via Calamatta: "*Quando, quando, quando?!*"

The man on the marble stairs didn't even bother to thank me. Neither was he in the habit of using a handkerchief. Perhaps he was like Weltfeind Flusser in the orphanage on Belgická Street 24, who detested underwear and bathrooms. (W.F. would say, "When someone wants to beg, they can't be fat, look happy, and want a strawberry when a cherry is being offered. Only an idiot wouldn't be able to beg enough to afford a mink coat.") If he would have invested those ten liras, his granddaughter could have been whistling a sweet tune of profit, but unfortunately not for long.

Drenched to the bone, I sauntered toward the more flamboyant center of Rome and pushed away all the pickpockets, pimps, drug dealers, rough and dainty adventurers, thugs, beggars, and slackers—homeless people with an occasional guitar or mandolin, pocket radio, or accordion. Proprietors of bottles filled with alcohol bulging from their side pockets, street thugs on a stroll after the rainfall, like me. Ladies of the street, some dressed better, some worse. Should I have taken bus 26 and had a Peroni beer at the Frantina Bar, where I already knew the headwaiter? I bought an orange at a kiosk. Adler's ears were probably ringing again. I slowly peeled it, eating it piece by piece. I ate the peels from the inside and threw them on the sidewalk.

In Prague during the war, along with Adler, W.F., and Luster Leibling, I saw the weekly news and UFY at the Cinéma Koruna. In 1940 actresses were singing to Italian soldiers in Somalia, while natives brought them baskets of fruit—*frutti per gli soldati*. We had tickets to see the Nazi films *Legion Condor, Das Gewehrüber, Es leuchten die Sterne* (we saw that twice), and *Heimat* with Zarah Leander, who sang the tune "Frau Wird Schon Durch die Liebe." Back then Luster Leibling, alias Black Pepe, punched a boy from the Hitler Youth at the coat check. We had to race out of there to the blare of whistles blowing as the boys' unit was sounding the alarm. We took the corridors and back alleys, all the way to Belgická Street 24. We knew Prague and all her shortcuts, as Little Narcissus's legendary cuttlefish knew its piece of the sea. We saw Jew-bashing films when the term "Jew bashing" could no longer be said in Prague: films such as *The Eternal Jew, Robert and Bertram, Rothchild's Stocks from Waterloo,* and *Rembrandt.* We ended up seeing *The Jew Süss* by Veit Harlan, who kept repeating in his postwar radio program that he never had anything against his Jewish colleagues. He just didn't want to get in a conflict with Goebbels. Had everyone forgotten what the Gestapo was capable of doing?

It occurred to me why I was able to forgive the Italians, but never the Germans. Was it because the Italians never slept on mattresses stuffed with the hair of Luster Leibling or Weltfeind Flusser? I guess

I would never feel comfortable in a German hotel, laying my head upon a pillow and a mattress stuffed with God knows what.

The German newsreels weren't as pleasant as the Italians', although they did have better music. For the Somalis, it never made a huge difference anyway. But perhaps I would see it differently if I were in the shoes of Enzo Vittorini. Enzo feared that all aggression was fascism, even if I changed places from the chair on the right to the chair on the left. The fascists needed to see blood on their hands, so they could sleep better. They liked blood better than a weasel that fed off of it. Albert Weltfeind Flusser—alias the Caveman—knew this fact. I had to give credit to some of his prejudices.

I passed by several parked cars with newspapers covering the windows like curtains from the front, back, and sides. They were bouncing up and down, their shocks screeching according to the make of the car or the passion of the couples inside. This not only confirmed what W.F. once told me—that the Italians would always, in every war, end up on the other side of the battlefield from where they started, usually at the eleventh hour, under the flag of any victorious power—but also explained why the world was filled with so many Italians.

On the corner of via Ludovici, I picked up the prior day's evening post from a bench under the shelter of a bus stop; I glanced at the headlines and threw it into a gutter. I was looking at a shop display for the company Bruno Magli of Bologna and noticed in my reflection that I needed to comb my hair a bit. As Grandmother Olga would say, "If you behave, little boy, your hair will grow nice and wavy." And then I remembered Porgess, who had similar curls. The last day of the war on the eighth of May 1945, before Porgess could cross the border to Germany, the soldiers paralyzed him, so he was subject to a bed since the first day of peace on Wednesday, the ninth of May 1945.

Porgess was blond with golden curls. He was the most handsome boy in Jewish Prague. I knew him from the summer of 1940, when France surrendered to the Germans with its entire Maginot line, including its freedom and brotherhood, not to mention its best cuisine and suspicion of the British and their modern military equipment, which later proved useful to the Germans. During the time after the Jewish Maccabiah gymnasium was banned, when Ping-Pong and sometimes even jazz (when the rabbi leniently turned the other way) was played in the basement of the Vinohrady synagogue, because

Jewish children were no longer permitted on public playgrounds, Bobby Lenta Mahler discovered Ibn Khaldun, who claimed that the less a person glutted himself and the more he hungered and lived modestly, the more courage he would gain, the more resiliency he would have, the better skin he would boast, the better figure he would retain, and so on. And vice versa. Did he mean the Germans? The more audacious the conquerors, the more they spread out, and the more they lived in the lap of luxury, which their stomachs were unaccustomed to, the sooner they would feel the demon of a bitter end. It was during these days that Bobby practiced hunger and read Franz Kafka and Baudelaire, not only to carry the "burden of the Time" but also to absorb the answers to questions yet to come.

Porgess looked as if he carried the head of a German prince, painted by Cranach from the gallery of Bobby's favorites, on his shoulders. Porgess didn't have to demand the right to be equal. If he didn't have a yellow star with black lining and the semi-Gothic letters spelling JUDE sewn on in the place of his heart, he could have enrolled in the Hitler Youth out of jest, or at least in the Czech equivalent, the Kuratorium. He had fresh light skin, golden locks, and a nose as straight as a ruler.

Porgess boxed at the Hagibor in the summer of 1940 under the guidance of Freddy Teveles, also known as TV or Teve-Sugar Face, and Kona Levit, who later hanged himself on a curtain string in a hotel room at the Grand Operetta. Teve-Sugar Face broke Porgess's nose during a training session, and Porgess's father, with his petite blond-haired wife, came to the gym to see the shady Jewish party of their son's friends. Porgess felt at home among the orphans.

For Porgess, as much as for Adler and myself, boxing meant the world. It gave us an element of confident beauty, since it taught us how to defend ourselves. Just before the transport to Germany, Porgess had a dream about floods. Perhaps it was because in '41 and '42, Prague experienced two massive floods, the second being worse than the first. For Porgess, it all flowed into one entity. He had dreams that he was the water, the current, the river, the trough, and the dam. He was afraid that he would fear the water, but it was because of something else. At the end, Porgess even dreamed of the water in the camps. All the water would be gathered in a basin. The camp was a basin and so was Porgess, every human being, guard, and prisoner—they were all a basin. Everything poured into the basins—water, blood, wounds, the voices of the SS, the prisoners, even their echoes. He dreamed about water until his dreams would stop, and even though it was only for a few hours, he would sleep like a dead man. In the camps, sleep looked like death, because there everything was so close to it. He dreamed of water until, once in the camps, he started a dream of boxing in which time was reversed. It started with him in a championship match and went all the way back to the moment he first put on a pair of boxing gloves. The bell, which was the first to initiate his career as a fighter, was at the same time the last one to ring in this dream. He would feel weaker than normal in his dreams.

Mr. Porgess had a store with leather products: purses, suitcases, briefcases, toiletry bags, belts, and wallets. It was located in the Arcade Praha, until its Aryanization, which took place around 1940. Then he became a gladiator in the Jewish religious community. The gladiators would empty furniture, books, and pianos from abandoned Jewish homes and take them to one of the six synagogues in Prague in which the Germans banned religious services. Under Gestapo regulations, the Jewish community was forced to transform these synagogues into storage space, until the Germans turned them into stables or, as in the case of the Spanish synagogue, a museum of an extinct tribe. And so Mr. Porgess was relieved of his obligation to be wealthy and, at the same time, virtuous, so that his little son with golden locks wouldn't be allowed to think that he, unlike others, was born with a silver spoon, and that everything that other people had to work hard for, if they could manage, would fall into his lap. If Porgess Jr. ever thought along these lines, he never showed it to his friends from the orphanage on Belgická 24 or the Jewish school on Jachimová 6. He had a good personality, a democratic heart, and a sense of camaraderie—that is, before the Nazis tried to beat it out of him, like during the Middle Ages, when people would try to exorcise the devil out of the body and soul of a sick man. Later on, when it came to women, Porgess would claim that he had a demon living within him. It would betroth and divorce him at the same time. It was enough to go out with a girl once; the demon would multiply her, so he could go out in the meantime with other ones as well. Porgess couldn't understand why a man could fall in love with one woman, and at the same time eye another. He couldn't understand how a person measured love and how love was pieced together like a mosaic or a puzzle.

"Love is a collage," Porgess said. "A boy and a girl are a collage. What you add to things that have already occurred and are still yet to come is a collage."

"Life is a collage," his father would say. "The way we put everything together, the way we glue it, that is the way everyone can see it, yet only sometimes it is a real work of art."

In the beginning of the occupation, such philosophy came in handy. He didn't look like those hungry individuals whose minds would start to grumble before their stomachs—echoes of past luxuries. He would dress extremely well. He would make an effort to wear something that would match his yellow star. He knew, and he would go much further than this, to hang his pants after wearing them, so that they wouldn't look wrinkled the following day. It was better to wear the pants every other day and to not fill his pockets too much, even though such tasks were taken care of by the Aryan servant (as long as they were allowed to have one), in case he forgot. He didn't take the occupation as hard as his father and mother. He created a table of numbers, which predicted that the Germans would win and then, later, lose. He combined it with his image of running water and the walls of the basin and how much pressure they could take. His blithe personality could nourish many people, like mothers whose bosoms are so plentiful they have enough milk for those infants whose mothers are barren. In the beginning, the Germans didn't succeed in ruining Porgess's mood. He made up a number system against them. In those days, he was still dreaming, night after night, about the water and not about boxing. What the water would bring, it would also carry away. He was one of the first to find out that the titans of occupation never enjoyed a bit of fun, just as they never appreciated the mystique of numbers, jazz, and abstract painting: German psychics would live off of other resources. Perhaps he lacked the confidence in a single dogma that would remain with a person once and for all. This offered the possibility for an individual to think on his own, step out of line, and change his marching pattern, and it forbade anyone to regulate his thoughts and actions; as if three, thirty, or three million organized people had more truth than one unorganized individual. Porgess loved to be unorganized, even though he never placed himself above others. He didn't like schools, the army, the police, and so on. He agreed with Franz Kafka that all institutions created by man in order to serve mankind sooner or later would turn against man, including banks, armies, the police, and, not to mention, insurance companies. Belgická 24 was an exception to that rule, but then again, he was only a guest there. He claimed that institutions destroyed creativity, even though they seemed to be the redeemers of humanity and individual willpower: a person would vanish in them like a sardine in the ocean. Where institutions were fewer, life was much more bearable. Woe to those who were grasped by the claws of an institution, including political parties and clubs, like the one where his father was a member (two-hundred-crown monthly fees, meetings every week, lectures, and theater performances). Besides numbers, Porgess loved jazz, which meant he liked Negroes. He would elegantly fuse with the existing energy of a melody, which illuminated a different sensation than the high-pitched sound of the Nazi whistles, though he never had anything against the sound of whistles. His father would tell him about a land where a ship was built in a day and a plane in a few hours. It was too bad that he didn't move to America when he was supposed to. Mother was afraid. If the Germans wanted to summon a duel against the land of Stars and Stripes, then they should have reconsidered; and besides, it was still bearable, at least for the Porgesses. He would whistle to himself "American Patrol," "St. Louis Blues," and "In the Mood"; hit songs by Glenn Miller, Tommy Dorsey, Count Basie, and Harry James. He considered jazz his private weapon against the Germans, and he seemed like a submarine that played and sang forbidden music. The submarine would just relax upon the surface of the ocean floor, like somewhere in Patagonia, far away from everyone's attention. He would invite us to his place and play us records. It would replenish something within him, elating Porgess and at the same time making him strong. The music had the sensation of a secret advantage, it accelerated time and enabled Porgess to maintain a reliable gauge of what was beautiful and good, and what could cheer up not only him, but also everyone. "It is great music for the soul," he would say over and over again. "A source of energy. A grave to hypertrophy. Only true persistence. Drunkenness to cure boredom." He knew the original orchestrations of Fletcher Henderson and Don Redman; the way Duke Ellington arranged it, clarinets, saxophones, drums, and wind instruments. It spoke to him up close, and even though the ocean or the difference of languages separated him from it, he felt that he knew Ira and George Gershwin and lyricist Lorenz Hart personally. He didn't care that he spoke broken English. He would sing as before and then quote Wolker's ballads. It linked him to people he felt closer to than the most educated Nazis. His theme was "String of Pearls." He would replace the new Nazi morals, which pertained only to the Nazis and treated the rest of the population like garbage, with his own sense of morals—to do what he pleased, not what was expected of him. He divided this world by those who loved him and loved him not. He turned everything inside out: what served Germany could never serve him. What was good for the Nazis was bad for him. Anyone afraid of freedom for all was a thief, liar, hustler, and weakling. If something belonged to someone, it belonged forever, like the treasures of sunken ships. How could anyone desire that all rights be based on the ratio of rights denied to others, or desire justice only for oneself? For the Germans, everything was a one-way street. No one could think about taking a step in the opposite direction. Since they were trying to break Porgess's will, they didn't have to look as if they were tickling him under his arms or claim that he was responsible for his own actions. He didn't want those brutes to think for him. He would repeat Bobby's favorite Descartes quote: cogito, ergo sum—I think, therefore I am. He could even quote it if he was awoken at four o'clock in the morning. Unfortunately, this logic never applied to the notion that the Nazis didn't think, therefore they never were. It made him wonder why so many intelligent people joined their ranks. Just the number of neighbors and colleagues of his father was more than a person could count on his fingers. He would notice that logic and nonlogic were sisters, both larger and, ironically, smaller than life. If only they had been kind enough to stop thinking for him. They could have saved some of their strength.

It would always sound so adorable when it came out of Porgess's petite, red lips. When he couldn't protest in an effective manner against the injustices upon which the Germans built the foundations for their future, he would spit, when no one was looking, on the

Germans' public notices, which contained the signatures of the Reich's Protector Reinhard Heydrich, Vice Protector K. H. Frank, and other officials, all shielded by the two lightning bolts of the Waffen SS and the Gestapo. During the last days of the war in Germany, Porgess ended up on a death transport, where the SS would transfer prisoners from place to place so they could slaughter them somewhere far beyond the wind. After the war, someone explained to him the events he had missed in Theresienstadt, when during the liquidation of the fortress, the SS, with their trucks, would run people over who were blocking their way of escape. (This was how the individual lost his relatives in the twelfth hour of the war.) Someone also managed to tell Porgess that after the war, someone discovered SS doctors in Chicago. They tattooed numbers from Auschwitz-Birkenau on their left forearms and practiced in Jewish communities close to the Standard Club, an establishment for descendants of Jewish immigrants from Germany. (Where, at least from the beginning, the more fortunate immigrants did not permit membership to the more impoverished European immigrants from Poland, Lithuania, Ruthenia, etc.) As a result of their assignments, the former SS men knew the geography of the camps even better than their American hosts did. They were silent when more intrusive questions were asked. Such silence would be acknowledged by those who were sensitive, giving the doctors an advantage.

Before the Germans surrendered in May of 1945, Porgess made an attempt to escape beyond the Chemnitz River by running from a freight train. All the numbers that he believed in seemed to be very good to him. He endured six days of hunger and thirst with only the rain to sustain him when it began to fall on the seventh day. Germany was already on its knees. He could see that even from the closed cattle car; he managed to squeeze his body into a tiny window secured by barbed wires when the train was at a halt. He watched the convoys of soldiers who, clearly, were no longer at their best. It was to his advantage that he was so gaunt, that, literally, his skin stretched over a skeleton of bones. One, two, three, he made a pile of dead bodies (three bodies), which enabled him to have access to the window and change the position of its barbed wire, expanded across in three rows. On "three" he would jump. He was alone, without his family. He had no illusion that his mother and father were still alive, but if they were, there would be three in the family. Even if they weren't, originally, there would be three in the family. He gave himself a speck of hope, because he wasn't certain. And since nothing happened to him up until now, then perhaps luck would stick close to him, even in this final moment. Some images of doubt lurked within, like hallucinations, because he had not eaten for so long and was on the verge of falling unconscious. He knew that if he did not escape, his body would join the hundreds of dead in his boxcar and the five thousand on the train. He was lucky to secure himself a place by the window where he could breathe. When it rained, he could gather the drops that fell into the boxcar with the palm of his hand and his lips. The others were suffocating, dying of thirst, and if they had just a bit of strength left, they would fight for a place along the sealed door. The people in the center were the worst off. Most of them were pushing toward the cracks in the walls, opened by those who were suffocating in the transports before them. Hundreds of people, with the dead among the living, didn't offer any comfort. The dead would steal the air from the living; the smell was unbearable. By the end of the journey, not only did the people hate one another, but also they hated the moment their mothers brought them to this world, perhaps they even hated their murdered mothers. It was just a question of time before Porgess would go insane—that is, if by then he would have not already suffocated. The boxcar turned them into animals. Many people desired to die on that train, so they wouldn't have to suffocate so long. Life was poison, just as poison was death. Time was poison, just as poison was timelessness. They slept lying, sitting, and standing on top of each other with their eyes open and their eyes closed, upon the living and upon the dead. It resembled the sleep of a sleepwalker. The train carried them toward a death comfortable for the German authorities. Someplace where the decay of their bodies would not threaten the population. And then the train stopped again and again, and there was death. Only in fever did Porgess hear the sounds of his music and see, in a picture long since destroyed, the Andrews Sisters; Benny Goodman, in his golden glasses and a black clarinet, the way he pressed his silver keys, his light mouthpiece; and Glenn Miller and his trumpet conducting his "Moonlight Serenade" for the soldiers, as he did for audiences before the war. It was surprising that it never left his memory. It was somewhere in the air, but he heard it from a distance, growing further and further away, as if the hallucination were fading, weakening more, until the brakes started screeching: the train jerked and stopped, and everyone awoke and prepared for the worst. Now everything was at stake. He depended only upon numbers. He knew only three addresses he could contact, if he reached Prague. The number 3 seemed good. It could always have its place in a fraction of a second, in order to see himself standing at the front door of his former villa, even if it were emptied out or some new tenants moved in. He didn't bother with such minor details, such as the restitution of property to the previous owners who survived the war. Three meant promise. Everything better comes in three, as he once enlightened us in the beginning of the occupation. Three was the beginning, the middle, and the end; the past, the present, and the future; the length, the width, and the height; the action, the inducement, and the consequences; an alloy of everything that was, is, and will be. It was also the number of members in his family: Mother, Father, Porgess. Number 3 was earth, water, and air; morning, noon, and evening; dusk, night, and dawn. And the rain meant water — a basin that overflows and breaks through the walls.

No matter how much he calculated, he would never reach the number 5, which he feared. He still had five fingers on each foot and hand, but he quickly multiplied it by two, not to mention the toes, which had frostbite, three to four on each foot. He was lucky: spring had started more than six weeks ago.

He would come across a few pairs that would make him nervous. That morning two people next to him died of hunger and two of hepatitis or typhus, but luckily that was four altogether. The number 4 was good: the four seasons, four directions in the world — north, south, east, and west.

Before he let go of the window, which he was holding on to for a while longer, before he jumped, he remembered the number 6, which consisted of two 3s. Numbers divided by three would satisfy him. Perhaps he heard segments of those zingy jazz melodies, from the land that can build a cruiser or a submarine in a day and a flying fortress with four motors in six hours. Germany never had a chance. It was his hour. Even number 5, in extreme circumstances, consisted of 2 and 3. He was in the camps three years. Three times he escaped the noose; three times he escaped a bullet. Three times he was not selected to enter the showers in Auschwitz-Birkenau. Once, he got three lashes from a whip and survived.

He didn't have diarrhea for three days, even though before he had been bleeding. He had survived three camps: Theresienstadt, Auschwitz-Birkenau, and Buchenwald. The Germans were transporting him from the third to the fourth camp, or perhaps to one of those "convenient" locations for a mass grave somewhere in the forest. There were more mass graves in Germany than village wells. Porgess took numbers seriously, because to take his life seriously in that moment would make him nervous. That was why he had jazz, to ease everything just a bit. He would blame everything that did not make him feel competent on numbers. He thought of the time he learned to swim, and how he would swallow air bubbles and mouthfuls of water, and then he swam across the Vltava where it was widest. After a long time, images of water returned to him: a huge basin that was beginning to burst, his modest place in all that water. He had never run this way, but it was good, the numbers were still there. That was what brought him to cards in Prague. He was holding on to the number 3, like a hungry infant to the embrace of its mother's bosom. He felt like a wolf cub, unfed for a long time. He had breathed the taste of life, which already had blown past him, beyond the boundaries of the train. Perhaps after a long time, he heard that wonderful song, a ballad, about how all ends well, the familiar melody that intoxicates a man before he moves a finger. He was just waiting to land on the pebbles along the tracks and then run. Each number had its good and bad characteristics. Some things it would permit and some things it would ban. Some things it would recommend and some things it would discourage. Did he count to three? He didn't break his legs—that was good. He held up. His legs were still holding him; that was great. He could always count on his soccer-playing legs. We were both similar in that way. Sometimes he would look at his legs and think that they were the most beautiful part of his body. He loved his body, but his legs were his favorite. A person needed something on which to rely. He ran across a field, all on the count of three—one, two, three. He reached three meters, and then another three, and soon he was thirty meters away from the train. He was almost cheering, if he only had the breath to do so. The field was deep and high. The sides of his body and his lungs were piercing through him. The air was hot. Every movement he made was hot. Hopefully, his lungs and kidneys wouldn't fail him.

"Halt," the commandant of the transport shouted. "Halt!" He didn't stop running. The officer from the booth of the last car began to shoot. Porgess could count the number of bullets. Three flew over his head. He could hear them buzzing by his ears—the first, second, and third. That was nothing, three shots. Three, and another three were left, until the officer would empty his cartridge and assess where Porgess was before reloading? He lowered his head as he ran. Then, the commandant lowered his aim, and the next two bullets, coming from his pistol, hit Porgess in the spine.

"*Scheisse!*" the commandant said out loud, in case Porgess could still hear. Porgess said the same to himself. Number 1? What number 1? Numbers were suddenly disappearing from his head—from his existence. He felt like the water, the basin from which it was overflowing. He couldn't stay in one place; he was in an open field. The commandant spared the third bullet, since he noticed it wasn't necessary. He watched Porgess render the obvious symptoms a person shows when he is fatally wounded. He started by slowing down, dropping, and falling to the ground like a pile of rags.

On Wednesday morning, the rest of the world was celebrating the end of the war in Europe; orchestras, fanfares, and drums were heard from everywhere, even Porgess's music was played—Harry James, Glenn Miller, and Russ Morgan. At the same time, German villagers carried Porgess from the field next to the railroad tracks into the house of the local mayor. The first bullet hit his back and went through the upper portion of his lungs, and though he bled very little externally, and most of his blood was soaked in his prison gown, internally he lost more than a pint. The second bullet hit his spine. He couldn't feel his legs. Could he have lost his legs? He never stood again. From that moment on, Porgess never made a single step with his dancing feet. His eyes questioned what would happen next. Part of him didn't care, and the other part was critical for trying to escape. He continued to have the feeling of water flooding his body. He clearly miscalculated. Did he not satisfy the numbers? Did he misread them? Didn't he know that there was the possibility for a person to both win and lose at the same time? Everything inside of him changed—his rhythm, words, pulse, and breathing. Even the image of water—the basin—was now shattered. Music suddenly stopped playing . . . thoughts . . . and most of all, hope; it streamed from Porgess's body, just as his own blood, though it streamed inward. It was drowning Porgess's insides, and his innards soaked it up like a sea sponge. Hope was dissolving in his blood, in the same way his blood was dissolving in the entity that was once his body. He was still conscious.

The German village doctor assured him that he would live: but how . . . with *murdered* legs? The doctor was eighty years old. He told Porgess that he had been sewing people up for sixty years. He mentioned to him that he had already known what Hitler was about, for twelve years, even though the Führer promised Germany a most glorified present and future with a heritage to the past, even though his people cheered him, because he could blind them into insanity, like a hypnotist or a magician-psychic. It had gotten to a point where the doctor felt misplaced, in the wrong era, erroneously born on this planet. The doctor had his own opinion about Hitler, even though everyone admired the dictator in the early days. Later the doctor was surrounded by more and more wounded Germans who would rather see Hitler and his henchmen in a straightjacket. Perhaps it would interest Porgess, the doctor thought, that the Czechs were involved in the assassination attempt on Hitler in 1944: Porgess didn't give a damn. Now that Hitler was dead, the doctor said, everybody knew that he had shot himself. Only the marshal, with a face scarred by smallpox, who, perhaps fearing that Hitler would find out, forbade any written account of his suicide. The doctor assumed Porgess knew what he was talking about, but Porgess was silent. He was in agony and groaning. The doctor confessed to Porgess that no one knew exactly what happened in the camps; no one knew how far it reached or the depth to which it sank, not even those who survived and were returning home. The hospitals were filled with such people. It was impossible to calculate all the knowledge the survivors of the camps had of those who put them there. Only the dead knew the sum of what happened. Only the dead could be *totschweigen,* or silenced. It was more than just a simple summary. From that time on, everything should make sense. Anyone who would destroy another person for being different or disagreeable should be judged, even those individuals who were just standing by when other people's lives were at stake: those who declared that a foreigner should not poison the blood of a German woman, those who disliked the shape of a nose, color of eyes, or accent of a people from the south, east, or very center of Europe.

The doctor's raspy voice assured Porgess that there was once a time when Germany embraced freedom of speech and religion. They didn't burn down the synagogues, which were once sated with congregations. They didn't always consider anyone who had just one Jewish grandmother to be a non-Aryan. They never burned books. They didn't inject needles into the eyes of the gypsies to make their eyes lighter. They didn't murder the mentally ill or torture the nuns and priests in Dachau, near Munich. It was a different Germany than the one Porgess experienced. No one knew how it got to the point where it could no longer be stopped. Nobody believed that politics would become an inescapable avalanche. The doctor was speaking through Porgess to himself, and he was quite unconvincing. He realized that Porgess was having hallucinations. He couldn't make sense of why Porgess would shout about his water and overflowing basins. Porgess would whisper the name of Woody Herman. The doctor had no idea whom he was talking about. Perhaps it was someone from his family? He also didn't know what the word "Caledonia" meant.

Porgess was aware that he was alive; however, he took no notice of the doctor or his speech. The doctor was old, at an age when people mainly spoke to themselves. He was struggling even when he took Porgess's blood pressure. One of the bullets missed Porgess's aorta by half an inch. A quart of blood was pressing upon his heart.

Just three days prior or, for that matter, even yesterday, the villagers, for fear of the Gestapo, or out of apathy and weariness, would have left Porgess's body in the field to be torn apart by the wolves and perched upon by crows. He wouldn't be the first anonymous death they had seen. The number of dead long surpassed the number of living. For the past three days, the doctor assured Porgess that he would have friends again, but only the best of them; that he would play games again, but those different from soccer, handball, or blind man's bluff. The mayor of the village disappeared westward toward the Americans, who were learning, firsthand, about Germany as the Third Reich was losing its battle. Times of German glory were now left only to the imagination. (Initially, the Allies addressed human rights violations, relating to the war, with only German prisoners and those confessing their crimes. It was only when the Americans were able to communicate with their own prisoners of war, and when General Eisenhower visited Buchenwald and Dachau, that they learned the whole ugly truth. They had never seen such terror beyond the boundaries of Europe and, in their lifetime, they had seen plenty. Porgess had seen it long before, and most Germans pretended they saw nothing.) The mayor left his home and his bed the way it was, so Porgess found refuge under the official's covers.

The first three days and nights, the German doctor engaged in a monologue with Porgess. He consoled him, told him he would live, hopefully, with his parents—they would be a family—only under different circumstances. Everything would have to adjust to his new lifestyle. In the meantime, they would have to carry him everywhere and, then, they would see. The doctor wasn't surprised that Porgess was not responding to him. He could read people's eyes, and the rest could be read simply by looking at Porgess's legs. He knew from the beginning that he could not pity Porgess, for it would make him feel worse. Eventually, Porgess was the only person in the village in whom the doctor confided. It was comical, this monologue, which the doctor was trying to explicate. The difference between a fanatic and a murderer was lost somewhere down the line. Only traces of blood were left behind. There were no extenuating circumstances. It was better to have a smaller country and a clearer conscious, a modest table and clean hands; to raise arms only in defense, not to conquer and suppress for one's personal glory. No single flag was important enough to murder, pillage, and occupy other countries in its name. No language was more superior or more cultured to step over others; this also included the geography and history of any country as well. The doctor was collecting his thoughts as if out of something scorched in ashes. The skin beneath his neck wrinkled. In the end, he began to whisper.

For Porgess, it went in one ear and out the other. It was all the same to him, whether the doctor was screaming or whispering. Germany lost the war, but so did Porgess. He wasn't thinking about what would follow after the war, at least not yet. He was battling against death. During the entire war, he was on the opposite side of the doctor's monologue, which was addressed to himself, under the pretext of speaking to Porgess. But the truth was he was speaking to himself and to Porgess. They both knew that the spine keeps a man on his legs. Without a healthy spine, even with a full recovery, a person has to recline in a horizontal position for the rest of his life, without any sensation in the legs. His left lung was punctured by the bullets and drooped to one side. He had a broken rib and a shattered collarbone. Yes, Porgess was battling, but he lost any sense of feeling from the waist down.

After the war, I visited Porgess in Prague. It was the least we could do, the few who remained. His room was clean and smelled of fresh air; he had four vases filled with azaleas, begonias, and yellow and red roses; a record player, a tape recorder, and a pile of records—Ray Noble, Gene Krupa, Charlie Barnet, and others. His parents took care of him: his father, tall and thin, and beginning to look rabbinical in appearance, who prayed every day, and his blond-haired mother, who wouldn't have had any problems arranging fake papers during the war. They survived the camps and, then, the evacuation, thanks to the Swedes in upper Prussia. Mr. Porgess no longer had to worry about being wealthy and, at the same time, being moral. He was just plain happy that he got what was left of his belongings and a roof over his head. ("The proletariat will deal with some of those peyote heads and bearded bastards," as they were described by a high-ranking official of the revolution, "and we'll send them back where they belong.")

By the ratio of family members who survived (all·three), the Porgesses were an exception for the reparation bureaucracy. In any case, the number 3, as the chairman of the citizen's committee once said, had to be their lucky number. In time, the water would wash away all the pain.

"How do you feel, Porgess?"

"Not bad. I don't have to go to the tailors and have my clothes measured, everybody comes to me. And how about you?"

"I'm fine."

"You look it."

"You know me, I never lie."

"You don't lie anymore?"

"That I still do," I looked at him, "and I'm also trying not to feel guilty for living." I was taming that idiotic subject inside, which forced me to emphasize that I was healthy and almost rampant, standing face-to-face against Porgess's impotence and sickness. It was subconscious and awkward and, for that, I found myself miserable. I had come across this feeling several times, and I wasn't proud of it.

"The same with me, I no longer count the number of people who were killed, so that I could survive." Porgess added, "I hope you're doing the same."

Did he still think about the water, the flood, and the basin? Did he still dream about boxing and his career from beginning to end? At least he returned to his jazz orchestras, to the echoes of yesterday's triumphs, to Orrin Tucker, Bunny Berrigan, and his beautiful black and white men, who were lucky to be born free from parents, beyond the ocean, far away from here.

"When I calculate from top to bottom, from back to front, I feel like the lucky soul who was the last to be rescued from the wreckage of the *Titanic*," Porgess also added.

"I heard that it was quite the high-society boat," I said. "Except for those on the bottom deck, but even they weren't weaklings. I heard that children were separated from their mothers and later found one another."

Porgess cleared his throat.

It was Monday. Porgess asked me whether the table hockey and soccer game machines were still in the arcade on Wenceslas Square, as if the last time we saw each other was yesterday. When we left for the great fortress of Theresienstadt in 1942, the BB gun and target stand were tended by twins, the nineteen-year-old daughters of a former fighter from the Prague "Mask of the Ring," which was in the local carnival tent at Meteor VIII. By then, the war was at its height. Hitler attacked Holland, Belgium, and Luxembourg without declaring war, and, on Christmas, a certain radio channel urged a church tower to ring its bells to the chants of "Hatikva," a Jewish hymn, which contained the most important word: "hope." The church's cardinal was not the first to be eliminated by German authorities. The girls at the shooting range would paint their nails and put on makeup like the alleged mistress of Hitler, the famous Pola Negri, an actress of Polish origin and a rival of Gloria Swanson. Apparently she presented an Aryan birth certificate to Goebbels and got a role in the movie *Forbidden Paradise*. Her photograph, from the film *Passion*, was one Porgess carried creased in his back pocket, next to the naked picture of Hedy Lamarr. Porgess also had a collection of pictures of naked ladies, from the Venus de Milo to the unveiled Maya to other anonymous nude women. It surprised him that someone was not embarrassed or afraid of being photographed in the nude.

"I hear that you claim that a picture of a tractor is different from a photograph of a tractor," Porgess said.

"The best metaphor is reality," I said.

"Do you have a pattern of some sort?"

"Yeah, one that creates a photograph that allows others to understand."

"I'm thinking some kind of secret."

"There is no secret. You simply have to uncover certainty."

"Give me an example."

"Ashes, chimneys, butcher hooks . . ."

"Without the flesh on the walls?"

He understood, and I understood that he did. We both understood.

"A rat," I added, before he could tell me to stick my theory up my ass. "Silence. Even though it means nothing more than the walls of a home, factory, or fence surrounding an old metal yard."

"Hmm," he said. "A scream is equal to immortality for just a short distance, because it will never work out for a long distance—am I right?"

I thought about the fact that from one record, he could hear all of America, or from the hit "Brazil," he could hear all of Brazil, which declared war against Hitler and, ironically, was the country many Germans took refuge in after the war. I thought about the things a person needs to learn in order to adapt, and that Porgess seemed to behave as if he were in the waiting room of a train station, waiting for a train that had already left or had not yet arrived. It was some sort of forgotten rush. A waiting room for an echo that was withering away or had already withered; and I thought about those who were selected or simply neglected by good and bad luck. I didn't want to look as if I had sealed my lips together.

"The games aren't there anymore," I said. "Instead, there's a perfume shop and a fishmonger right next to it."

"The fishmonger was an arcade downhill. Am I right?" Porgess asked.

"There are two fishmongers now, in two arcades. People love fish."

"When will they open a third?"

"Why?"

"That's what I'm asking you."

"Well, when do you think?"

"People are being born again. The war is over."

"Yeah," I agreed. "How is it that good or bad luck never depends on whether a man is good or evil, whether he strives for something or is apathetic?"

"Do you still steal?" Porgess asked, saving me from too deep of a subject.

"I never steal from an individual," I said grinning.

"How can you tell now what is bad or good?"

"I decide."

"How can you tell?"

"I do what I can."

"Does this include justice?"

"Aren't you asking a little too much?"

"Can you stand the truth?"

"I can deal with a lie much better," I said. I refused to give in.

"Does everything seem strange to you, as if you just arrived from Mars?"

"It's more as if I were still there," I said with a sneer.

"Do you have all your teeth?"

"With the exception of some."

"Do you remember those two beauties at the shooting range?"

"They must have dumped an entire bottle of perfume on themselves in a single afternoon. If someone told me that, out of the entire war, I remembered those two most, I would think that he was babbling. So they are no longer there?"

"That's too bad, but I also think of them sometimes."

"Everything has really changed."

"Faster than you think."

"I stopped thinking about it."

"It almost surprised me."

"People here had a different experience."

"It went through different brain cells than those you and I have."

"Different, but identical at the same time."

"What do you mean by that?"

"More likely, you and I are the ones who have changed."

"I got used to it."

"Everything goes on," he said.

"You have that right."

"Even if I didn't," he admitted.

He started to hum the tune "Caledonia," and then the version of "I Can't Begin" he had on a record by Bunny Berrigan. He had a few notes on each record, but they never amounted to five.

"I won't be forced into anything," he said.

"I'm not forcing you into anything," I said.

"You wouldn't succeed."

"As if we didn't know each other."

I wondered why Porgess never liked the number 5. Did he blame his five senses—sight, hearing, taste, touch, and smell—for all his misfortune? I had no desire to criticize him or myself, for that matter. Some people do not like the shade at high noon and some dislike the sun. Weltfeind Flusser disliked water and soap; perhaps he blamed the soapsuds, because W.F. would blame anything fresh and clean. The number 5 also meant the five continents. He didn't care that there were actually seven of them. Porgess would have to incriminate the entire planet. Five also meant the game quid, which was played with five cards of the same suit; in which his father once won a thousand crowns playing it. According to Rabbi Citron, it was forbidden in Palestine to pick fruit from trees younger than five years. The number 5 ... 5 ... 5 ... why? What was it to me? I would remind myself. This was not why I came to see Porgess. Even with Porgess there, I felt alone, as if I were on some remote railroad track.

During the war, a lady affiliated with the Salvation Army once told Porgess that 3 was the number for heaven and 4 the number for earth. Three was a female number and 4 was a male number.

"Why?" he asked.

"According to the basic laws of the universe," she replied.

Number 4 was about dynamism, stability, understanding, and endurance. She was blond, with gentle, white skin, large breasts, a bit short of breath, with greenish gray eyes, an angelic expression, and a neck slightly thicker than most (she probably suffered from wens). She never had children and wanted to adopt, perhaps from Romania.

"Number four embraces God, man, woman, and child," she said to Porgess.

There are the spiritual and physical parts of existence. Everything that grows has the same traits, both internal and external; every molecule, particle, all the way to the smallest atom. According to the lady from the Salvation Army, 1 was the number for goods; 2, for brotherhood; 3, the number of perfection; 7 consisted of two 3s and a 1. Was he following? Ten had three sets of 3s and therefore 1 perfection, or something similar. Twenty-one meant three sets of 7s. He was following. He was thinking about cards: blackjack. Forty was a complete number. It had almost everything. Every time God starts war with Satan, it lasts forty something—days, weeks, years, minutes—but it is always the number 40.

"What do all the numbers consist of?" the woman asked.

"Giving and taking, understanding and misunderstanding," Porgess replied. Not giving in to anything, Porgess thought.

Porgess remembered that when the lady was long gone; or more likely, the lady stayed and Porgess was long gone. Ten was a dynamic number. Seven was the number for uncertainty, even endurance. That didn't rhyme with Porgess. He once spoke with a Hasid, a Jewish sectarian, who came to Prague from Poland and looked to the numbers, searching within them for the connection between intuition and cognition, between passion and reason, between love and hate, and between all the above and desire. On the peak of everything stood desire. Everything embodied numbers; he could not understand. How could Porgess at his age possibly think he could understand them? He claimed that it was probably because he wasn't forty yet.

Everything that pertained to Porgess's immobility reminded me of motion; an interplay of all his body parts, stability that petered out with a mutilated spine. It was quite a shift, this immobility, like a stone frozen in a piece of ice or an air bubble in glass. It reminded me of the possibilities that healthy people have, and yet they lie in bed on their belly all day long. The essence of why a person often loves his body above all. Bobby Mahler used to tell us about Pythagoras, who considered the number 4 the basis for everything. Pythagoras's famous theorem was one of the things we learned by heart for Bobby Mahler. Pythagoras also invented the five-pointed star. (Five apexes with a strange mission throughout history.) He also considered number 1 the father of all numbers, 2 the mother, all even numbers female, and odd numbers male. Porgess once claimed that somewhere in the sixth century B.C., the five-pointed star represented a human: the head, arms, and legs. He wasn't surprised that the Whale chose the five-pointed star as its symbol, or that Americans adorned their flag with such stars.

"Symbols can penetrate very deep and reach even further. They cross eras in time, the borders of lands, civilizations, and religions. Everyone loves to hide away in secret and act more mysterious than they really are, so that no one can see their cards."

Porgess had connected to Pythagoras long ago, as if they were friends.

The broken nose made Porgess look older. It had been more than five years since 1940, when we met each other for the first time and still had no idea what our futures might hold. His features had roughened, his face had grown longer, and he had begun to grow a reddish beard. He remembered our common acquaintance, Leda Freivilig, also known as Puberta, who was sent from Theresienstadt on a transport to the east along with the feebleminded, including Miss Herzl, the daughter of the "Father of Zionism" and "Jewish King," as he was called in Poland, and the sister of previously mentioned Franz Josef Kafka. From the beginning, Porgess told me that women needed to be handled like indestructible treasure chests. The key was to discover the proper place, using the pillow of your fingertip, so that she would open and you could get inside.

In those days, Porgess looked up the theory of French doctors, who, in 1905, were contemplating whether the heads of aristocrats, cut off during the reign of terror and later, could still sense the world around them, and, if so, what they sensed and for how long. (One doctor-criminologist declared, with the agreement of his distinguished colleague, that they do still sense things.)

Specialists of the guillotine, similar to those who, in the future, specialized in all that had happened to Porgess and millions of Porgesses alike, proved that a decapitated head has the ability to see, think, and God knows what else, for a few more seconds. It is an ability pertaining to the dying, wounded, and victims of accidents and battle—crystal clarity, understanding, keen sensitivity, and an ability to reason. The above-mentioned doctor did an experiment. At the second when the guillotine cut off the victim's head, the doctor called his name. The head apparently gave the doctor a clear and conscious look. It could be possible, Porgess thought. Undoubtedly, a pair of eyes that were still alive could be answering his call. Apparently, death isn't immediate and sudden with the separation of the head from the body. A head can be consoled with the coming of death by a rapid motion of thoughts, and then a gradual (yet, at the same time, rapid) peace takes over, almost a dreamlike sleep that puts you in a state of bliss, like a mother's embrace, and then nothing. That is all that awaits us, Porgess would say, laughing. He took an advance on this. He knew what was at stake.

Porgess would bring it out to raise the mood, like the joke about the two dogs that met at the veterinarian.

"I saw her, when she wasn't all that well, in Theresienstadt on the train platform," I said. "You wouldn't believe it, but she actually got fat from the hunger."

"She was probably swelling."

"Yeah, she was losing weight, but she kept on getting fatter," I attested. "Perhaps she was swelling. I don't know. She looked as if she were pregnant. She looked like a ball of meat. She was already no skinny twig when we knew her. She did love buttercups, as I recall."

"I met her kind many times," Porgess said. "She came from a family where cousins would marry their cousins. She was pretty, but a bit vulgar. When I first met her, every day, in both summer and in winter, she would wear a white blouse, white socks, a white hat, and white gloves all the way to her elbows."

"She was very sincere, I mean, for a girl," I said, "but too submissive."

"Sometimes sincerity is extremely vulgar. The difference between the underdeck and first-class dining room of a steamboat."

Porgess was silent about the venality of Puberta—Leda Freivilig. They had their affair, but I didn't want to reproach his conscience.

"Did you ever take a trip in such a steamboat?"

"Yeah, on the *Titanic*," Porgess said with a sneer.

"Once our family took a trip from Genoa to Venice. Father thought it best that I see the world, so that I wouldn't think I knew everything just because I had twice taken a round-trip from Prague to Počernice. It was morning; the night was already behind us and dawn was soon approaching. I will never forget that moment. It was like the beginning of earth. Perhaps the world truly had begun from the waters. Venice just pushed its way through the mist, and all of a sudden it was there. We couldn't keep up, and in a moment the sun, an enormous circle, a flame harnessed by distance, made its way through the mist to take control of the rest of the morning. Father was a bit afraid of cholera. Luckily, they cleaned it out before we arrived. I also didn't know that Venice once belonged to Austria. The Italians had to wage war to push them out. I remember the large amount of water. Except in a dream, neither before nor after, had I ever seen so much sun and water in one place."

"I could deal with that."

"It can't hurt. You see, there are other worlds on earth, and in some places they aren't afraid when someone knocks on the door in the middle of the night, because it isn't the Gestapo. In some places, people live comfortably, without fear."

"That must be really far away," I laughed.

Porgess laughed back. Did he remind me of his past, because I was afraid of his future? I probably would not have wanted to photograph him; perhaps only if the picture returned to a time before or during the war, but still in Prague. We saw a lot, though we didn't see everything, and we would have preferred not to see anything.

What he said about Venice and the Austro-Hungarian empire (which disappeared from the face of the map) reminded me how every "today" was suspiciously addicted to the past, and how little it had to do with the future, which was clouded by a shadow cast by "yesterday." The future was always a maiden; no one ever knows what becomes of her. The past is a mother, from which everything is begotten—a "grand" grandmother, a public and private affair, a little lady of loose morals.

"Leda Freivilig," he said.

"Yeah," I said.

"Yeah," he answered.

A memory consists of common nostalgia and common guilt. No one, after what had happened, could understand the other person, and vice versa. Why was I here? Each and every one of us was carrying his own private, inexplicable ration. His own yes and no. Why does a person need a memory, when it makes him suffer? Did Porgess want to be faithful to his memory, or did he want to lose it and give priority to unfaithfulness? No false understanding, just a blissful thanks. Was that also why Porgess had his own yes and no, a shadow that cast another shadow? In a place where memory could have been a blessing, it was a curse. Where it was a curse, it transformed into something different. Did he blame everything on himself, while at the same time not blaming himself for anything at all? To remember and to forget were beyond the category of good and evil, the horrific and even more horrific, but it embraced them all nevertheless. A question occurred to me: Was a person brought closer to life by memory or by oblivion? What can and cannot be forgotten when the past pervades a person to his final present? Porgess probably had to solve this every day, both when he woke in the morning and then when he went back to bed.

"I'm lying here like a snake," Porgess said.

"That agile, huh?" I asked.

"Annoyed and lazy," he added. He was looking at me, even though I was still far away, like someone who already knew the difference between a glutted and empty stomach.

I once read an article by Adler in *We Shall Return!* about snakes. A villager in Borneo once went to gather wood in the morning and a thirty-foot-long boa constrictor attacked him. He later showed the doctor the cuts made by the snake's teeth, which were separated by a distance of sixteen inches. How could he have survived it? He was cutting twigs for a basket, with his arms raised above his head, when the snake bit him. With a knife in one hand, his reflexes drew his arms immediately downward and, by chance, he cut the snake's tongue off and half his head. It was a coincidence that saved his life. He was able to tell the story so that the doctor could write about it.

"I'm not afraid of anything, and I don't regret a thing," Porgess said. "Mornings are the best, in the afternoon I languish, and in the evening I wither away."

In that moment, I was sailing during the time of exploration, when we were all Columbus, sailing on our own private sea. We would set off for India to begin new eras by discovering the Americas of our youth, including such novelties as the fact that people used to bite each other rather than kiss, or that only three girls out of ten were made for games of love with all its consequences, whereas the other seven were pretenders; the explorer still could never tell which one was which. It was old hat that Columbus, like us, would never know what he would discover; what existed, exists, and will remain existing in the mystery of a woman. It was all coming back to me sitting next to Porgess. I guess I remembered some things more than others.

"What are those other women doing now?"

"How would I know?" I answered.

"Leda Freivilig—Puberta—was quite a character."

"For a long time no one really could make any sense of her, and that's a fact."

"You know who really understood women, don't you?"

"Yeah, I still remember," I admitted.

"A woman is something different than a man," Vili Feld once said during a poker game in the Café Nizza. "She wants the same things a man does, but she wants them in a different way, and yet she wants them the same way as well. Most of the time a man can only imagine what it is. Women perceive themselves differently than men. They even perceive men differently than men do themselves. Men are presumably lost when they try to explain a woman from their point of view. No one could ever explain this phenomenon, even if a person spent half his life as a woman and half as a man. You see, it's a well-known fact that the essence that is most womanlike within women is also what they least understand about themselves. A woman, for instance, believes that marriage is more beneficial for a man, because the man gets everything he wants: food, a roof over his head, and companionship in bed. He will go about his own business while the woman has to strive for the same things she did before her wedding, as time flies by faster for her than for a man. The man can only try to convince himself that marriage is better for the woman, because it will guarantee insurance against everything worse than being with a man, including getting old."

That day, Porgess came up with the question in the Hagibor locker room: "Was it Columbus who discovered America, or was it the sailor who was on duty on the mast?" I was trying to guess how much energy Porgess had and how he replenished it.

I was embarrassed a bit to speak with Porgess about the mystery of women and the way they were in the old days, especially ones like Leda Freivilig, alias Puberta, before she lost her mind; before Porgess's spine was shattered. We only spoke of how many women disappeared and how many were left to whither away alone—an end they feared so much. It was better even not to speak of such things, but to avoid the subject seemed unfair. What is the unknown inside a woman? What energy, extenuating biological dynamism, is hidden in every cubic inch of a woman's body? But it didn't matter anymore. Through his amorous experiences, which he would share with us no later than the first Saturday afternoon of the month, Porgess became famous at the age of fourteen. Why is masturbation so pleasant to those lonely riders with their palms lathered in perfumed soap and washed in warm water? (As if all of us in Belgická 24 had baths with perfumed soap.) He started to speak to me on his own initiative, so that I wouldn't catch him off guard.

"A woman is something that comes out from the darkness, when we're still lost in it," he said.

"That sounds complicated," I answered.

For some reason this all reminded me of an echo, which distorted the fact he was once fourteen or fifteen, and that on Sundays we would eat leftovers together on Belgická 24. I had respect for what was going on in Porgess's mind. He spoke of darkness and I transported myself to another murkiness, a tone of gloom, obscurity. I could only touch the surface of what Porgess could touch inside. It was a feeling within, as if in some way I was touching his insides, some sort of center, where only I could get lost; or a darkness where only I would do damage. He seemed to me like a person whose stomach and intestines had been cut out and put back in with his own hands. He was lucky that the German doctor, who was present, stitched his back, stomach, and spine. He seemed to be surrounded, and nothing would permit him to get out—an existence under a pressure that no one would lessen. Something in Porgess frightened me and, at the same time, fascinated me. He would invite me into his world, but with a politeness and beckoning stemming from a different logic than that of a host. I noticed that I, too, had a logic different from that of a guest. Were we eating out of the same bowl? We were both discovering special codes, which separated us because, although we were one, we were divided as well by the realities of the postwar world. I wanted to ease things up a bit. I pretended to have other interests than those inside of me and pretended to retreat when I failed to move a single step. Luckily, Porgess came to my aid.

"Women are like Christmas tree ornaments," he said. "Some will amaze you, others are just right, and some you never notice. However, you will always accept the Christmas tree as it is. Expenses, pleasures, complications, and advantages are all included in the price."

"Yeah, but sometimes I'm just not smart enough," I answered evasively. "I still can't remember that infamous woman's shoe size or bra size, not to mention her bathing suits."

I gave into a voice of passivity, even apathy, similar to the way Bobby Mahler explained the art of ancient Chinese war: to pretend that one was far away when close by; to stand as if at a disadvantage when you are at an advantage; to render order as if there were disorder; to seem as if you have taken the shady side of a mountain when you have the sunny side, or that you are in the valley when you are in the watchtower on the hilltop.

"Don't tell me that!" Porgess laughed.

"You were always better at these things," I lied.

"Yeah, a regular stud."

"It's always harder when it comes to women."

"Now I belong to the putrid ten thousand, for a change."

"You're pretty bold to say something like that."

"All you need is to crash once."

"You're holding up," I attested. "As little Bobby Mahler would say about ancient China, there are five ways to find out who would win: those who knew when to engage in a fight and when not to; those who knew when to add a lot of force and when not to, and so on."

"Yeah, and so on."

I waited to hear what else he had to say.

"In some places, they consider the biggest women the prettiest. Before they get married, they stuff themselves. The Arabs consider a woman beautiful if she has many jowls." Then he sneered, "I don't have to burden someone with something I can get on my own." He reminded me of what he would say in Hagibor: "It was easy, like scratching in a place that itches or like yawning for a while, or stepping under a shower."

I cleared my throat. I was trying to say something.

"Do you remember Sonya Utitz?"

"She was famous."

"That she was."

"No one could say that she was quiet and passive."

"She was a great gal."

"How could someone possibly forget such a girl?"

"Not a chance."

"Yeah," Porgess sneered again, "she once told me that the best thing a woman could do for a guy was to listen and observe, because men have huge egos; a woman could do anything, but she would not be able to please a man the way he could please himself. She really thought that and based the opinion on real-life experience. The fact that she wasn't even sixteen speaks for itself. She was probably blemished by the Mesmer twins, Helmut and Verner, who were both sharing her, or should I say, perhaps with whom Sonya was sharing herself. And then later, Adler played along. She claimed that before girls can become sisters, they must bark like bitches at each other. She also mentioned that nothing gave a man greater pleasure, including making a woman happy, than making himself happy. It bothered her that men felt this way, even if a man were head over heels in love with her. It seemed unfair that men were not ashamed of this, but that women were hesitant to admit doing the same. Nevertheless, the fact is that this is easier for a woman than for a man. It's easier for them than doing it with a man. Women don't feel good afterward; they are alone and emptiness falls upon them, even more so than before and during the act. That is what kept her around the boys from Belgická 24. She told me that, for a long time, she didn't know that women could do this. She felt guilty. All she needed to do was to put a towel between her legs, and then she would feel good and sad. She needed someone to hold her little hand while it was happening. She complained that Little Narcissus, even when next to her, preferred to observe himself. Perhaps he was excited with her close to his own body. He could look at himself for an hour, even though she was next to him. She didn't understand why he was so pompous. She pitied him for being an orphan until she realized that that was a lie, but, nevertheless, she searched for him when the Mesmer twins went to Palestine."

What was he remembering? I noticed that his eyes were embraced by a shadow. Only Porgess could say what it all meant. Did he see the end of the winter, the way everything began to melt and the icy and soiled water began to flow through his valley?

What about jazz, his wonderful Negroes—Louis Armstrong, Nat King Cole, or Ella Fitzgerald? Or was it something else? What did he imagine when he had no visitors? How do gullies gather water high in the mountains and how do currents adjoin, when they flow without obstacles into the valleys or perhaps somewhere far away where they link to a river and then to the sea? I imagined Porgess's basin. Did Porgess think about the girls with whom he had little romances? Over time, his basin would burst and the water would free itself. Did he dance in spirit to the music of the great orchestras: "Caledonia," "Sentimental Journey," and "The Skyscraper"? Did he sing "Oh, Johnny, Oh" in its original tongue? The "Eastern Sun Serenade"?

"So, how are you doing these days?" I asked him as casually as I could. "I mean it."

"I'm struggling."

I looked at him.

"With boredom," he continued.

"And how is it coming?" I smiled.

"I'm in training. Lying down in the meantime."

"You know you could win."

"It's a piece of cake," he agreed.

His eyes showed something else, a challenge for a fight, where the opponent was himself. Perhaps it was the thought of how he looked or, rather, how he wished he looked, or an echo of something left over from the war. Did he remember every hour of the war, what he did, what he said or thought? Simply, what was here and now?

"You have to be a champion," he said.

"Of course."

He was looking around the room. That I could understand.

"Do you know who else survived?" Porgess asked.

"One out of every four."

"Four is good for me. Three is better. Everything worked for me on the number three; well, almost everything. As I once heard Rabbi Citron say, 'Eve had covered herself with a four-leaf clover when she discovered the feeling of sin, and also the feeling of shame and humiliation.' Those three out of four have nothing to regret, but I don't know whether they are worse or better off."

"Nothing hurts them anymore; it's number four that suffers."

"Yeah."

"I guess in those days the four-leaf clovers were larger," I said. I passed over the rest.

"Or the people were smaller."

"Yeah, they had smaller balls."

"That was probably the way Bobby Mahler imagined apples or gooseberries."

"Cranberries," he corrected me.

"Yeah, or apricots."

"You forgot to tell me whom it was that survived," I reminded him.

"Oscar Schizka. Someone hid him in an insane asylum. Apparently they haven't told him that his old man, old Abraham Rothberg, flew up the chimney. Oscar took up lodging in the loony bin just as if it were a hotel. Perhaps he thought that it was a depository for luggage and that the bars were there so the wind wouldn't take away the suitcases, so he'd have something to hold on to."

"He looked very Jewish," I said. "He had to pretend that he was a Frenchman or an Italian or a Romanian."

"He was a number seven. I think that was what saved him."

For Porgess the number 7 embraced the seven winds and the seven sins about which his Catholic girlfriends spoke. The seven strata of age, if a person assumed that he would live seventy years of life. The seven plague wounds of Rabbi Arnošt Citron, at least from the Jewish side. In a pamphlet, Porgess read that Babylon believed in the creation of earth by the seven winds, the seven storm spirits, the seven deadly diseases, and the seven levels of the underworld, secured by the seven gates and the seven levels of the over world and heaven. If it really came down to it, Porgess would be able to do his doctoral dissertation on the number 7. Meanwhile, in my mind I saw Oscar Schizka Rothberg, his body swaying, his head frantically turning to the left and then to the right, up and then down, his hands constantly in his pockets. Anyone could figure out what he was playing with. The way old man Rothberg would look at him, never knowing what to do with him, and then go and write his incomprehensible verses, like his final (not too original) rhymes about the Golem's saber. Abraham Rothberg was a character. Whatever was missing in his talent he would replenish with fervor and, unfortunately, an unbearable disposition. He presented an image that conveyed a comprehensive understanding of everything, but, ironically, he couldn't understand himself, not to mention his little son.

I brought two playing cards for Porgess as a good luck gift — a king and queen of hearts. (I gave them also to Belle, Hana Kaudersová — my wife — as a wedding gift in a golden frame.)

"Today is the eighth; it's a good day for visits," said Porgess. He didn't mean to infer that the world looks different when a person has something to look forward to — that the unformed sense of matter is formed and the emptiness in which a person loses himself is replenished. This probably included visits. I could even imagine, from my perspective, how it really was or, more so, more like how it wasn't. How many people have been rediscovered, only preferring to keep their addresses forgotten?

"What was the joke about the two dogs at the veterinarian's?" I asked.

"The first dog asked the other what brought him to the vet. He bit a boy on the street and now they were going to castrate him. 'What was the second one's reason?' 'Passion,' said the other dog. His lady undressed to take a shower and he couldn't control himself. 'They'll probably castrate you, too,' said the first dog. 'No, they just want to file down my claws.'"

"You would never say that in front of a woman," I said.

"No way," Porgess agreed.

This flattered him. He caught on to it. I felt as if I could share something with him without taking away his prey. Porgess always knew a few jokes, which would tickle our tonsils in Hagibor.

Porgess no longer had an angelic face, as he did before he left for the transport. I did what I could to seem calm. He asked me if I still could, as in the old days with Erwin Adler in the Achermanc or in the Cellar, win fifty crowns each week just for spending money. I said that these days I would probably lose the fifty crowns and then smiled. I carefully fastened my belt up a notch, so Porgess wouldn't notice. I was a bit nervous after all. I was guessing what it was lingering inside Porgess—the wind, fire, or dust—that made up the road upon which he walked, that made the flatlands, valleys, and swamps. Porgess already knew that I was a photojournalist for the magazine *We Shall Return!* and what gave me, along with Adler and representatives of the Whale, the hope of more equality, democracy and a thicker piece of bread, butter, and God knows what else (before it started to fall apart). In the beginning, the Whale seemed, for people like us, the all-promising woman whom a man woos, marries, and then discovers is an ill-tempered old bitch, a dragon that swallows her daughters alive. Porgess recognized what it took to hook us like a fish. (A building without the idea of the rich and poor, the exploited, the ones who exploits the blond and the blue eyed, those with aquiline or crooked noses, those with hair, those who were bald, and, most importantly, no one would be put behind a barbed-wire fence and then put into the ovens without being guilty.) It was in the aftermath of the defeat of Germany that an elated surface of grand illusions appeared, upon which a person could keep afloat without knowing how to swim. Who wouldn't want this? Porgess would replenish my old tendencies with new ambition. (As Erwin would say, "Give a hungry man something to eat, a roof over his homeless head, and desire nothing but gratitude, and he will die for you, because gratitude does not cost anything.") Porgess had echoes in his voice and his eyes—the German village doctor; the Hauptsturmführer who pulled the trigger of the pistol that shot an unarmed Porgess full of two bullets in his spine; swamps, hills, woods, and words; millions of people who didn't have food, money, or anything to wear. I could only imagine what Porgess wouldn't accept, with what he could never come to terms. Was he a strict judge? Did he turn his verdicts against himself?

"The king and queen of hearts—I like that," Porgess said, as he was looking at the cards.

He had a wrinkle entrenched above his eye. Considering Porgess's relatively young age, it was a wrinkle set deeply into the pores of his skin. Was it a mark of inner tension, describing what was burdening him? What troubled him? Besides that wrinkle, there were also two other wrinkles in the shape of a sickle on both his cheeks. He also said that the blood was not running through his legs and that he didn't know what could be done. Porgess was known for sorting out the system of games; he was a fourteen-year-old who never got thrown out of the worst of joints. He became acquainted with the system of probabilities, which had to interest any gambler. "How many socks do you have to buy in order to have at least one pair of the same color?" His favorite number 3 served him well. I could try it out. If I reached into a dresser for three socks, I would have at least one pair of the same color (that is, if I buy only two colors, of course). He had his own personal system, even though he kept it under a tight lid. He would take twenty-five halliard coins, throw them in the air, and count how many heads and how many tails would fall on the ground. He would repeat this several times. In the end, it would follow a pattern. What was the essence of this trick? For instance, when nine heads and eleven tails would land out of twenty-five halliard coin tosses, could one assume that the next time it would be the other way around, that out of twenty-five halliard coins, nine tails and eleven heads would land? Why was this? It was just a simple "because." Porgess was under the impression that a gambler had to develop his memory to remember three thousand attempted plays. I begged him not to show me all three thousand times—I believed him. We had something that bound us together. We caught each other's eye immediately. We had a common understanding: cards, girls, friendship, his love of jazz, syncopation, piles of records, and the selflessness with which he would greet us in his home.

It occurred to me that I could invite him to the circus, if only I knew a way to get him there, but I immediately reconsidered the idea. Yesterday, I was at the circus with Adler. (I thought about Tanga the whole time, and then about Porgess, for whom I took the day off in order to visit. He made me think, and I pondered over him long before I arrived at his bed. Perhaps even Adler thought about Porgess as well, though probably not the entire time.) There were three rings. Each of them was competing for the attention of the audience: tightrope walkers, acrobats on bicycles, and dancers accentuating their physical abilities, flexibilities, and perfection (at least when it came down to using their muscles). A threesome of clowns was doing somersaults to get and put on two hats, but because there were only two, one of the three was always without a hat. By the end of the performance, the crowd was laughing so hard it was crying. The laughter was followed by sadness, and vice versa. People always imagine themselves in the place of a clown. (Although in Porgess's case, perhaps, it was the other way around.) Finally, the grand finale came: flying acrobats on the trapeze. Under the circus tent, they swayed on the trapeze higher and higher until they jumped. Each floating seamlessly through the air, like flying fish or birds. They caught each other's trapeze and then, on the second time, the first caught the arms of the second as the audience gasped. What would Porgess have to say about that? Why was I thinking about the circus in his presence without even mentioning a word to him?

Porgess's fame as a gambler reached all the way here, thanks to his presence.

"Do you remember how the Americans would bomb us during the day and the English during the night?"

"Yeah, I would watch them drop bombs on me. We couldn't seek shelter anywhere, only the Germans could. That was quite an overwhelming sensation."

"That's what you got for making shells for German airplane machine guns." A well-informed Porgess added, "Likewise."

"In the last three months of the war, I made millions of bullets in that German armory, but in doing so, I felt like a brother killer and a felo-de-se: it was a strange combination. The Germans loved this concept. Those bombers from the ground looked like silver flies that couldn't be killed by the long arms of the German antiaircraft artillery, so they were able to spit fire and steel upon them. The pilots probably had no idea of the hope they were instilling within us down below, even though, at the same time, it all seemed so hopeless."

"Yeah, it was certainly a paradox. The better they would hit their targets, the sooner you were dead."

I only added, "It was good anyway, that's all I have to say. It seemed destiny wanted us destroyed, but this time, the Germans were going down with us. I remember, as if it were yesterday. A couple of times I was waiting, almost anxiously, to take the hit."

"I know what you mean," Porgess said. He was probably thinking about Samson, about whom Rabbi Citron used to tell us, but I wasn't sure whether he was recalling this in a different manner.

The cards made him seem as if he were wearing a suit that would always bring him luck.

"I hope we'll be able to meet those pilots someday," I said.

"Likewise," Porgess said again.

Porgess's personal system was based on his theory of waves. A huge wave was made out of several small waves. When a person was on the pinnacle of the large wave (happiness), by the law of gravity he had to go down (misery). When he was at his lowest point, the law of the wave would elevate him upward and then vice versa again. Of course, it was necessary to determine the difference between the motions of the larger and small waves. The small wave could go down, while the large wave could continuously rise in the opposite direction. At every moment, a person had to pay close attention to his location; to the status of the wave and its motion; to his time for victory and his time for defeat; and in which section of the large or small wave he could win. In the game of baccarat, Porgess recognized the principle of two days and two nights.

After the war, he added to this a theory depicting the fall of civilization, which, according to him, had begun a downward process in the time of its greatest triumph. The only difference was that, unlike a gambler, it never managed to get out of its misery.

Porgess also once pulled a trick on Bobby Lenta Mahler and Leon the Bald, when they forbade playing poker for money in Belgická 24. He wrote the names of animals on leaflets. A gorilla was worth a crown, an eagle ninety halliards, a falcon eighty, and a vulture seventy. A giraffe was worth a five-crown piece, a zebra ten, a bear twenty, and a mammoth a hundred. Porgess also discovered that no game system could work if every player knew it. At the end, even the best system would destroy the individual, because a majority could not always be beaten.

"To win or to lose is better than to not play at all." Adler and I both thought this.

"What is our trainer Talisman, from the Maccabiah, doing these days?" Porgess asked.

"He flew up the chimney."

"It seems that all of them joined the paratroopers."

"Yeah"—I understood his irony—"upward."

"Where did they land, in heaven or hell? Where did Bobby Mahler end up?"

"Probably torturing some poor SA or SS officer, trying to explain that all men were created equal and that he could prove it by the existence of the same myths in Egypt and the land of fire, and in areas below the North Pole, though none of these myths could possibly have been influenced by the others. And how this should have proven more about the cognitive similarities of the human mind, regardless of the origin or place of birth, than any of Doctor Alfred Rosenberg's theories."

"Don't tell me that Rosenberg was a doctor!"

We trained with Mr. Talisman in the gym on the wall bars, ramp, pommel horse, and the giant's stride, and he tortured us on the horizontal bar and the vaulting horse. Porgess competed with me on the rings. We were proud of our bodies.

After training, we played cards. Porgess was never against having girls in the room during a poker game. He would never spit on the cards; he would only blow on them. In the beginning, his mother didn't like to watch him play, but then she would sit in with us. When I visited them, and old Porgess wasn't at home, there were many times when I took them pretty badly. She would always be inclined to take Porgess's side, but at the same time, she didn't want to insult me. There was a modest dignity within her that only mothers have, a sad courage to strangle one's only child, to renounce a victory for the sake of her son.

In those days, Porgess was as pretty as a peach. He didn't have to think how awkward everything concerning him and his bed must have seemed to his mother. He still didn't want to unburden her from such a feeling by engaging in a decisive and drastic action. He didn't bother to ponder over the worth of vegetating like that. And he was embarrassed to look his father straight in the eye, just as his father was sometimes embarrassed to look straight into his eyes.

Porgess wore a white sleeping gown that was unbuttoned down to his chest, which was emaciated to the bone. He had long hair that had become frail, like that of old men. His voice also changed from that of a child to that of an old man. He wore a golden necklace around his neck. In my mind, I journeyed along the trails of his lower body. I didn't want to admit to the distance that was separating us, and that could create a trench that was much longer and deeper than the differences in psychology.

And what about Porgess? Suddenly I felt ashamed to stand or stretch, because Porgess could no longer do such things.

"I heard that they were testing ways to revitalize the spinal cord in laboratory rats."

"I hope a few rats will stay alive to see some results."

"All they really need now is the father of Herbert Weinberger-Winedresser, alias Little Narcissus."

"Is he a rat catcher again? That's a really big break for the rats."

This was the only comment I heard Porgess say about his spine. I noticed a camber in his eye until it withered away. His eyes were speaking a different language than that of his tongue. He was friendly to me, nonchalant, open, spontaneous, witty, mordant, and defiant, but something was missing. Something was stranded in the world of a person who could never forgive, and yet forgiveness would be to no avail. He had his own opinions on Germany. After the war, everything was different, but deep inside he didn't budge a bit. If someone would ask him what his biggest fear was, besides his spine, he would have probably said Germany and those who lived on its soil. It would be difficult to find someone there who had nothing to do with what had happened. Did he include everyone? Even those who were yet to be born? I found that unlikely. And yet the Whale started to claim that it wasn't a war between Germany and the rest of the world, but a war between Hitler and the Nazis and the rest of the world, as if someone other than Germans wore the uniforms of the Wermacht, Waffen SS, and the Luftwaffe, with a few exceptions. At the same time, Porgess would ponder over whether this could change. His life, once active, was pacing in one place. Women, like everything else, were a question of memories. Echoes. A song that once sounded as if it were never meant to end.

I wanted so much to cross over that distant trench or dam lingering in my mind. We were both on the same wave. I almost didn't want that. He always looked like a doll, even when his nose was broken in the ring, or when he got wet from the rain, or when a car sprayed him with the water from a puddle on the street. He would always open the door for a lady. In the bathroom, he would turn on the faucet and continuously allow the water to flow so that he could disguise the other sounds he made while in there. He knew at the age of fourteen that a man walked on the side closer to the street with a woman, so that a car couldn't spray muddy water from the street on her. He never asked any questions that were not his concern. He had the blue irises of a fourteen-year-old whose curiosity could never be justified. Compared to the audacity of Weltfeind Flusser, or Little Narcissus, or Renate Oschler-Salus, he had a friendly prudence that would win him over with others, especially when it came to playing cards. Inadvertently, I would use him as an example without it being forced upon me. (I guess I would allow that task just for Vili Feld.) He loved to share things with us, including indecent pictures and photographs. He looked like an Aryan. In 1941 and 1942, when we wanted to go out in Prague without a star, we would bring him along to the Orinoko, the Café Sterb, to Mišák's place as our escort. Sometimes he would go to the pastry shop at Berger's, where he was not afraid to go on his own. Once in a while, he would go there just before we would arrive, when he knew we were coming. He wanted to see the expressions on our faces when we would see him there. This also included arcades in Meteor VIII, with game machines, table hockey, soccer, and pool, where the two sisters born from the same egg tended the guns and the targets. He had been wearing a hat from the age of thirteen, and it was a pleasure to watch him doff it from his head, like Cyrano de Bergerac. For a moment, I realized what was cruel in him; what probably happened to his generosity, which would encourage him to pay for the boys; to his gentleness, which gave him the ability to win the race for a girl in a time half as long as, for instance, Renate Oschler-Salus and the others. What made him always beat us, with the exception of Luster Leibling, at courtship, a quality that never resembled a bull in a china shop. (L.L. considered Vili Feld the king of the saloon. He claimed he had the look of a tiger. He noticed the luster in his eyes when he would look at someone, as if he were grasping that someone in his claws.) In that moment, Porgess had eyes like two metal coins. How did Porgess imagine a tiger looked at a person?

He would lie upon a lowered bed on wheels so that he could reach the knobs of the radio, the record player, and the tape player without the aid of anyone. He still didn't have a phone in his room. His father had one installed downstairs at the main entrance. He lifted his pillow and, not by coincidence, he had a pistol lying beneath his head. He took out a full cartridge. I saw a golden bullet, which he must have frequently polished. Then he put the cartridge back in and, once again, placed the pistol beneath his pillow.

"Impressive," I said.

"It's better than kicking one's self in the head," he said.

"Who left it for you?"

"Left it? That sounds a bit too generous," he laughed.

"Who is missing it?" I restated my question.

"Nobody anymore. I would be the only one at this point."

Porgess came across the pistol after being transferred from the mayor's bedroom to a hospital, because he developed a blood clot that pressured his lungs, which made the German village doctor nervous. Porgess was placed on a cot next to a fatally wounded SS Hauptsturmführer.

In the German hospital, the captain would polish his pistol and holster next to Porgess. He couldn't sleep because of the pain. He thought no one would notice. The captain kicked the bucket with the revolver in his hand. (The last nail pounded into his coffin was the facts his family had told him: at the end of the war, the world was unrecognizable; two hundred and fifty divisions were in Europe, arrived from the east; they were sharing the world with the Americans; Germany fought and lost to two countries that came out of the war stronger than when they entered—it looked as if they were going to have the main say for the next fifty years. The war changed everything.) Porgess took the pistol out of the captain's hand in the morning. It was still warm. The relatives from Chemnitz didn't come for his belongings until later that evening. Were they wondering who had emptied the leather holster?

The pistol had VATERLAND engraved on it, and the initials FJK (Franz Johanne Kaiser). Porgess showed it to me.

"He had it shot off below the waist," he said. "He had a hole in his belly. He died because of that hole, and because they shot off both of what he had down there. He felt like a sea sponge."

I tried to imagine how Porgess would practice shooting while lying in bed. In the summer of 1945, Europe was full of old German weapons, ammunition, and other military surplus. Adler knew a girl who went out with a boy whose hands were blown up to his wrists by a hand grenade while he was playing with it. (It made the girl crueler than the boy.) Everyone was looking for payback. A weapon always seemed like a good reserve and guarantee. According to Adler, some of the weapons that were found after the war helped several former officers regain their confidence, even though they couldn't even lift a finger during the war.

Two weeks after the doctor placed Porgess in the hospital, complications began. The bullets caused an infection in his chest. The German doctors and nurses in the hospital had experience in dealing with severely wounded patients. Would it have been better for Porgess to have half of his lung removed? His medication was destroying his vessels and his veins. He had a fever. Six weeks later he was feeling better. The German nurses would turn him over every two hours. They would wake him up and help him with whatever he needed. In the meantime, two scars were slowly growing from gunpowder, smoldered rings of skin that were located on his back. It turned out that his shoulder was shattered quite nicely.

The German doctor would never smile, not even to his colleagues or Porgess. It was strange that the first one to smile at him was actually Porgess. One morning, the old doctor visited him and sensed that Porgess was too embarrassed to ask him, because Porgess had no one else to ask.

"You will live, young man," he said. "You must live. You must want to live."

It sounded different in German. That was the last time Porgess saw the village doctor. I guess the doctor didn't want to live. He didn't have to live. Someone said that the doctor was shot in the back on his way out. Perhaps he shot himself. Sometimes the doctor would inject something in his veins that would make him stronger. From the beginning, he seemed as if he had one foot in the grave. Everything must have been eating him up inside.

"No one will ever get used to anything so easily as they do to people dying."

"As long as they're not the ones to go," I laughed.

"We all have to die someday."

"Well, don't rush into it," I said.

"It's like when the weather changes," said Porgess. "Next to us, the nurses would leave the door open to a room where a German girl was lying. During the night she would cry out, 'To the Elbe! To the Elbe!' What was she dreaming about? She was caught and raped by fifteen men: Russians, Tajiks, Ukrainians, Mongolians, Armenians, and Georgians. They made her vagina bulge. Thistle was growing on her literally everywhere, especially in that one area of her body. She was no longer worth it to any of them. She was just bleeding on them. She froze to an iceberg. Finally, someone fished her out. She was torn up inside. She saw the Elbe in her dreams—the water, the ice—either in front of her or behind her. She will probably never have children again."

"The war," I said. "I didn't start it. You didn't start it either."

"Yeah, the war," Porgess agreed. "We didn't start it."

"Absolutely," I said.

"That would be too easy," said Porgess. "When something occurs, I would like to know where the source is and how it sprang. What had to precede? How could everyone be involved by not being involved? It is an invisible essence, like the undercurrent. That woman was afraid to look at herself in the mirror. The nurse would comb her hair every morning and hold a little mirror in front of her, as if it were reflecting questions she didn't want to answer. Perhaps she kept reminding herself of the way she looked before—what she wanted to accomplish in life and where she wanted to accomplish it. And it was probably for the better that her family had not survived to see what had happened to her. I guess she would dream at night about how it used to be: going to school, to dances, and things that she could no longer even consider doing. She was avoiding her friends and those she knew. Who could ever love the likes of her in such a condition? She had to feel like a sunken ship. I began to wonder what songs she probably heard. What songs were sung when she was still untainted?"

I didn't have to ponder over whom Porgess compared himself to perhaps more so than to Adler and myself. I managed to give a weak smile. It occurred to me why Porgess was telling me all this; what linked him to that unknown rape victim from Germany.

"The way that woman would scream throughout the night was contagious, as if it had happened to me," Porgess said. "In the beginning, I was angry at her, because she was waking and disturbing me so that she could always bring attention to herself. Then I began to understand her. During the day she never mentioned a word about it. During the night, it would rage out of her on its own. I have a piece of that German girl within me just as in that German girl there is a piece of me. We don't even know each other's names. Perhaps if I write to the hospital. My nurse's name was Monika Blech. But it's more than likely that we'll never see each other again."

"Probably not," I said. I spoke with no purpose to my words.

"And so I ended up with a crippled woman, who didn't know my name, and we're together all the time, everywhere: when I'd go to the bathroom, when I'd eat soup with a spoon. Every time a song by Marlene Dietrich is played, we revisit each other."

"You mentioned that her vagina was bulging."

"Yeah, it's really hilarious."

A wrinkle of reluctance made a mark on his forehead and around his lips.

"You're probably right," I acknowledged.

"People are strange creatures, that's for sure."

"It's quite a devilish story," I admitted.

"They say the devil is just an angel's older brother, but that's nothing new to you or me. People don't like to blame everything on themselves, so instead they always find someone else to take the heat."

I didn't respond to that. I was thinking about Tanga.

"The third war is raging," Porgess suddenly spoke. "Now it's all about who is going to win, though the war is already over. The Hauptsturmführers will probably cash in on it, if a tank didn't run over their legs or their insides don't look like a sea sponge and they can still serve. Who cares about uniforms? They were given some time from both sides to have a pillow fight, and the best brains and soldiers can even choose the side they want to serve. The rest of them found their paths, either in some cozy place at home in Germany or perhaps in Argentina, Brazil, or Paraguay, and they didn't leave out South Africa, Australia, Syria, and North America. You could bet your life on that. I'm keeping track of what's going on, and I cannot cease to be appalled. In the east, they pin on a different emblem. In the west, they ask for forgiveness and equality for everyone under the shadow of remedy. The truth comes out only when in the west they publicize which general, Gestapo officer, or murderer was rehabilitated in the east. The east, on the other hand, with great enthusiasm, counts the number of miracle weapon inventors, Gestapo colonels, and assorted company who are running freely on the western side of the Elbe. They have scientific cities in Siberia, where German is spoken more than Russian, and America has the El Dorado in rocket production."

"Yeah, I no longer believe that history has ended with me and that everything will be better now," I said.

"It's just another round. It keeps on going even with us on board," Porgess said.

"Yeah."

"For a moment, I actually thought that it would start all over again."

"More like it would continue."

"Just read how many times per day a woman thinks of sex and how many times a man does," Porgess said. "A man in his prime averages a thought every five minutes."

I was observing Porgess's wrinkles. I didn't want to correct him. I guess there were different statistics elsewhere.

"That's a fairly bold statement," I said.

"Should I lose my appetite over so many anti-Semites trying to outdo themselves so they could save the lives of those beasts and warmongers, because they want to save themselves as well?"

"Likewise," I said.

"That would destroy us all," Porgess declared.

"As Erwin Adler would say, 'There is a big difference between a man and a woman. When everything is underlined and summed up, the woman is the one who always complains the most. Why? For nothing.'"

"Do you remember that little brat in fifth grade who got a beating from the boys for no reason at all because he wasn't the brightest light in the harbor? I wasn't too thrilled about joining in, so I threw crumpled pieces of paper against his head. But why? He was slow, always a step behind—different. It bothers me till this very day. I don't believe I have thought of anyone more than that boy. He would always appear before my eyes. That stupid fool who was never capable of answering quickly to anything. I knew not only that I would never do it again, but also that no one would erase it until I was erased along with it. I knew what it was. There is a devil in every one of us, and then you spend the rest of your life ashamed. We have to control ourselves. That is all, we just have to control ourselves. But it will never go away, as long as we're alive, even if we lived for a very long time."

Porgess laughed so that I wouldn't feel the same guilt he did for beating up a retarded kid in a forgotten classroom.

"You know why I'm telling you this, don't you?"

"You're just pouring gas onto a burning fire," I answered.

"I'm not so sure about that. What if some sort of invisible justice existed that, sooner or later, would sum up everything?"

"I wouldn't add that onto the flame either," I said once more.

"Will you be the one to sum it up yourself? If you know what I'm talking about?"

But he never waited for an answer.

I never knew whether this would do any good or bad, as long as this was true. I was afraid that it wouldn't be.

Porgess must have guessed my thoughts, because suddenly he said, "Do you remember the girl from Hagibor, the one with the older brother? She looked as if she really took care of herself and seemed easy to get, but no one could get close to her. Well, she once told me that when her body would start to tease her and she was just about to land some boy in the bushes or the grass, she would close her eyes and do what her brother told her to do: engage in something he, too, would spend his evenings doing to extinguish the flames of his body. Her brother would ask her why she thought she had a fantasy. He told her she could imagine everything that she would have wanted to do as if it had already happened. She should play with her imagination. This was the purpose of fantasy. It was the reason why people were capable of dreaming and imagining anything they didn't have or didn't do as if they did have it or had done it. Fantasy was, for her, a safety net into which she could softly fall. She wanted to be a writer of those romance novels, because her fantasies actually worked. She literally enumerated everything with fantasy, without even touching herself, because her brother and sister convinced her. And you can believe that I know what I'm talking about, because I have to use a lot of fantasy since I'm forced to get along with myself. She told me that a boy didn't have to worry about getting pregnant; such a worry would never leave a girl, not even for a fragment of a second, like a shadow. A girl could lose her virginity only once, and it wasn't only because of what she'd have to carry in her belly for nine months; it was the eighteen years of responsibility for a child who would be born. She told me that I should imagine girls, single mothers, and that I should know that all girls, before they would give themselves to me, would have this thought go through their heads."

"I remember her; she was the girl who claimed she would never blame anything on anyone," I said.

"She looked like a girl who would end up in your bed within an afternoon."

"You're right," I agreed.

"When she was still young, her brothers and older sister would tell her she had the face of a boy, not a girl, but she would be beautiful as a woman. She couldn't wait to grow up. By then, she was already more beautiful than her siblings claimed, a long, thin face like Greta Garbo. Too bad we'll never find out how she would have turned out."

He didn't mention that when she flew up the chimney, she must have been beautiful with her long, thin face, as her older sister had predicted; and that by chance, he managed to talk to her from across the wires that bordered the women's camp, when she told him the Germans were child killers. She never had children of her own. She flew through the chimney as a virgin, though no one would think so, the way she had developed: full breasts, hips, and a maternal smile, a smile that some girls possess, which seems as if it could embrace the whole world, all men and children. She probably thought of how many children she could have had. She had heavy breasts, full of jiggle, before they started to look like two dried melons. Who could have known what her final thoughts were? I always linger over that question of what was happening that final second, and then what was no longer happening. I remembered her well. Her spirit, with her long, thin face, was unfurling above Porgess's bed along with her fantasy.

Porgess was looking at my shoes. They were carefully polished. They were shining as Black Pepe once described it, "like the balls of a dog." I always liked the luster of a polished pair of shoes, before the war and after, even during the war, whenever it was possible.

"That's quite an arsenal you have there," I said, retreating to the topic of the gun with which Porgess was playing. He was aiming the muzzle sometimes toward me, sometimes toward himself, toward the ceiling, and toward the bed.

"She's an insurance policy," Porgess said.

"It's better than nothing," I admitted.

"She's quite heavy."

"A perfect piece of work. A real killer. You can't beat the Germans in such things."

I didn't tell him it wasn't worth the admiration because I didn't believe it myself. (In Hagibor, Porgess once told me that it seemed as if I admired only the things that I could criticize, sort of like a Renate Oschler-Salus turned inside out.) I liked having a revolver at home after the war, despite the laws and regulations, orders, and punishment, yet seeing one in Porgess's hand did not thrill me so much. It was all linked to the old German doctor to whom, in the end, Porgess probably wished the best gift of all, a normal death. He already knew that life and death were a gift, and what existed in between. From the age of fourteen through seventeen, he would accumulate experiences that some would need a thousand years to amass. I imagined the German doctor, the way he would stand in the corner of the hospital room, with his head lowered forward, as if he had just matured at the age of eighty. (The same way Porgess connected with the German girl in the hospital room next to his, I suddenly connected with the German doctor who had one foot in the grave, without even meeting him personally, before someone shot him in the back for saving the life of a Jewish boy.) By then, Porgess had already known that every war looks like all wars, and why after this war every peace would bear the child of a war, without the next generation being able to change a thing. It was obvious that the image of the hunched doctor, who after six years was the first person to speak to Porgess in German without evoking terror, was engraved in my memory. (Under normal circumstances, someone having a conversation with him in German would probably flatter him.) He realized that, for the first time after the war, he was wishing the best to someone born from a German mother, in spite of what had happened. Despite all this, did he have a pistol under his pillow to answer the most unrevealed of his questions: to be or not to be? According to Adler, a person should have a revolver either to shoot from or . . . I was looking around at the pictures and the decorations on the walls.

"Hitler was a fool," I said suddenly.

"Absolutely," Porgess smiled, "a fool and a genius, an idealist and a pervert. I heard that he was once offered three German actresses to enjoy, but two of them shot themselves because they saw him lying on the rug, wanting them to piss on him and crying that he wasn't born to satisfy a woman. He could only rule a country."

"Yeah."

"No one can ever push you in the mud, place you on a wooden pillar, and give you a hundred lashes with a whip or send you to the showers and then make glue out of you."

"You can bet on that," I said.

He owned a pistol and, suddenly, he had a thousand years within each of his blue eyes, in addition to the last five or six years as well as the one final year after the war had ended. (Yesterday, when Adler and I were at the circus, he heard about a young boy who was shot somewhere in Silesia. He was on a bridge covered with the bodies of dead Germans, and he ended up dead in the middle of a bridge, in no-man's-land, among the bodies of dead Germans.)

Porgess knew how to watch and listen carefully, and he never forgot a single thing. Just as for so many people, for Porgess, the war never ended and never could end. If someone wanted the meaning of infinity explained to them, then they should have asked Porgess.

"Do you think that it's a defeat when somebody ends themselves?" Porgess added.

"In some tribes, I once read, they do it to each other in the blink of an eye, even children, and no one is surprised by it."

I tried to keep my voice from trembling. I had a knot in my throat. I didn't want this to show, and so I didn't let it.

"But there is no victory in it," I answered slowly and nonchalantly. "Perhaps it brings relief, but only for one person." I smiled, though I really didn't feel like doing so. "Surely you're not going to let those who prepared a feast for you scrape the bones off your plates and then throw them in the garbage?"

"Don't tell me that you do the dishes at home. What else did you read?"

"That Eskimos offer their women to their guests."

"Did you also read that a turtle has to live twenty to fifty years before it can breed for the first time?"

"Yeah, and how long a cat is pregnant before she gives birth to her litter?"

"Three weeks."

"And an elephant?"

"Two years. Twenty-four months."

"Are you testing me?"

"And you, me?"

"How long is a horse pregnant?"

"How long do you think?"

"I happen to know," I said as I remembered Tanga. "Eleven months."

Porgess's blanket slid off of him. He no longer bothered to mention the things a revolver could replace for him. I noticed his legs, two sticks completely without muscles. He had strength only in his arms and the muscle that lay behind his forehead.

"I heard that you finally popped the question."

"Yeah, finally."

Porgess already knew about Belle, Hana Kaudersová, my wife, though I wasn't sure whether he knew about the details. We were at that moment on the same wavelength, yet we were on ten different ones as well. Porgess's eyes were sometimes weary and sometimes alert.

For a moment he looked as if he were half asleep and vice versa, as if he were a dying man who could see like an eagle and whose cognition was fast and clear. We didn't have to play hide-and-seek with each other. The world was full of ruins and old weapons that could still be used.

"Everything that was drastic has already happened," I said. "Perhaps it will happen again, but right now, luckily, it isn't."

"A bed is a beautiful thing. The first thing you see and the last. Before, I had to go and visit someone. Now, when someone wants to see me, he has to put in the effort and come on his own. It's never too crowded, but never too empty for long. I can kick anyone out, but no one can kick *me* out. When the other party gets tired, I rest. All you need to do is listen when others talk or talk when others ask in order to seem properly mysterious. It's a lot of fun. Any old fool can put on an expression that would save you, if only they knew how to save themselves."

Something overcame the both of us. Perhaps I shouldn't have spoken. It would have been better for him to speak about it himself. Porgess could read my thoughts and I could read his. I simply could not speak for him, as he could not speak for me.

"She's a bitch," Porgess said to his pistol. "Her heart and insides are made of cold steel. She will arrange without a drop of love and passion what only a few have the privilege to receive. She can sleep with me. She doesn't have to declare her love to me, and I don't have to declare my love to her. We have a mutual understanding of love and passion and reason. You don't have to worry—a barrel is just a barrel and nothing else. One can think about a lot in a relationship with her. I can bargain with her. I sometimes ask her: Are you sad? You're not murdering anymore, you're not threatening anyone, you're not cornering or blackmailing anyone. You're taking care of my beauty rather than my safety. You're capable of killing with or without a cause, but it doesn't depend on you. It depends on whose hand is holding you. You always come to me on time. You're ready to do anything I want: like scratch me on the ass. You keep me company when I don't have any guests."

"It was a good thing you took it from that captain," I said. I lied as much as I could.

He let me turn everything inside out. Porgess had the touch of something or perhaps of everything that was unobtainable and incomprehensible, and, at the same time, he maintained the rest of his philosophy from the time he was fifteen. It was in those days Porgess accepted decadence in the same manner as L.L., from a distance, with an apathetic expression toward everything that seemed horrific and disgusting, everything that was beyond normal. We lived with a condescending sigh for what the Germans were and what they wanted to be, in both Prague and elsewhere, and with a passion for the land of jazz and swing. Of course, in those days, like Little Narcissus, Porgess would confuse the struggle to accomplish something with craziness or, like L.L., he would mistake unruliness and debauchery with openness and courage. Did it come back to him in the form of the ability and disability of his body, plans, and actions? Or perhaps in a form of inability to do what would otherwise seem logical if he weren't lying in bed? I was looking out the window upon the full colors of the trees, flowers, bushes, and grass. His father or mother probably planted some tomatoes along the fence. Some looked as if they were overripe.

"Even in bed you can outrun anyone."

"Sure."

"And hold your own ground when someone thinks that the destiny of a man is a formula from nursery school."

"Sure."

"You don't have to be an athlete to run to the finish line."

"Of course."

"Did it ever occur to you what the difference is between the sluggishness of a snail and death?" Porgess asked laughing, with the pistol in his hand. "What's the matter?" he added, as if he were fifteen again.

Porgess possessed something darker than death, something suave as well. I was angry with myself that I would end up adding and subtracting him the whole time. It wouldn't help him even if he had a machine gun with ammunition belts over his shoulders (if he could carry them). He would have had to believe in spiritualism, and so would I, in order for his body to rise and begin floating. It occurred to me what was happening to Porgess, from the end to the beginning. (Including the time when he was eleven and joined with the other boys to beat up a mentally slower boy.) I remember how he used to play cards in the Cellar, in the Achermanc, and in the Café Nizza. How he would worry about what he was going to wear. He could never again sit in a chair with a backrest toward the table, with his legs spread out to face the whims of Lady Luck. He could only examine his hands so that they wouldn't be dirty before he put the cards in them. A great memory was probably the only thing that was left for him. But what comes back can be encouraging on one hand and devastating on the other. He remembered the words that someone once mentioned, and where and when they were said, though they had been long forgotten by the rest of the world. He even remembered the name of the last guardsman from the Jewish police unit in Theresienstadt, also known as Ghetto Wache, and the retired Jewish captain of one of the German submarines during the First World War, who couldn't shake off the superstitious respect for the ancient German pillars of the Reich, which both made us laugh and cry at the same time. (They sent him to the east when he organized, without permission, in the fortress, a parade of the Ghetto Wache, so that they would march like German units. Eventually the Nazis, at headquarters, forbade them to sleep more than two in one room and to carry wooden clubs.)

Porgess must have had quite an experience in the German hospital. The Hauptsturmführer's aunt said what Porgess would later remember: "People will realize one day that Fritz was not such a bad person." Then, with his own ears, he heard her mention that Hitler was not entirely wrong.

"This one idiot, in a cot from the other side of my bed, told me when Germany was on its knees that all that had happened was a misunderstanding. The gas chambers were only an experiment to convert people to the proper religion, which, in our case, was unsuccessful for the past nineteen centuries. We were the chosen ones, he said, and now we are not. Others have long been chosen. He meant himself and his *Volskgenosse*. I would stare at him to see how he became, unlike me, a chosen one. His own tank cut his legs off while it was backing up. He was writing a long letter to the Vatican. I didn't bother to question whether he wanted to ask the pope something or whether he wanted to give the Holy Father some advice. He was a murderer, but also a religious man."

"What did you say to these comments?" I asked.

"I started to pity him, but only because his legs were run over. I told him that I even pitied myself. That he probably understood."

The Hauptsturmführer's mother was a widow. But she managed to remarry during her son's stay in the hospital. She married another SS man. His hearing was very poor. He would mainly speak about a soldier's honor. A lost war meant a loss of land, matériel, manpower, and soldiers' honor. It could be erased only by the next war, the closest battlefield. If they couldn't save Germany, then they should have destroyed everything beyond Germany that could be destroyed. As if they could or hadn't already done so, wherever they had the chance. They should take his word for it. They would not remain empty and silent for long. One day, the victor's units would disperse. The enemy would split into opposite camps. Once again, all would be dependent on who was stronger, faster, more capable, even though it would no longer be determined by quantity or size of territory. Readiness was everything. A long arm span meant nothing. The enemy had too many positions to hold, and one day it would take just a little to destroy a lot. *Sieg Heil!* At the end, victory would be theirs. And what was he afraid of? The lost war meant that his son, even his grandson, without even knowing, could marry a half-breed, a quarter, eighth, sixteenth of a Jew. No one would keep vigil over undesired grandmothers. Such a union would no longer be possible to erase. In peace, a person could no longer take such a monster by the throat and strangle it. The widow gave him a look, because she didn't know who was lying in the hospital and who was listening. And she was right. There was no use in trying to tell him anything because he could not hear, and since they just got engaged, she didn't want to destroy their marriage with confrontations. But even she didn't like the old German doctor. Her new husband was of the opinion that he himself would be willing to place a noose around the neck of people like the doctor in order to teach them a lesson about how to express their Jew-loving minds. He was willing to do this to his own father, son, and grandson, as Hitler did when the relatives of the participants in the assassination against him had to watch their loved ones hang on a thin wire, and as they filmed the executions to discourage potential candidates from committing treason.

"That was how we ceased to understand each other without even engaging in a conversation," Porgess said. "She would claim to the nurse, when she thought that I was asleep or unconscious, that Hitler didn't know everything. He never signed anything that might incriminate him. He was not guilty of the worst atrocities. He had no idea of the horrible bestialities that took place. Soon after he had poisoned and shot himself, when they rolled him up in a rug in front of the Berlin bunker and set his body on fire, so that his teeth were the only thing left to recognize on him, they secured him a status of immortality. An immortality that only the martyrs and the butchers of history have; but only in the eyes of such ladies as the captain's mother. She would have liked to see, as she accosted the nurse, another leader who would manage to stabilize the mark and give every German worker, farmer, soldier, or bureaucrat a job. She asked the nurse to show her a Führer who would wash away a humiliation, such as Versailles, off the body of the nation. She wished for all Germans, those yet to be born, a will like his. She had a purse made from crocodile hide, and it had to represent something, because she would caress that old skin as if it were some good luck charm or as if it were someone or something strange about which only she knew. She got it from the Hauptsturmführer when he returned from general headquarters. It didn't bother her that it was most likely a purse taken away from some smelly Jew. Then she claimed that he should have kept cracking his whip and everything would have ended differently. 'His will was granite,' the angry widow would say as she kept pestering the nurse. 'He never feared anything. He never looked back, never regretted a thing. Now they had to deal with those demons on their own. He didn't make a clown out of himself, and he didn't grit his teeth as nowadays everyone does. He kept his dignity and the respect of others until the last second, without making faces and throwing himself into the mud like some dried-up senile doctors from the old school.'"

"Nobody understands these types, but I don't know whether that is good or bad," I said.

"The relatives who visited the Hauptsturmführer looked down upon the German doctor before he died. The SS man who married his mother spit on the floor. 'You pig,' he muttered under his breath, and he wiped his phlegm on the ground with the bottom of his shoe. The old lady told him not to spit on the ground like somebody in France or in Russia, and that the doctor would be insulted and that wasn't good for her son, since the old man was taking care of her little boy. 'Sepp, you should apologize!' she said. He never apologized to anyone, he said. It was his principle never to apologize. Never! Under no circumstances! Never to look back. And then he said, '*Damals in Krakau.*' Those days in Krakow . . . It's in their blood."

Porgess continued, "When they told the SS man, who married the captain's mother, that I was there lying in bed but I was getting worse, he muttered, 'So we didn't . . . enough of them.' I put two and two together with what he had said before—*damals in Krakau* . . . He served in the Kraftfahrschule, where the loading trucks were located. He never dared to mention the words 'Auschwitz-Birkenau' or 'Gleiwitz.' That all was *damals in Krakau,* when he served in the Kraftfahrschule. He thought that I was sleeping and didn't hear him, or he just didn't care."

Finally, Porgess said, "They lost the war, but he still believed that they were the chosen race. They. Him. *Sepp.* The old woman. The Hauptsturmführer told him that it was an *alles vernichtenden Krieg,* an all-destroying war. Yeah, they sure could look at themselves in the mirror. And I really didn't care much for them looking at me."

"My eyes are still sore when I think about this," I said.

"The Hauptsturmführer would babble in his sleep, something about him being in school again, and his teacher would give him a problem to solve. There were a hundred people on a ship far out in the ocean. If one person would be sacrificed, ninety-nine would survive. What would he do? Without discussion. He would not search for a solution for himself; he wanted a yes or no response. He liked it more when someone else came up with a solution for him. He was arguing with someone in his hallucinations. He would scream out loud, 'I'll show you! I'll break you!' Probably he was saying it to some woman. Then he would scream, 'You partisan slut! Old crows should stick to their own kind.' He screamed the morals of the Third Reich, about motherhood and women with twelve children for the army, the regular jargon. An order solved everything for him, only it didn't give him back his legs. He was bound to what his environment recognized. He would dream that he was making a triangle out of dots. It had some kind of strategic military significance, I never could make anything of it."

Porgess slowly took a deep breath. He could feel the pressure weighing on his chest. He continued, "He thought that I was asleep and he would begin to talk about race. He would say, 'They would get more and more audacious, and now they're all dead. They would arrive already dead, even before they were unloaded from the box-cars. I saw it with my own eyes. *Damals in Krakau.* You can believe me, I know what I'm talking about. Those who were still alive would mate for the last time: the chosen and the reprobated. They didn't care if they had witnesses. They did it as if it were the lower and higher multiplication table. He would also say, 'Wasn't it their destiny? An end to monstrosity. Horror! Have they not begged for it themselves?' Finally, I didn't leave my eyes open or closed, so that he could recognize that I wasn't sleeping, but that he no longer interested me. I could only ask later, when they all left, because it was past visiting hours, how could it get this far? We end up wishing death to the others—only death, nothing more and nothing less. Neither you nor I pushed it, except for the fact that it landed where we are now."

"It's possible," I confirmed.

It occurred to me what he had just said: people after a three- or five-day trip to Auschwitz-Birkenau would still make love for the last time. Of course it was true. Some were dying and some were embracing themselves. Perhaps it was because they didn't know where they were going, or perhaps it was they knew precisely where they were headed. Someone once said that in a spasm or in hysteria and primordial terror people would begin to make love, even in the dark, down in the underground dressing room next to the gas chamber or even inside the chamber. What if they did? It occurred to me soon after, as if someone asked a question that Porgess wanted to explain.

In Buchenwald, where we both had the honor to reside, as well as Adler, the inheritors of the concentration camps used the facilities to get even with nearly thirteen thousand ex-Nazis. Even though we never pitied them, there was something destructive about the whole scene. Buchenwald was placed in a beautiful landscape. It was on the hill where the Germans favored shooting people in the back of the head (and where it was paid back after the war). On one side the SS had extreme luxury and on the other side the prisoners were barely living. It was all so close to each other.

ARNOŠT LUSTIG

"If the Nazis were the lowest of the low," Porgess said, "how can we define what followed after them? And what will come after them, when on the Buchenwald hill they'll be selling roasted bratwurst on slices of bread?"

"A lot of mass graves will be found," I said.

"We'll all end up being archaeologists," Porgess said laughing.

The room was full of light, and I felt the darkness seeping out of Porgess, except for the fact that Porgess wasn't the one and only source of the darkness into which we were born. He ranked his pistol in the category of the cheapest whores but, at the same time, one of the most expensive ones. She linked him to the Hauptsturmführer from the German hospital, his aunt, his mother, and the captain's new stepfather; and if she couldn't keep silent she would link them together like an echo.

"People usually want something from you that they don't have; something that no one has," said Porgess.

"Do you mean men or women?"

"Whatever you like."

"That would be hell on earth," I said with a sneering smile.

"I have an article from the newspaper here. The former concentration camp Sachsenhausen near Berlin was passed into the hands of the secret service NKVD. Fifty mass graves were discovered there. They were twenty-three feet long, eleven feet deep. According to the Badenburg Bureau, approximately twelve thousand five hundred people lost their lives, among them old men, women, and children. It was hard to determine how they died. Nothing could be ruled out. So, as you can see, one camp can serve the purposes of both sides very well. No one had to rebuild anything. They just took over the facilities the way they were."

"Can you give me something else on women and men?"

Suddenly all the spilt blood was with us, no matter where it came from, whether from one side or the other. The last day of the war. And besides linking us together, it was linking one Hauptsturmführer with another Hauptsturmführer, and both of them to all the Hauptsturmführers who were in Germany and who were yet to come. For a moment, Porgess's eyes were sad. I pretended not to see them in that state.

Porgess still had enough time to realize what can weaken a man and then completely destroy him. But I wasn't sure whether Porgess would lessen these burdens with his famous "What's the matter?" as he liked to say when he was fifteen. And also, he had enough time to realize what determines things, in the end, even though at the time they don't seem so determinate. He went over everything that he saw, heard, and felt in life, the way it progressed, one after another and backward and a hundred times over again. The weaker his body was, the more determinate he was toward himself.

He had a hole inside, a hole that could never be replenished. It was the indemnity that occurred. Did he dream, like many of us, about a time when no one would kill without punishment? What brought back the humiliation, as if it had never disappeared? In reality, it never disappeared. It could only be condemned, because a person would defend himself against it, even though he could not stand on his own two feet.

"I feel like that clock on the old Jewish town hall on Maislová Street," Porgess added.

I imagined the two clocks. A face with regular numbers was located above and below, another face with Hebrew letters, with hands that went backward from left to right. Porgess transferred all this into his head and everything moved straight ahead, and at the same time it would return backward, where it already once was.

"Yeah," I answered carefully. "It's either moving too fast or too slow. And your head is banging like bells in the tower."

"Until the spring breaks," he said sneering.

I noticed Porgess. He was like that smallest particle of something greater, somewhat like a grain of sand in the desert, a drop of water in the sea. And I noticed the way he would look at the clock that rushed him forward with every second we were together, and at the same time rushed him back to where he began, back to something that he already knew. It was a component of every word, thought, every yes and every no; a component of something that kept growing and simultaneously disintegrating; something that was being born and simultaneously dying; an essence of all that crossed over to another side or perhaps even didn't cross over, and yet it created the tangible out of the intangible; something only nature could do to man or only man could do to other men. I felt this essence that was destroying Porgess's being so slowly, though somewhat faster than my own minuscule self. I felt that as it was destroying Porgess, it was destroying everything and everyone, or at least a great part of everything and everyone. It was a second, a split of a second, a small fragment of Porgess's and my dual time by which it strengthened and weakened, encouraged and deceived, and sought revenge like an echo that created a lie out of the truth, hope out of hopelessness. I was noticing my spine. Was I convincing myself that the bullet actually hit Porgess's spine and not mine? I would bet my life on the fact that what that idiot did to Porgess he also did to me for the rest of my life, figuratively and literally. Yes and no. Fortunately? Unfortunately? I knew that he crippled me just as he crippled Porgess, even though only figuratively. He crippled all the healthy people, including the ones yet to be born.

Porgess put his revolver back under his pillow. He fixed his pillow from behind his back. The revolver was close by. Where were Porgess's golden curls that had made him look like a girl? I remembered how he would dress like he was straight out of a magazine. He would always look the best out of us boys, even if he were only wearing a potato sack. An image of Porgess dying suddenly came over me for a second, quietly, like when someone pours out water.

"That raped and tainted woman from the German hospital, for God knows what reason, reminds me of the women from Ravensbrück who were experimented on by doctors. They would infect them with gangrene, which was caused by the gasses in the battlefields, and then they would grate their bones and wait to see what happened. But when I say 'reminds me,' it never has a beginning or an end. All I have to do is look at a forest, a road, or an injection needle and you would not believe what it brings back. Sometimes I look through this . . ."

From under his bed, he took out a pole that had strings and a movable mirror on the top and on the bottom of it, like a tiny periscope. He angled them both accordingly. I saw what Porgess could observe, if he wanted to. Then he put the pole and the mirror back under the bed.

"Not even the worst taste has a law against it," I said. "They'll have a lot of problems in Germany with that."

"The only thing I have to do is wipe my mirrors, so that I don't look at the world through a dirty glass."

"Of course," I agreed.

I never saw a dirty thing on him; even in school, he had immaculate fingernails. He smelled good and always looked clean. What did it matter that he didn't grow up in poverty like the boys in Belgická 24? He knew how to behave. He never ruined any fun. He would show me pictures that would make my head spin and my blood flow from my brain to my waist. He was driven by a logic of numbers and stellar objects. His father urged him to consider that having enough of everything didn't necessarily mean having enough truth within oneself. He taught his son that the law was morality and morality was the law, but then later such rules didn't apply. Porgess saw how wrong his father was. He was liked everywhere, and everyone would invite him to come again. (Little Narcissus always envied him for this.) Once someone asked why he liked his father so much. He responded that it was because, even in a room full of people, his father always knew the most about everything. (Except, of course, for the things about which his father knew only very little.)

Porgess's cards lay beside his bed, along with cutouts from German newspapers and anti-Jewish reading books, Rosenberg's *The Myth of the Twentieth Century*. Under the bed, there were three thick volumes of Robert Briffault's *Mothers*, a book about everything that a person could discover about his origin through the development of the woman. It occurred to me what Porgess wanted to gain from the cards. He had a bed, but he only could use his hands. Would he play with himself, against himself? What would he look forward to when his cards and his numbers would work out for him? Here, he had a comfortable pigsty—old newspapers and books with pages folded in the upper corners to mark passages to which he wanted to come back.

"The cards are in your blood," I said

"And what about you?"

"I guess my luckiest of all is the number eight, but I don't quite know why," I said.

"It is an infinitive number or it is the number of infinity. It is also the number of justice. For some people, it represents reconciliation, solution, and conflict. Anything that is added by the number eight or that comes out even in combination as the number eight is good, or at least it can't be or doesn't have to be bad. Only when you slice an eight from top to bottom will you have two threes facing one another. Do you know the one when two zeroes meet an eight and the one zero says to the other, 'Look how that bitch got thin in the waist?'"

"I see that you haven't given up," I continued to lie.

"Sure, everything is still the same," said Porgess.

By structure and by comfort, Porgess's bed reminded me of the iron baskets that bricklayers and road workers used to keep warm. I was guessing what Porgess made of this realm that rendered both its frame and its discomfort. What had he been missing since he was fifteen? What could he only distance himself from? He had twenty-four hours a day to figure it out. What was in his dreams? Was he boxing, playing tennis or volleyball? And once again, was he first in everything? Or perhaps he was boxing and pushing his opponent into the ropes with punches made of shadows, before the referee raised his arm. What sort of gong did he hear? What did he think of luck? He was up against a maliciousness he could only fight alone. Porgess was emerging and submerging into inner darkness. He was dissolving into waters that were pouring here, around him, and into him, from all seasons and places, and they were creating, out of his body, his thoughts, his room, and everything, a basin that was about to burst. Nothing was happening. He just laid there. I felt magnetic fields in which waves of energy were prevailing and igniting a storm. I could easily put myself in his skin.

The sun was piercing through the window from outside. I heard the sound of birds. I understood that all of Porgess's principles had failed, even though Porgess himself had never failed. Luckily, cowardly thoughts last only a fragment of a second. Both Porgess and I knew that there was a dual time that fit everything, and everything was simultaneously next to everything else: water and fire, silence and screams. Who needed two clocks? All the principles of calculating probability were too small in comparison to the two bullets that penetrated Porgess's spine. The Hauptsturmführer must have known that it was the last day of the war, that he would not get an iron cross with an oak sprig and a sword with diamonds for killing Porgess. Within an hour or two, for decades, even centuries, Germany would be different; divided into pieces, under surveillance, as long as memory serves generations yet to come. And it would be different when reunited, because there was something known as the memory of Europe, or the memory of the world. What ordered him to stop the escape of one prisoner out of twenty million prisoners of Germany, even in the last minute?

We both looked at each other. In my mind, I saw myself, instead of Porgess, lying on a low bed with a spine shattered by a bullet. I glanced at my cards. The radio was playing quietly in the background the entire time. On the short waves, he heard about the incoming and outgoing tide in Australia; about underwater earthquakes that occurred somewhere on the ocean floor, where the city of Atlantis was supposedly located; about the mountains of ice along the Falklands; about the status of the water level on the Czech rivers. He would collect newspaper articles that spoke about the mission of our paratroopers and the assassination of the police general, Reinhard Heydrich. He had them in two separate piles: one where they commended this action, and the other where they condemned it. And a conclusion? It caused too much unnecessary blood. Porgess sensed the ancient conflict within a man: to defend or not to defend oneself. To him, it seemed too easy to disembowel the matter. Silver A and Silver B. Everyone was already dead. They could no longer participate. Certain things would never be explained. They would probably still sparkle in the next ten thousand years.

Besides these things, he also had a pamphlet about the harems in Turkey and the eunuchs in China. Was he interested in the eunuchs? There are three types. Did they still maintain their desire? Their hair falls off, their voices change, and then they grow fat. Their memories grow weaker, they sleep poorly, and they are shortsighted. They enjoy money to treat themselves to candies, perfumes, and pastries. They love music and dance, and they secretly crave revenge. They are allowed to marry, and sometimes that which was so essential grows back. (Really?)

On one pile of books, Porgess had copies of Lermontov, Pushkin, Dostoyevsky, and other books that carried names such as Chekhov,

Andreyev, and Whitman. A bit farther away, the name Hermann Hesse was printed on the binding.

"You must be fairly well read," I said.

"Do you think that I'm such a fool to be reading about aristocracy?" Porgess answered with a question. "I study their patterns of gambling. There are three systems: the French, the English, and the Russian. The French implement passion and reason. The English— logic and cold blood. With the Russians, the cards are playing with them rather than vice versa. I'm studying Russian roulette. Where did it come from? In the czar's army, they took more heed to it than to maneuvers. It was the proper etiquette. They must have been extremely pompous and bored, but I can't say that they invented it themselves."

"You're really living it up," I said. "Adler took all the fun out of Russian roulette when he calculated that the chance of getting a bullet was one out of a thousand. The key to the problem was the weight of the bullet—that is, if you are dealing with a six-round revolver. And after you put the bullet in and spin the cartridge—sometimes you do spin it three times, sometimes up to nine—so that no one could remember where the bullet lay, in which position, even if they had the greatest memory of all time. But, according to the theory, which Adler dug up from somewhere, the weight of the bullet drives the cartridge downward, so the bullet is usually below and not ready to kill at the same level as the nozzle. Perhaps there is some truth in this theory."

"Perhaps there is, but, regardless, it still remains a dangerous game."

He looked up all sorts of statistics and came to the conclusion that, perhaps it was not one against a thousand, but, rather, one against good old-fashioned luck.

"They play it out of boredom. I guess life never had as much value to them as it did, for instance, for the French or the English. Mother Russia is what they value more than their individual lives. After all, they can enjoy themselves any way they please. According to Freud, from the day of birth, everyone carries the craving to exist and the craving to destroy oneself. Not everyone was made to aggravate the hormones and graze the abdomen. In some, the adrenaline just rises up to the heights, and in others it's just a small stimulus."

We changed the topic.

"Don't forget, most of my life, I was the victim of Bobby Mahler on Belgická Street 24. He really made my blood boil."

Then he said, "Do you remember when Leon the Bald would say that I looked like Freddie Bartholemew from *David Copperfield*? During the war, he served as a mechanic on one of those B-17 flying fortresses."

Who knows what was circling in Porgess's head? What rationale had he used in terms of himself and his parents? He never spoke of it.

"They have other games," he said. "They take crates with twelve champagne bottles, uncork them, and put cyanide in one. Then they call a servant and order him to pour each of them a bottle and everyone has to drink, bottoms up. In another game, one of them enters a dark room blindfolded with a pistol in his hand. Another keeps him company with his eyes uncovered. Then, the lights come on. The first one has to shoot the other one in three shots. If he misses, they switch. You're allowed to walk on all fours. You have a minute for each shot."

"They can prove that hearing is more important than sight," I said.

"In America, the students have a game: the Prince of Wales. In this game, life is not at stake; perhaps only by alcohol poisoning, and this would sometimes occur. On a certain day, they meet at a house that usually belongs to one of the married students or a professor where, with the exception of fellow students and certain ladies, no one is permitted to enter. It all begins in the afternoon, and a winner is proclaimed in the later hours. After an initiation ritual, they gather around the table and one of them calls a number. The other has to repeat it and add his own. That's how it continues all the way around. Whoever makes a mistake has to drink a shot or a pint of beer. The game continues with new numbers that one person records, so that no one argues. Most of the players are drunks and have a memory for numbers. The list has up to twenty or even more numbers. As the game continues, the players become more rowdy, audacious, and profound. You're allowed to stay in the game as long as you don't fall down like a log. Puking is permitted, though not in the room. Then you're allowed to return to the table and continue. At this phase of the game, people can stand by and watch. This is the point when just a few of the players are still remaining. The rest are lying on the floor, the couches, and so on. Guests may indulge in champagne, ham sandwiches, and cheese. Girls are also allowed to join. The guests dance and socialize and avoid the fallen brothers on the floor. A girl once won this game. Her name was Sheila and she would travel from coast to coast. She would make the others drink to near death. Apparently she was fat and ugly, but she earned respect among the men because she could drink them under the table. It was supposed to look really ugly. The interesting part of it was that the smartest and the most diligent students participated to demonstrate how stupid they were capable of looking. It was a ritual in which they could prove their masculinity."

All I did was clear my throat. Why do people in different parallels and continents of the world beg for condemnation and destruction when they are threatened by nothing? I was waiting for Porgess to say something else. Did he want to keep vigil over such things in all parts of the world?

"It had to come from somewhere. The more people are on this planet, the less they value life, and it will never be different," said Porgess. "Like ants, flies, or grasshoppers, but don't ask me about the way it was when there were just a few of us around. In those days, why would the rabbis say 'Go and multiply'? Nowadays, they would probably think it over. Just look at how many Chinese we have; so many that they're afraid to save another man's life. They have a proverb that says anyone who saves a man will later be robbed, injured, or even killed by that man. Have you read about what the Japanese are called nowadays? 'Economic beasts.' They don't have to build an army, and you'll still live to see great surprises."

"It's all just a bunch of bullshit," I said carefully.

"When it comes to bullshit, I just keep seeing it pile higher and higher," Porgess said. "So I read that Herzl, that self-proclaimed Jewish king in Poland, announced that anti-Semites were right in almost everything they said about you and me. He made up the term "Zionism," so that both of us could be converted. And for this pur-pose, we have to have our own country. And in this country, as much as possible, we have to convert children, especially our own. We have to give them a chance to convert. Both the Jews and the Germans in reality are dangerous—just as they are dangerous to the entire world because they constantly want to change that world. Another bunch of crock was that the Germans began to believe that you could barely spot a Wehrmacht soldier in the camps, even with a magnifying glass. Someone in Germany was now cleaning the slate. They claimed that if the Wehrmacht in Poland and in Russia were in on it, they were lured in by SS, but they never were directly involved in the Nazi crimes, unless maybe by entering the foreign territories, as if this, itself, wasn't a crime. I have a document stating how before Plan Barbarossa, the Oberkommando of the Wehrmacht, General Wagner, made an agreement with Heidrich. Then the Wehrmacht and the Einsatzgruppen collaborated, hand in hand, as they shot to death one and a half million people. Along with the SS mobile killing units, their intelligence service provided important information and material. Without the Wehrmacht, the SS would have lost a sea of valuable time and many people would still be alive. We can't say that no one within the Wehrmacht ever raised any objections. However, it never happened during the war and perhaps only occasionally before the war. The Germans are devilishly dangerous, I'll tell you that. As I always say, the Jews and the Germans are dangerous by being stupid."

"I tell you it's all a bunch of crap," I repeated, but my voice was directing the conversation elsewhere. "You're slowly but surely becoming more like Erwin Adler. Adler, on the other hand, believed that a drowned man resurfaces three times before he sinks to the bottom, and you'll never be able to convince him otherwise."

"Adler always had an addiction to water," Porgess took over. "In this regard we're similar."

"He still hasn't come to his senses, but nowadays he's into beer. He believed in the orphanage on Belgická Street 24 that the more water he drank, the faster he would grow, and that when his stomach shrunk, he was more elegant and handsome. You're not going to teach me how to know Adler, are you? You have a good memory. Adler would drink water from the latrine in Auschwitz-Birkenau. Everyone else would have gotten typhus. Besides this, he believed that lightning could never hit the same place twice, and that he had a magic twig within himself, with which he could find water that would not make him sick. He's on good terms with water."

I picked up a book.

"That's Knulp," said Porgess. "It's about a tramp who didn't know what to do with his freedom or what to do about dying. At the end, he developed a guilty conscience that ate him inside out. He was terrified of how little would be left of him, of what he could have done for himself and for others, but he never did, and of what he did wrong. He left an illegitimate child somewhere. It was printed on bad paper. I heard that the book will be printed on glass."

"You're really well informed," I said.

"I have a lot of time. My education is so minuscule that I discover something every day."

"That's good," I said. "It's the same with me."

"Everything that a person experiences will make him a killer—in theory or in practice, but it's the same."

"The worst thing is to blame yourself for something that you didn't do, or something that you're not."

"No, the worst thing is to allow others to decide for you. How often do people ask you why it was that you survived?"

"I quote Einstein to them: 'Imagination is more important than knowledge.' In time, I could have imagined what they had lined up for me, as could everyone. You know the way it was. You know I'm not going to tell them that I'm living because someone else was killed instead of me."

He had the latest copies of *We Shall Return!* and the *Jewish Post*. They were writing about Mr. H. from Ruthenia who, in 1943 in Auschwitz-Birkenau, took a book of prayer from the hand of his brother and handed him a piece of bread instead. He stomped the book into the mud and pointed toward the chimneys to show his brother the smoke that was rising from them. How could he pray to a God who was allowing the Nazis to kill children? He couldn't understand. His brother punched him in the mouth. He had a stream of tears coming out of his eyes. It was flooding his brain like the high tide. He couldn't understand that without faith he was more fragile than fragility itself."

"You have to read Weininger," Porgess said.

"Who is he?"

"An Austrian, a fag, and a Jew who committed suicide at the age of thirty-two. He declared that all people were a mixture of both a woman and a man. According to him, a woman was no more than sexuality. It was up to her historical basis whether she enjoyed it or not. He claimed that a woman was a mixture of a mother and a whore. People had to decide between the male and the female entities within themselves. The ideal scenario was to get rid of your own sexuality."

"That reminds me of someone," I said.

"It reminds me of a lot of people," Porgess said. "It must have tortured him greatly."

"Who isn't tortured by something nowadays?" I asked, in general.

Porgess began to think out loud. "He came to the conclusion that he could rid himself of sex only if he killed himself."

"If a person can choose."

"Some people never do."

"Yeah," I said, so that even this would not seem so hopeless. As the Japanese would say, kind words can keep you warm all winter. Porgess had that old flood in his eyes, as well as patience that would change places with impatience; passion, which he held on to, because otherwise he would vanish in the air like steam; lamentation, which turned all apologies into aggravating circumstances; desire, whose echo was reproach; and experience, which had already eliminated desire. I sensed a weakness that once was strength in Porgess. Ninety-nine percent of all that made him happy. Perhaps a twin lived inside of him who remembered him as a different man in the same body. Did Porgess want to forget what his twin was reminding him of? Did the twin wish to remind the original Porgess that survival was not the ultimate triumph? In Porgess, I sensed how he was answering the questions, which a person could, yet didn't have to answer for himself. Why was he born? Why was he living? What did he come to do or not do in this world? What was the sum of reasons for which no one in his final moment eats with a silver spoon? What has changed? What never changes?

"There are some mistakes in it," Porgess said. "It's a translation. The meaning gets lost and thins out in a translation. A word that hits a nail on the head in two places can have two or twenty meanings even though it sounds the same. It would have to be translated at least twice. Once in the language, and the second time in the psychology. Many things can simply never translate. They are understandable only in one place, and somewhere else the meaning will change. That's old hat. The same holds true the other way. Some things are the same everywhere. I can say with confidence that *Romeo and Juliet* was written several times mainly for money or for the purpose of setting a threatening example. Even Little Narcissus recognized this, though he couldn't recognize the difference between being smart and being shrewd."

And so we were both killing time. We exchanged gossip. Max Faltz, the headwaiter at the Jewish Cellar on Rybna Street, who, in 1942, the Gestapo sent to be reeducated in Sachsenhausen, returned with a wooden leg. He was a bouncer at the Orion. In November 1942 he was turned in by, of all people, an unsatisfied Jewish patron. They knocked out all his teeth. His teeth and gums were like solid rock. He thought that he was undefeatable, if not immortal, because of his teeth. Now he bangs an empty beer mug when he wants peace and quiet in the pub. The man who turned him in survived the war and came in for a drink when Max Faltz was on duty. They looked at each other and remembered everything. The snitch embraced him around his neck, and he began to cry."

"You're going to laugh," I said, "but before Faltz was hired, he had to bring in a certificate of preservation."

"I hope they gave it to him."

"Yeah, but he had to go there three times and pay for the revenue stamps."

"Austro-Hungary will never die here."

"Why is it so?"

"It's in the blood. A love of seals."

"Yeah, especially round ones."

It didn't matter what was said. I could have started an interplay or even an argument. At times it was all right, at times it was interesting, and at times it was just plain boring. Were we like a train that derailed because it crossed the wrong shunt, or more like a train that a person boards and gets off immediately? I was afraid that the basin through which Porgess envisioned the world, full of dirty and clean water, was about to explode. I sensed a silent and gradual sensation of coldness. There, between us, lay all that had and had not happened to us. The past was a mirror and a hammer in one. When he looked into the mirror, did he see himself cry? What did he see with his mirrors attached to a pole, when he looked through the windows at the world, as through a periscope on a submarine? Did he see all that was between the broken pieces? Did he see himself drowning in the basin or, perhaps, the water overflowing? I was handling everything that came up in a conversation like a spark that would ignite a fire if it were to be blown upon. According to my needs, I have already learned to make larger things smaller and smaller things larger. It was probably driving Porgess up the wall. It also bothered him that ninety-nine times out of a hundred I could see things in a better light. Perhaps it was; perhaps it was not. His eyes were gathering impatience and were muffled by humiliation, and humiliation was being pushed away by anger, and I knew it was neither pretentious ambition nor envy. He locked his right-hand fingers into his left hand and cracked his knuckles. I didn't say anything.

"There are two reasons why people are pigs," Porgess suddenly said. "They want something, and they go after it no matter what the cost. Others don't want it that much, but they go after it anyway, and they don't even realize that they're like the first ones."

I didn't tell him that I had known that since kindergarten, as if he were to say that I had to wash my hands after a meal or that I had to clean up after myself.

Then he asked, "What can the Whale give to you or what can it give to Adler?"

I replied with an answer that explained the price of a live gorilla. (We were doing a story with Adler about the zoo.) A tiger cost just as much as a lion. The rhinoceros was the most expensive—for the price of one rhino, a person could buy five giraffes. The giraffe, on the other hand, was more expensive than a lion. Porgess started to laugh. Did I ever see a giraffe run? They run as if they were rising into the air. They are the most beautiful when they are running. When did Porgess see them run? I kept my mouth shut.

"How long does a rhinoceros live?" Porgess wanted to know.

"I think until about forty."

"I read about a lot of nonsense during my stay in this bed," Porgess said. "You would not believe what interests people who never experienced the camps, except, perhaps, after it was all over, when the camps became a place for a weekend excursion. In Buchenwald, they serve the best sausages. In Ravensbrück, you can buy a postcard, charms, or trinkets, like in the best souvenir shops. In Auschwitz-Birkenau, they sell first-class key chains and colorful pamphlets depicting the ovens and Zyklon B. I heard that the Carmelites wanted to build a church over there. They have school trips to visit and tourists as far as Brunei come to see the place. There is no sense in explaining to them when memory is death, when forgetting means existence, or when living means not forgetting. No one better tell me that justice has to arrive quickly and that a criminal without a judge will be punished by his own guilty conscious. Justice to me seems more like a snake that crawls very slowly until it strikes with its venom, except somewhere down the line someone cuts out its fangs." I guess he thought that he was getting too serious. "I have one advantage. I can't get hit by a car on the street."

"You should ask me what price a can of sardines is nowadays," I said with a sneer.

"Is it the same with you: the more you return to the camps, the less you understand?" He didn't wait for an answer. Was he thinking more about revenge than justice, because revenge was a faster solution? "It was as if I needed to understand the laws of gravity in order to walk, or why a rock doesn't fall upward—until they send you to the camps and everything is the other way around. Who would understand this?" I asked.

"I also have a copy of von Clausewitz and a brochure about why the Germans and the Russians do not have any love for the Jewish race. They keep singing the same song about how all that is rotten in the world is because of us (you and me). The Japanese didn't forget that during the Russo-Japanese War of 1905, when the Russians sank half of their own navy by mistake. (The other half was destroyed easily by the Japanese.) Japan received a war loan given to them by the Jewish banker from America, Jacob Schiff, to put them on their feet. That was why some of our people could save their skin in Shanghai when the Japanese were still there. It was the only place where my father could have received a visa, if Mother would have agreed to move out."

"I know a Japanese proverb: Don't forget the people who dug up the well when you're drinking out of it."

"Do you know any Chinese proverbs?"

"Yeah, a centipede never falls, even after death."

"Isn't it wonderful how proverbs can explain all the pain and solve all the riddles? They have the capability to cover everything."

"I don't want to look at the world through a dirty window. You probably know how it is."

"I have dirt sometimes in my eyes, ears, and nose, and my eyes are running," Porgess said. "Sometimes I wash my soul in it."

I didn't get up yet. Porgess no longer asked me anything that didn't require a simple answer. Those were answers that didn't need an explanation. Except that not even for a second was it true. (I was thinking about Leon the Bald from Belgická Street 24, who was the meanest during the hours of ten and eleven o'clock in the morning, when he would smack most of the boys. I remember Eli Pepper-Del kissed his hand with the ruler still in it after he had gotten a beating. For the teacher, Eli rendered ideal cooperation.) Did Porgess still recall the girl who fantasized that she had a harem in China or in Singapore and that she performed in Hong Kong as snake woman? And how they wanted to destroy her career because she could remain a virgin? She swore that she would be naked at her wedding along with her groom and maid of honor. The guests would arrive naked or in a bathing suit. We would see. And what about the rabbi? The rabbi would have to come with a long beard and with his prayer book placed in the right spot. Or she would let him wear a white veil. Was Porgess accumulating, by the magnet of his memories, all that he could play over and over again in bed? Yeah, that little girl who let Luster Leibling know why some boys enjoy access to a woman from the other direction. She didn't have to think about it for even five minutes. It was more comfortable. She didn't have to control anyone but herself. She didn't have to try that hard. It was fast and easy, and it was hot and moist. She probably kept the other hundred reasons to herself. She had a big tongue with taste buds spread out in the proper manner, mostly up front and almost none in the back so she could bear the taste. Some people enjoy it because they were never breast-fed. Some people portray the most devout loyalty to this, because the boy wants it or they want it themselves, either for calculation, fanaticism, or love.

Porgess knew what Oschler-Salus was doing. He was doing nothing. Only that everyone owed him something, and he owed nothing to anyone. He remembered how his drunken father, a musician, would beat his mother. He would become more and more unbearable, but he didn't care. He would come up with all kinds of sicknesses and guessing games for the district doctor, who claimed that Oschler-Salus was a fraud—that is, until he discovered something thanks to his diligent study of medical books. Like a pain in the back, you simply could not prove that it existed or deny it. Dizziness was a similar ailment. How could the doctor prove that his back wasn't hurting or that he wasn't feeling dizzy?

It was clear outside, nice and sunny. Spring was in the air. The sparrows were chirping in the garden. Porgess was happy that I came to visit him, even though in a while he was unhappy for the same reason. First of all, I didn't visit him immediately after the war. Then, I didn't consider announcing my visit in advance. As Adler said, all those who survived the camps survived them in a different way, just as everyone was different in the camps. They viewed the world they lived in differently, and no one would look into their souls, emptied by those who no longer lived. They dwelled more with the dead than with the living. The only thing that connected them to one another (though the connection was never complete) were the dead and all that the dead never took to their grave, because they had no grave. There are two types of people: the ones who turned their backs on the camps and the others. Some people think that it should be discussed so that history does not repeat itself, even if it were someone else or in a different place. Others prefer silence, because they already said everything and were afraid that someone would change the picture or they wouldn't understand because they weren't there. Sometimes, those who were there didn't understand it, anyway. The third type believed that through the most horrible events a person gains experience that will strengthen him. To some it was little, to others it was plenty. For some, it was a privileged experience; for others, it was a truism. We both brought back experiences from the camps, experiences that go beyond words. All laws, the way they were known, changed in the camps. Those entities we called "morality," "rules"; only a few had the time to fulfill them. It was a new system of coexistence between the worth and worthlessness of human life (before a person would turn into ashes). I didn't like the silent types who thought that because they were there, they had the last word, as if they were the only ones who survived. Porgess read that memories are the key to discussions about the camps, not poetry, fantasy, or inspiration. A few survivors would try to close everyone else's mouths, if only they had long enough arms. The more he thought about this, the less he knew. He wasn't the only one. He had enough time to find and search for all sorts of comparisons. Some people, always and everywhere, want to have the final word, and others just keep their mouths shut.

The past is made of layers, like rolls of fabric in the tailor shop of old Mr. Kafka, the father of Franz Josef, whom Porgess deciphered from the beginning to the end. Even by skipping from part to part, each layer had a color pattern and secret of which no one could make sense. With boxing, Porgess had everything in his hands: the better of the two wins, the weaker is counted down or loses by points. He had to share neither victory nor defeat. When his nose was broken, he was no longer satisfied with seeing his opponent hanging on the ropes with his eyes popped out or lying on the ground. He had it much easier with the girls, when he didn't have any bruises and black eyes. In the past, he was like a roof, under which the girls could seek shelter with the illusion that no one would harm them next to a ring fighter. Porgess mastered the difference between Don Juan and Casanova at the age of fifteen. One searches for prey and the other for love, the most love possible in the reality of many women.

Porgess took a letter from a pile of paper that was written by an acquaintance from Hagibor, a cousin of a boy from Belgická Street 24. She survived and moved to Caracas, and she wrote a letter to Porgess in a green envelope with a stamp containing a picture of a gorilla, saying how girls grow up by listening to boys speak about their dreams. "In the eyes of a girl, a man is someone who feels responsibility for others, no matter what the obstacles are. If he fulfills his goals in some way, he helps a woman fulfill her goals just as a woman helps a man fulfill his goals and accomplish her goals. The woman connects her hopes with a person beside whom she is free to dream, precisely because he fulfilled what he had dreamed of out loud next to her. His dreams must include decisions, which make a man out of a boy. If he manages to accomplish such a task, he has her respect, because he has become a man, even though he looks like or behaves like a boy." (There was no need for her to write: "or if that boy is bedridden.")

"What do you think of this?" Porgess asked.

"Sounds good," I said, handing him back the letter, which smelled of lavender. "We know what to think of women, and what a man is, that he, too, has a thousand faces. How often do you write?"

"Once every month or so. She sometimes sends me magazines with pictures in color that are a bit faded to make it seem like a drawing, but they reveal everything in all its natural beauty, for which I am most grateful. It must be because we are not so far apart from each other. Sincerity from a distance can never hurt that much, neither her nor me."

I could imagine a beauty in the sand. As beautiful as an entire body could be, a torso of a body, many bodies, all that it evokes, the wonder of shape and complexion, the colors. But it is all far away, accessible only on paper, a dream that is made out of reality, memories of darkness.

"You could make a couple of bucks on the side doing this, you know."

"I still have time, you know," I said, trying to avoid the question.

"If you do, don't forget about me."

"Don't worry."

Porgess didn't mention the doctors that came to visit him, who probably sat in his chair, the very one I was sitting in; where the ambulance or taxi would take him to be examined; or the thickness of his medical record. Suddenly, I flicked Porgess across the tip of his nose. I was thinking about those girly magazines. He was startled, but a second later, he began to laugh. We started to laugh out loud. Everything began to release itself. Tears were coming out of my eyes. It took everything out of Porgess. His voice became raspy and he was wiping his eyes. We crossed the barrier of murkiness and uncertainty.

"If anyone ever dares to tell me that everyone gets what they deserve, I will break his nose."

As he laughed, Porgess said, "Stop crying, do you want to play a game of poker? Shall we prove that both good and bad luck are siblings?"

"Only if your cards aren't marked."

"What's the bank?"

"Should I draw some leeches, skunks, or hyenas on a piece of paper?"

"Don't forget the snakes."

"How much should the whale be worth?"

"Don't leave out the lice, fleas, and the leeches."

"There are still plenty of them in circulation."

"Yeah, mainly rats."

"I hope you don't have anything against those cute little animals?"

"Of course not, only the fact that they remind me so much of people."

"But perhaps we reminded them of something or someone."

We laughed again. It was like a new game built on the ruins of an old one. The worst was behind us. Someone was standing behind Porgess's door. Were Porgess's parents listening? Someone knocked gently—once, twice, and then a third time. Mrs. Porgess brought in some tea and a plum cake with powdered sugar sprinkled on top. She was probably happy that I wasn't asking questions about the doctor, and that I didn't tell horrifying stories about what happened to our common friends. She asked me what I was doing, and I blushed when she told me that I have become a "handsome young man." Porgess gulped and then sneered. I was grateful to him for doing that. She was looking at him as if he had never grown out of his boyhood pants. Porgess would look at her in the same way, if it weren't for the fact that it made him feel uncomfortable to need a mother as children do.

"Do you like cakes with poppy seeds?" Mrs. Porgess asked me.

"I would sell myself for one just like that," I answered.

"A poet or a gambler could never be a match for a baker," Porgess said.

"Have you ever noticed that the greater the number of bakers there are, the lesser the number of poets, but such ratios never apply to gamblers? I would like to know why."

Mrs. Porgess laughed, as if she had done this to Porgess herself. As if she sacrificed her child by giving birth to him. It occurred to me that children without mothers think this about the world.

I was careful not to let Porgess win. He mentioned Belle, Hana Kaudersová, and it occurred to me that it was ordained for everyone to know everything about everyone else.

"Would you like anything else, lad?" Mrs. Porgess asked when Porgess was looking through the window.

"Let some of that spring in here," he replied nonchalantly, "some freshness."

The cards were going my way, as if they wanted to spite me. I have long given up the notion that it would be better for some people if they never existed. We were what the Germans considered *Der Überlelbende*—one who outlives—in spite of the Waffen SS and the Wehrmacht's cooperation. The English and the Americans called them "survivors"—castaways. The German language probably cannot be blamed for reminding me of such words as *Genickschuss,* a mercy shot; *Sheistorder,* an order to shoot; and *Arschlock,* asshole. We both learned German in the camps. Porgess had something in his eyes that the blind would have. It allowed him to look within. I ate a couple of slices of the cake, poured tea from a tall pot, and added some sugar. Porgess drank his tea bitter. I wouldn't bet a dime against the fact that Mrs. Porgess was listening with her ear glued to the door.

"When Max Faltz returned, an opera singer told him that it was hell during the war. The lights were being turned off; you couldn't even see your own nose. During a blackout, she walked into the glass display of a store on her way to the theater, and it ruined her whole performance of *The Marriage of Figaro.*"

I could barely hold the food in my mouth. We started to laugh again.

"Her brother used to make chassis for German tanks in the Czech-Moravian Kolben Danek for extra cash," Porgess dragged out of himself. "And stop spitting here. My mother is going to think that I made this mess. You're spraying like a cat. I couldn't swallow another bite." Porgess straightened out the golden chain around his neck. (He read somewhere that gold wasn't just a precious metal and a good luck charm but it also had a healing effect on the bones.)

"I dug bunkers for a German hospital with a fellow named Kolben back in Theresienstadt," he said, "but I guess they weren't relatives."

"You never know."

I reached out for another piece of cake.

"Now that you mentioned those girls from the shooting range," Porgess said, "I'd like to know where they disappeared to. Where they are now. What they are doing, but we'll probably never see them again. What can you do? Isn't it comical and strange how people disappear. Do you remember those two beautiful girls in Theresienstadt: Fanzi and Lizzy? In Auschwitz-Birkenau, their mother apparently looked out of the boxcar, saw the chimney and the SS Oberkommando Kanada, who unloaded people and things as he shouted behind her in the wagon, and stated, 'It will be good in here. This place is watched over by a bunch of invalids; they're all walking with canes.'"

Porgess's mother was pacing and listening behind the door. We were making noise. We were laughing as if everything were just a comedy. I thought that Porgess was going to fall out of his bed. And right after that, I felt foolishly healthy. It didn't make any sense to criticize the world for being restless and merry every time we had a chance. Something in our subconscious forced us to laugh at all of this. I guess under no circumstance would I exchange my health for the existence of someone else's sickness. I'm not of such material. After the war, I knew a rabbi who had a kidney taken out in order to save his son's life, but the operation was unsuccessful. Porgess pushed some book off the side of his bed in order to make more room for the cards. He took his legs into his hands and handled them like a foreign object.

"I have to have strength in my arms," he laughed.

"Yeah," I said.

"Cut the deck, so I can head for my doom."

"As if it already happened. Can't you see how much I trust you?"

"You can't even trust your own brother when it comes to cards."

"What can kill time better than a deck of cards?"

Porgess adjusted his pillow and the nozzle of the revolver showed a bit. He had five decks of cards close by, and we were playing with the sixth. They were first-class waxed cards. We didn't have to lick our fingers to shuffle them well. He nodded. I topped off a clean, well-shuffled deck, cut precisely, and began to deal.

"The Germans suffered the greatest losses in the U-boats," Porgess said. "They had 1,170 of them, and they lost 630. Out of 41,000 sailors, 25,870 drowned or were pronounced missing in action." Then he asked, "Did you ever wonder what happened to the German communists, besides the quarter of a million whom Hitler ordered to the slaughterhouse? You forgot to say what they dissolved into. Why do you think that NSDAP was so big in numbers? Who is building a new Germany in the east and the west?"

Porgess caressed his cards like the skin of a woman. It was a pity that he never created a reliable system that ensured he would never lose. He lost fifty crowns in five minutes. I sensed the possessiveness, the submission, and humility coming out of him and the strength to suppress and endure it all at least in some ways as he used to. They were the kind of emotions that only the severely wounded or invalids know, those who were healthy not too long ago.

"Just a second," I was holding off on the bet.

"We have all the time in the world."

I was looking at the cards, breathing on them. I squinted my eyes. I pretended to be concentrating.

"Do you know that you still owe me a copy of Pitigrilli from Theresienstadt? *An Eighteen-Carat Virgin.* Just because he was a corrupted bourgeois writer didn't mean that he didn't write about interesting things, including why some girls would do it with their legs up in the air so that they wouldn't get pregnant. A communion of the heart and tongue. I shouldn't have lent it to you. I wanted to know if you could read. You already knew how to steal. You were no beginner in lying either. What would you trade it for that couldn't be found in the library? Some sort of minor murder ritual? A little blood on the shoes? Are you playing or not?"

"Just a second," I repeated.

"One of the boys from the sulfur compound was hidden in a Catholic monastery," Porgess said. "He probably had to live it up. I hope they taught him the Ten Commandments, since he didn't manage to learn them at home, as well as the New Testament. He never knew how many sins there were in the world before they explained it to him. All a person had to do was look around. They divided people by those who sinned and those who had no idea that they were sinning, and then they pitied and envied them at the same time. Just as people were divided by their race and their group, by the standards of those in that monastery, people were divided by their sins."

I was holding the bank. I had just won sixty crowns. Porgess started to nonchalantly criticize my pictures in *We Shall Return!* Not even the smallest of captions below the photographs won his approval. He wanted to know what gauge I used to measure the quality of a photograph.

"When I shoot a hundred pictures and don't like them, I shoot another hundred and hope to like at least one."

"You don't measure the pictures by whether someone else likes them?"

"It all adds up," I said.

"Why did you decide on doing this?"

"We wanted to find something in common with Adler. It was like writing, but I wouldn't be good at that. Writing takes a long time and people prefer to go to the movies. You end up enjoying it; you work on it, you improve, extract, edit, and once in a while, it comes out. You can hold on to something, catch a moment, and enjoy it later when you're no longer there. You meet a lot of interesting people. Every day is different. I have a reason to visit places I would normally never be able to see. It's interesting and continues to be even when it no longer exists."

Did Porgess expect that I would write like Rainer Maria Rilke, Franz Kafka, or Hugo von Hoffmanstahl? Was he waiting for me to give a comparison, as when Rabbi Citron in Belgická Street 24 concurred that for Jewry, the queen of all virtues was justice, whereas for Christians it was love? Did he want a portrait of every average face or did he want me to play Titian, Michelangelo, or Leonardo da Vinci? I was careful, raising the stakes higher each time. I was waiting for the worst card. (When my big wave and my small wave would go down.) I had already won seventy-five crowns. That was a fairly hefty sum. I wasn't going to strip Porgess bare. He wasn't going to bet his golden cane or his shirts with pockets. At least I hoped he wasn't. As for captions and well-known cultural values, all I had to say was that if I were given the chance to choose between Beethoven, Goethe, and all of Germany's culture or the American and English boulder, for which the most important was first and last individual rights, including the right to open your mouth, I wouldn't hesitate a second. With their culture, the Germans created the gas chambers. The partisans in the mountains of Montenegro would wipe their nose on their sleeves and their asses with their hands, but they never lowered their heads when the Germans tried to stomp. Whoever could hold on longer to what was good was the better man. The Germans invented the printing press, and yet they burned books. They would have themselves killed for music, and they would send Benny Goodman to the gas chamber. Armstrong would be let out like an ape in chains. Count Basie would be considered of a lesser race. The entire jazz era and all its supporters, whom Porgess so staunchly endorsed, would fill up a complex of freight and military trains to Auschwitz-Birkenau. The platform, next to chimneys, would be the last piece of ground and sky they would see.

"I bargained well," I said looking at my cards.

"Less is often more," Porgess said nonchalantly, and I had to determine whether he had the captions below my photographs or the cards on his mind. The old card jargon, I thought. Little fish are fish, too. Porgess never compared people to the cards—a seven, joker, and ace—but rather he compared them to the way the game was played: carefully risky or boringly. That was something he had in common with Adler. I surely couldn't have seemed impatient to Porgess.

"People like to pay attention to something other than the last war. They want to have fun, just like you and I; to make money and spend it; not to worry about how deep in the ground the next anti-aircraft bunker should be," I said.

"How many cards did you take?"

"Three on a whim."

"I was under the impression that everyone kept writing so much about the war so that everything today would seem as if it were just moments after an experience that has passed, making the present seem better and more beautiful. That the world wasn't just something that was scorching us deep underneath our skin. And probably so that no one would complain too much. You know, to have something to compare to. Perhaps there's some truth and some lies in it; some righteousness and some falsity. Someone could seek it out, go over it, and then choose."

"I could bear that for the next fifty years or so."

Porgess was in his groove. He had the face of a playboy who, after some wild party, played an undeceived game with destiny, capable of holding out long enough to win something back. I understood why Porgess compared people to card games. There had to be two or more participants. No one could play cards by himself. Perhaps only solitaire. Cards would bring companionship to Porgess, a spark of life. They would force a guest to sit down with him on his rear end.

"You have beautiful flowers here," I said.

"Azaleas tell a girl to be careful. Begonias are refusal. A rosebud can tell even a whore that she is too young. I'm only missing a cactus in here."

Porgess's twin wandered in again. I was playing against two Porgesses. He was speeding up the game and raising the stakes. I knew that the more tired he would get, the worse he would feel. He lost two hundred crowns. I was almost angry that he let me win so easily. Was it so that I could feel guilty? Did he want to turn me inside out? I probably had the expression of a woman who had been dumped or a girl who was going through her period. I felt impotent.

"That's enough," said Porgess.

"Shall we stop?"

"I'll go tell my mother."

"I could lend you the money."

"My God!"

"You're not superstitious, are you?"

"Out of principle, I don't borrow."

"All right, we can take a break," I said cautiously. I felt like a girl who had been guarding herself a long time, until she began to regret what she had missed and not what she failed to protect.

"I have such a hairy chest," he said. "I'm studying myself as Darwin studied squirrels. You should know what I've been dreaming about for the past few nights. I'm flying, falling, and saving people. It's incredible. You would find it incredible. It is definitely better than when I dream about the floods or when that basin full of all the waters of the world burst."

"I like to win at cards," I said.

He knew that I was lying. He saw it in my face, even though under different circumstances I would be telling the truth. Once when we were fourteen Porgess and I went skating. We were skating in one direction, but we felt that it was the wrong direction, because the music was mixing it up. It confused the cells for equilibrium in the ears. He asked the caretaker of the rink to play some jazz. Now that was skating.

On the window stood a candleholder that looked like one of those silver towers designed to determine the position of the sun. Porgess had already known about the prize I received for a collection of photographs in *We Shall Return!* that I named "Moments." .

"Do you comprise them with Adler?"

"I've seen better photographs with more intelligent captions," I said. "I'd often prefer photos without the captions. But some pictures become unbalanced without them. It's because those old-timers underestimate the power of words. They don't believe that a picture can speak louder. They don't even believe in words. I guess they know each other too well."

"Hmm," said Porgess, "you're pissing in your own nest."

"I like people who live on the edge. Most of the time, people don't get appreciated. People with a story to their face have their own philosophy written in their eyes. I like to take pictures of workers, inventors, pilots, young workers, and boys, like you and me; every-day stories, in which thousands of people are recognized or like foot-prints created by thousands of people. They are the salt of the earth. They represent the truth. For me they are the truth. They look at you and everything in them says, 'I exist, therefore I act,' or 'I act, there-fore I succeed—or did not succeed,' or 'I have nothing to regret,' or 'I argue, therefore I am.' You can catch the identity of a person in a split second. You take a picture of him from his 'outside' and then feel what lies within his 'inside.' You take it in a moment that he doesn't even notice. And if you're lucky, you can unveil that person's essence from his expressions and his features, his face, stature; that uniqueness that defines every human. A lot of times, I don't catch it. I throw away a bunch of untrue pictures as soon as they come out. Unlike Erwin Adler, I don't have to read into stories that are not my own. It's a race, even though you're lying in bed."

"What's in those cutout articles?" I asked at the end.

"They're about how Napoleon believed he was protected by a homunculus that would shine a white sphere, and, in a moment of danger, would render the color red to warn him."

"And what is that?"

"An artificially made man and a fetus in liquid from which you were born. Something in the egg that is beginning to look like an adult human being."

"You can say that again," I added.

"Hitler, on the other hand, believed in psychic powers . . . This one is about how the dinosaurs were wiped out six million years ago by a tiny planet circulating between Mars and Jupiter. The planet, which was about five and a half miles in diameter, vanished com-pletely during its entrance into the atmosphere and impact into earth, except for particles of dust. They consisted of the element imide.

It was the dust that rose above earth after the impact, darkened the sky, and froze it. Then it rose up again, so that the trees and the food for the dinosaurs disappeared. It proves that the discoveries found within earth's surface, fossils and fuel, were what existed in the past and then died out. This one should interest you: in Paris, during the Middle Ages, our people were chased away from the main synagogue; it was made into a cathedral for prostitutes. The whores would pray to Mary Magdalene. That's interesting, isn't it? There's nothing like a pious hooker. And here I have an article showing that today people know of ninety-four elements; the last is plutonium for bombs. Eleven ounces of that stuff is enough to knock the world out of its socks. Or here it says that, in Hebrew, the devil hides behind a number with three sixes. Except for the fact that Hebrew, just like Latin, has no numbers. I just go crazy and cut these things out. Stone never gets withered away by the wind. It endures even the sun—the most powerful of flames—yet submits to the human hand. They castrated boys in Vienna in order to maintain their high voices and use them for singing. The fact that, to seek pleasure, faggots put gerbils in their asses was something that I heard from you when you caught Finderlind in the act, but you read about it everywhere nowadays. Somewhere down the line, the animal rights activists protested. Then I read about a general who gained victories by postponing all his battles. He let the enemy wait—a Roman. I also heard how the Romans elevated their favorites to the status of gods, and when these favorites grew old and tiresome, they simply drowned them in the Tiber. (Like when Dr. Mengele gave his personal favorites pastries, and when they would bore him he would shoot them or send them up into the chimney.) Someone once proclaimed that it wasn't 666 that was the devil's number, but rather the number sixty-nine. Are you grasping this? There are still people who believe earth is a flat plate and beyond its edge lure the flames of hell."

"I'm sorting it out," I said.

"By all means, sort it out. I never managed to."

"What else is there that you can tell me about?"

"In America, they are trying to create a car that works on compressed air."

"Really?"

"It'll surface on the market as soon as they run out of cheap oil."

Then he said, "I'm studying how many people are getting married and how many are getting divorced at the same time and what their average age is. I'm studying how the ratio is getting closer."

"I hope it calms you down."

"You'd be surprised."

"Why would I be surprised?"

"What does time do besides the things that even time can't do?"

"I hear you."

"I never managed to understand time, even though it would tear me to pieces."

"Take your time," I said in jest.

"What do I know about time?" he asked.

Then he said, "I also often wondered about the difference between a woman and a man. Why could no one truly understand it? Perhaps it would be better if it remained undefined. Perhaps a definition would destroy everything."

Porgess didn't wonder why I no longer answered his questions. He had photographs on the wall. Pictures that his father hung around the room. Pictures of when he was a boy: Porgess with golden hair and a jockey hat; Porgess with a blue sailor uniform and golden buttons. There were no longer questions, only answers, and these answers didn't need words. This could explain, but not justify, his existence. I didn't want to envision the Hauptsturmführer's face; the way he spread his legs when he shot Porgess in the back; the bed of the mayor who ran off to surrender to the Americans and, in the last minute, opened everyone's eyes.

"The Austrians have gotten off easily so far. They proclaimed that the Anschluss made them the first victims of Hitler and that the Nazis were not greeted enthusiastically. The best is to mix up the first with the last, so that the world could analyze it. People have a short memory. Adolf Eichmann was an Austrian, as was General Ernst Kaltenbrunner. Arthur Seyss-Inquart, *Qualetier,* he was from Holland; Odilo Globocnik who has anti-Jewish operations on his conscience that cost the lives of one million seven hundred thousand people. Hitler was born in Braunau, Austria, even though he lived in Germany since the age of twenty-four. Seventy thousand circumcised Austrians went straight to hell, one hundred twenty thousand emigrated. The Germans didn't even allow them to take extra undergarments. They even left behind their shoelaces."

I was silent.

"Then over here I have an article about a retirement home, consisting of people who decided, in their old age, that they would no longer postpone anything in their lives. They came up with this concept too late. Nothing should ever be postponed. That is obvious."

Porgess frightened me somewhat by this. What was it that shouldn't have been postponed?

"I'm starting to like the number twelve," Porgess said. "It is a complete number: twelve months, twelve hours in a day, twelve in a night. Did you know that executions used to be carried out on Friday the thirteenth? As if executions weren't carried out throughout the rest of the month, and the rest of the year, from Monday through Sunday. The next three Friday the thirteenths in one year will be in 1998. How old will you be? Be careful!"

"Well, we'll have to have a repeat next time," I said. "Either you'll win it back, or you'll lose your shirt. We can play for that revolver of yours. I still have to go to the barber today."

"Old Rozenkratz comes and cuts my hair. For my revolver? I don't think so."

By the length of Porgess's golden hair, I assessed that Rozenkratz hadn't visited for at least three weeks.

"I'd say you're living it up. Who has his own barber these days?"

"It's still no good," Porgess admitted.

How did old Fillip Rozenkratz survive? What did he tell Porgess while he was cutting his hair? Whose hair did he cut in the camps? I guess he didn't dream about the king and queen of hearts and how they kissed each other and breathed heavily. In some camps, the barbers were better off. In some, they were the only ones to survive; yet in other camps, the prisoners hated them. I didn't like the barbers either, but if I were a barber, I would probably do the same. The Germans always wanted to get the most hair to fill up their mattresses, blankets, and work vests, not to mention for insulation and rope ladders used on ships and U-boats. Also, they always came up with something to lure the prisoners when they promised to let them live longer than the others. He would brag to Porgess that, before they were sent to Germany, he slept on bags filled with hair and under a cover also made of hair and bristles. Rozenkratz returned alone without a wife and three red-haired children. He was making a pretty good living by cutting people's hair from house to house. He would constantly repeat to himself over and over that all that had happened was not true. As if he could succeed in denying everything that he despised and that probably haunted him both day and night. Perhaps he was able to endure such an approach. What a person doesn't remember is good.

"I hope you don't envy him," Porgess said.

"It's usually pointless to envy something," I admitted.

"It's like slapping the palm of your hand against the surface of water in order to find out which is harder, your hand or the water."

Perhaps, I thought; if Rozenkratz were capable of thinking of something more horrific than what happened to him and what he had seen as a barber in the camps, he could hide the truth. Nothing more terrifying could be imagined, not even by the greatest of fantasymongers. Rozenkratz killed memory in him as people kill love, greed, or desire within themselves. He never counted on the future and never saved anything, because he didn't want to mistrust tomorrow. He would cut people's hair, as he did before and during the war, and that was enough for him.

"It's like when a fire is burning inside your head, but it's only the size of a hazelnut."

"I don't know whether I should like him or hate him, but I don't think that he will ever leave my mind."

"Maybe he never found peace, because he's unable to focus on anything else."

"Yeah, until it hits him at once."

It was pretty outside. The leaves had the right green and golden colors. It was a pleasure to look out the window. It occurred to me that there are three kinds of people: those who think it will always be beautiful like this; others who cry, because they know that it will not always be this beautiful; and those like Porgess, who can only watch.

He talked about a few acquaintances who returned and a few who didn't. It was all coming to him, as to the center of a spiderweb. Some news came to him about a girl from the Hamburg circus who, in Theresienstadt, acquired a fairly infamous reputation, even though Porgess knew that reputation equals only one percent of the truth.

My heart stopped for a second.

"Really?"

She worked in Auschwitz-Birkenau in the delousing station. She made friends with a friend of mine from Theresienstadt. I think her name was Schnicková or something like that. Three female German Wachmans came into the laundry barrack for inspection, but without the Oberaufseherin. The Hamburg circus girl was boiling the laundry in a pot. She would tell the girls stories of Salta Mortales on a white horse, which was kept at a proper pace by the ringmaster snapping his whip, while standing on a round, black pedestal in the center of the ring. She would then blow kisses into the audience and the music ended with fanfare. She dreamed about the horses and about something to put in her belly. The guard tore off Schnicková's scarf and discovered that she had grown hair underneath. She smacked her hard. According to the legend, Schnicková returned the favor by slapping the guard back. I heard that silence spread through the room, but the other two Wachman guardswomen did not like the first. According to another version, Schnicková got slapped and nothing happened. There's a third interpretation suggesting that the circus rider was counting on the Scharführer, who had the delousing unit under his wing, so she gave the Wachman a smack and all three of the guards took her out to the bunker. In three days, the Scharführer brought her back to the laundry room on a stretcher with her hair torn out, toothless, fingers loosely spread out to hold a heart that was still pumping next to an eye. The second eye spilled out during the final round of her torture. They did this to show the launderettes in the delousing unit what would happen if someone were to lay a hand on another German Wachman. They left her hanging upside down, like a bat, until the Scharführer decided to take her down and throw her in a pit of hot ashes.

"I didn't know," I said gasping for breath. I felt pressure upon my chest, as if I had swallowed a dog, similar to the feeling Headmaster Freudenfeld had when he suffered a heart attack.

"Who could possibly keep up with all that? You have to have at least six million questions and six million testimonies; six million pieces of evidence; and six million eyes and ears. It is something no one ever will be able to explain. It's like the Germans—no one ever has been able to explain them, not even the Germans themselves. The Germans, as a whole, are the most limited and, at the same time, most intelligent people in the world—at least the majority, who voted for Hitler. Did you see the movie *Triumph of the Will*? You have to take them all to trial, one by one. Where would you find so many judges? You have to murder en masse to get away with it."

"I agree," I said softly, and it sounded as if it came out of the dark and immediately went back.

I didn't mention to Porgess that I liked when a photograph in some way rendered the ability to appreciate a human being; when it captured the most important and most determinate of human features, or the magic of the human face or action—an essence that anyone could erase along with the person. I didn't want it to sound cheap. A photograph was the body, the stature, and the work that a person did. Everything that made him useful to himself or to others. It rendered a point, face, and substance even beyond the given moment. It told us what made a person or didn't make him so dangerous. Words would have only made it sound strange. Perhaps it could never be expressed by words.

I was watching Porgess and thinking about the unapproachable essence that a human face has. Sometimes actors have such a look. It brings up thoughts of the best in a man as well as the worst. The better in a man attracted me, just as it did Porgess and Adler, ever since we discovered that it took no special effort to crumple a human being. To put him back on his feet was worth much more.

Porgess was still handsome. His face carried a spiritual illumination that created pain, though bitterness as well as anger for all that happened to him in the last moments of the war.

It was within me like a carousel of the heart and the mind. Where do they meet? Where will they never meet? Where will they meet with me? It lasted a second or two, perhaps even three. I was glad that we were alone in our thoughts and each on our own. When a person doesn't know what to do, the first thing he does is smile. He had his own share of the inexplicable, just like every person. He allowed me to be presumptuous, as I allowed him.

Suddenly, I felt his memory traverse from the past into the present; everything he tried to support when he could no longer secure it. It was like a tunnel in which he wanted to elongate and connect all that had happened to his past character and personality, when he was healthy, happy, and joyous (at least most of the time), or when he would hang out with us. He couldn't forget those days; a time when he had springs in his legs, the speed of wind. Endurance, reliability, simple thoughts about food, clothes, and entertainment created equilibrium within him. Those days when he thought about boxing. Happiness and misfortune—how can a man make peace between two conflicting memories? How did he intertwine the misfortunes during the war with the misfortunes after the war? When he almost fifteen, did he think it was easy to grasp life and squeeze the most out of it, as if everything in life were to improve gradually from the time he was born until the time he closed his eyes forever? I guess it wasn't pleasant for him to recognize that life was the greatest teacher. Perhaps it wasn't always the case that intercourse, between a boy and a girl, would result in the birth of a child. It was as Headmaster Freudenfeld would say in Belgická 24, about not having any illusions or making any mistakes. From everything in life something was born. It was not always a child. I sensed what strangles a man, even though he is not yet paralyzed. Why does it sometimes stop in certain places and no longer continue? I began to perceive what connected Adler and me to the Whale: the desire to change the world in order to live comfortably in it. Porgess's memory must have caused him pain. It must have lied to him. A source of endless complications toward a better or a worse existence. He showed me a large school photograph and then one of his family: two uncles who left on time in 1938. Porgess was still tiny in the picture, with platinum curls.

"The other uncle didn't get a visa from the Americans because he had a hump," Porgess said. "The council in Lisbon told him off. We can't go against our rules. Don't try any other embassies."

"What did he do?"

"He swallowed a capsule of cyanide."

"Hmm," I muttered without any purpose as I thought about Porgess's gun.

"So far, the uncle that survived hasn't kept in touch."

"That might happen later," I said. "The world is large."

"Perhaps he had an advantage. He was color blind."

I hoped that the story about the circus girl wasn't true. I wished that the story arrived to Porgess warped by time, distance, and the unreliability of messengers. Perhaps it wasn't true. One day, when nothing will be able to be proven, all the heads of the camps will bet their futures on it to cleanse their past like a dress faded by the sunlight that hadn't been worn for a long time. It would be a clean slate for the Wehrmacht, which, compared to the Waffen SS, was like water and fire. This was just the beginning. It was as if the far more horrific actions of one component of the army justified the smaller crimes committed by another section. At least there are a couple of crumbs for us to swallow, at least for me.

"How did you ever decide to become what you are?" Porgess asked me as if I've never explained it to him before. Did he not have the desire or strength to stand up and arrange an adventurous life for himself or to have something that lends a sense of purpose to his existence? Doesn't a person distribute, at the very least, a few privileges to himself, which he believes he deserves? This includes all people, those who have all their body parts in working order and those forced to lie in bed.

"I guess I have the personality for this. I probably will never be good for anything else."

"How can you tell that something is very harmful to you, or just a little, or not at all? Who is beneficial to you?"

"To tell you the truth, I still can't tell, not even after the camps. Sometimes I think something or someone is harming me a bit, but, in the end, it turns out they are harming me a lot, and vice versa. Sometimes obstacles seem very far when they're just around the corner. Too much seems a little and a little seems too much. I never want to underestimate or overestimate a person. Everything is a test for me that I hope I can pass. A challenge that would make me stronger and smarter. I think that I understand people when I don't even understand myself. You know how it is. Something gets mobilized in me when I should be at ease. Something disarms me when I should be fighting tooth and nail. I would prepare myself for something, though it's not even worth an old penny. Any other thing, I simply let go when it's exactly what I need. I don't worry about it for too long. I can't get angry for a long time. I don't suffer that long. Perhaps it's the only case of shortsightedness that is actually helpful."

That was a long speech, and Porgess probably had his own opinion.

He asked, "When do you like a photograph?"

"When I find no mistakes in it. Actually, perhaps it has mistakes, but I don't see them. That is my peak."

Porgess just spoke of things that came to mind. It was something like when old men decide that they no longer need to tell a lie, either because they are tired or simply have had enough. And Porgess, just like those old men, would sense when a person was lying to him or not. He didn't have to think about Rozenkratz to realize that the truth is heavier than a lie, time, earth, and all the stars in the sky. He was never too religious, so he never considered placing the truth against God a sin, but neither did he wish to insult his mother or irritate his father.

"He prays ever since this happened to me," Porgess said about his father.

I didn't know how to leave. Porgess wasn't holding me up, but he wasn't throwing me out either. There was still something that kept me from getting up.

"In the *Vjestnik* they wrote about David, when he became a judge, before he was chosen to be king," Porgess said. "He would impose the highest fine to the poorest of paupers. The people could not believe this, and then he paid the fine himself. First he made amends with justice, and then he showed his true nature."

I hesitated to say anything. Porgess continued.

"Sure, they're writing about the mind and the heart, anger, greed, understanding, and all sorts of other garbage. People must really believe that when they ask questions that have not been answered, something will change. When pigs fly. No one can admit that some things just do not have a solution. What about character?"

Porgess knew that he had cornered me. We both knew that there was more involved to these questions. When Porgess ran from the boxcar the Hauptsturmführer no longer had to shout that, in the end, the revolver was always right. A person should never forget where they are. Did Porgess forget that he was in Germany?

A person's character outside the camps was, just as in the camps, more important than reason. It was more important than the heart and the rest of what could be considered the soul, intelligence, or gluttony of a human. Character was everything, for the rest was nothing compared to character. It was much later that everything was divided into single virtues and vices by the usual standards. This included extenuating and aggravating circumstances. During the war, character was an amalgam, the only thing that kept a person together. They could kill him, but he didn't fail if he maintained his character. He survived and would have shown himself to be a black sheep if he lost his character, even once, for just a second. The word "apology" disappeared from the dictionary and vanished from the sphere of silence. Even though there were no witnesses, because they were all killed, their consciences would eat them alive. There was a rabbi in the barracks where Porgess dwelled, who prayed not to God, but for God, because he believed that with every person that went up the chimney, a piece of God was taken. But it was with him, when he went to the gas chamber, that his God suffocated once and for all. Well, I'll be a monkey's uncle! Porgess would no longer bother to do what his mother and Rozenkratz did: to question God. Let God, if He is still capable, ask Porgess. Sometimes he amused himself with God like that.

"They also write that David fell in love with a woman and sent her husband to the front lines to get rid of him and marry her. That's old hat. We're only human, you know. Who's perfect these days? Somebody then brought up the case of the rich man who had a lot of sheep, who managed to take the only sheep of a poor man. David was angered by the fact that the poor man had lost everything. Who dared to take his only lamb? Who was that bastard? I want to see him! A certain prophet told him, 'You are that man.' Do you get it? There is always someone who wants you to eat out of his hand. I also tried to avoid people who were always fine and will be fine with listening to orders."

"Where do you have a bathroom here?"

"Next door. Don't forget to lift up the toilet seat."

"Do you get to see Vili Feld from time to time?"

"I've heard about him."

Was this, perhaps, an echo that pondered over the foundations of manhood? A dilemma whether to succeed or not to succeed? That question of being or not being what you want or no longer can be or, perhaps, not doing the things you don't wish? A question of being measured by the best of men as well as the worst?

"I'll tell you something about him," Porgess said.

"When you want something from him, he'll say, 'Yes, but . . . ' It's the secret of any business relation. 'Yes, but . . . ' Do you get it?"

The radio played "The Ships Sail into Triana," which was sung by the famous singer who was later banned by the Whale. Then the box played "When We Stood beneath the Stars at Night." There were suddenly many people with us, in spite of their absence. For some he felt life was worth living, and for others it wasn't as much. Who was with him in spirit when I was sitting next to him?

"We know a lot about each other in spite of our youth," I said.

"Luckily, it's still not enough," Porgess answered.

We were twenty years old, everything was moving in some direction. I noticed that Porgess had a mirror on the wall so that he could see himself when he wanted. Perhaps he needed to assure himself that he existed once in a while. It occurred to me that he had risen from the dead. His complexion was almost crystal clear, like people during the war, before the transports or before they flew up the chimney. How many Porgesses did he see? It was as if he had a double. The Porgess with a shattered spine remained the same. It was only the other Porgesses that were changing inside Porgess. They were not growing older or they were randomly disappearing and then reappearing. Perhaps they were even growing older, but differently. Then Porgess saw himself in very different ways: first younger, then older, and in various costumes and masks. His own image was always a passage from darkness. It was harder than lading your mind with questions about infinity or God, harder than asking questions such as where infinity begins or who created God. Couldn't he just ask Him the main question that tormented all people: How to live? Why doesn't luck or loss reach people according to what they deserve? Why does destiny serve everything on a silver platter to some, while others receive nothing?

"I often wonder why people sometimes forgive each other and sometimes don't," Porgess said. "Where is the truth in this? It's like that ridiculous story about Joseph and his brothers, which is for some reason stuck in my head. What would have happened if he hadn't forgiven them, or perhaps he didn't forgive them, but the authors changed the truth? There are always at least three variations to every story. One day the people will forgive the Germans for inventing Nazism, and they will pretend to be objective. Didn't they always forgive people involved in such things, even before the Nazis? If Nazism could be chemically dissolved, the world would be terrified of the stuff from which it was made."

"I hope you're not so serious all the time," I said.

"Not really, only when it gets to me. I reflect on everything I have forgiven in others and myself, as well as what others had to forgive me for doing. What can be undone and what cannot. There is enough to make your head spin."

"I don't even try to do something like that."

"Sometimes I think of Germans who were kicked out, as the Germans kicked us out before."

"You could play this game forever."

"What comes around goes around."

"Yeah."

"The longer it takes, the longer it gets devilishly personal," Porgess said. "It's like getting screwed in, or like a spiral, if you know what I mean. It's hell, constantly returning, even there, where you've never gone before."

I had a feeling that one visit with Porgess was a lifetime of everything that had happened.

It was like the pieces of an endless chain connecting Porgess to a past and all its reasons with everything that was yet to come. It linked him together before it all disappeared with him in the universe, like so many human destinies before Porgess and after Porgess. A something that no one will ever truly recognize, that one can and cannot prophesize until it happens. It has no boundaries, like the boundaries between forgiving and not forgiving. It's beyond redemption. Porgess wanted to live, but living for him meant making amends with invisible debts while lying in bed. That was only half of his story. Did he need to forgive himself? To pay his debts to someone else? He was like Joseph and his brothers, I thought, but I kept silent. Perhaps it was a bit of everything at once?

"Sometimes I kill time by talking to myself, and I feel as if I'm speaking to the devil himself. Do you know the joke about when the devil visits a lawyer and asks him whether he would sell his soul and the souls of his wife and children for a million a month, all written down in black and white? The lawyer thinks about it for a while and then says, 'I'll sign it for a million a month, but tell me, Where's the catch?'"

"I sure hope that the two of you understand each other."

"Yeah, I'd ask him what he did with Sonya Utitz or whether he's happy."

I could see Sonya in his eyes. The way she would groom herself for an afternoon in bed with one of the boys from Hagibor or Belgická Street 24, before she unleashed on Adler that blessed girlish laughter, equilibrium, and patience of hers—the kind that only girls have.

"Ask him how hot is it down below."

"Down below or up above?"

"Down below and up above, just in case. Who is keeping his books in order? What do they do down there on Sundays?"

"Next time, I'll tell you about what they talk about with Hitler, Himmler, and Heidrich. How they cope with nonaggression pacts, general friendships, the usual."

"I'm really looking forward to that." Then, on another note, I said, "What would you never do, if it came down to it and someone asked you to do it?"

"I would never steal anything from a friend. I would never like to overestimate or underestimate a person. I wouldn't claim that everyone gets what they deserve or that the more things change, the more they stay the same. I don't believe when you finally want to find yourself you have to first lose yourself, or when you release your soul you'll be born for eternal life. You don't grow wiser with age. Guardian angels don't protect children, drunks, and the feebleminded. Beauty doesn't lie in the eye of the beholder. Like when my father used to believe that you had to have money in order to make it."

"We're in the same boat, you and I," I said.

We ended with that note. He reminded me of those individuals who would speak to the devil as a joke or perhaps even seriously, and it appeared as if they were saying something to themselves, like some unsuccessful ventriloquist. One could easily read from their lips what they tried so hard to say with their stomachs. The next couple of times I avoided their house. The Porgesses lived in a small villa with four apartments on a street that was later changed by the civic commission to Rosenberg Avenue. His room was painted in a happy tone. It had a light blue ceiling, the front walls were painted yellow, and the back walls were painted pink, like a room for a girl. Mrs. Porgess came up with the colors. Her hair had long turned gray. She would comb it every day very carefully, and she was always so neat. She never wore anything dark, only green, red, yellow, or blue, and sometimes orange as an accent color. Perhaps she had a guilty conscience for fearing departure before the war. There was no point in trying to catch up or undo what already had been done. Just as Luster Leibling, alias Black Pepe, tried to avoid, as much as possible, the places where misfortune occurred. As Adler would put it, don't take any advice from anyone who's in a slump. According to Vili Feld, you should never tell a person who is down to his last breath that miracles do happen. If they do happen, he'll find out for himself. He also claimed that it was better when someone envied you than the other way around. Vili wasn't impressed by the compliment that a weak man gives to a weaker man. He wasn't moved by the reproaches of the weaker one. Porgess's existence dug deeper within me like a worm burrowing in an apple. Even in his absence, to him, Vili Feld seemed like a spy who worked for both sides.

Porgess's mother asked me on the staircase, "Did any of the girls who knew the boys from Hagibor ever return?"

Porgess inherited his ability to blush from his mother. Somehow I slipped out a few names with whom Porgess had a good time. I told her that we envied him a little. He was the most beautiful of us. Tears were coming out of her eyes. She was smiling. Her chin was trembling. She suddenly knew something about her son from the time when he wasn't entirely dependent only on his hands—or on pictures of girls. I could imagine their family life when all three of them were together, or when Porgess was still in the hospital. Mrs. Porgess would reprimand her husband for taking her advice and not moving to England when there was still time—to America or even to the North Pole. And the way Porgess, when he listens, imagined a view to the ocean, somewhere along the coast, where he would walk under the sun during the day and the stars at night. What rules does he abide by and what rules does he break? What lies in between? Did she know what Porgess thought? Did she blame the rabbi with whom Porgess shared a bunk in Au-Birkenau for saying that with every man who died innocently, a tiny piece of God died? That with the last victim who lost his life innocently, the last piece of His holy tissue disappeared as well? Or was it only the last man?

"Where do you live?" she asked.

"On Sacco and Vanzetti Street," I answered.

"Will you come back to see us again?"

"I will be glad to."

Mrs. Porgess was constantly apologizing and asking me to keep in touch. I felt like a driver who hit and ran.

Porgess's mother had light blue eyes, just like Porgess. When I was leaving, I was careful not to ruffle the blue rug that was in the hallway. Mrs. Porgess shouted, from behind closed doors, that each week, every Friday, Porgess awaited the publication of *We Shall Return!* Also that he looked for Adler's and my name, as well as the names of Herbert Weinberger, the winemaker, Little Narcissus, who wrote verses about the way he liked to drink tea on the east bank of the Elbe and about the tomb on the Red Square. (In those days it was still unknown that there was a gym and a café under the mausoleum, where the secret police indulged in caviar and crabmeat, and the tailors changed the clothes of the embalmed statesman every year and a half.) I remembered how the women in the Orion would offer Porgess ice cream with fruit, and how he would surprise them by paying for them. Didn't his father tell him not to allow anyone to pay for him who had less than he did? Why didn't Mr. Porgess want this?

In the meantime, Porgess began to play his American big band orchestra music from the jazz era, his bridge with no pillars or chains upon which he could walk forward and backward without leaving his bed. Beautiful, frivolous, and massive music from the records. "Caledonia," Chopin's "Nocturne in E Major," "The Train," "Snowflakes," "I Got Rhythm" by Glenn Miller, "All or Nothing" by Harry James with Frank Sinatra, and "Sing, Sing, Sing" by Benny Goodman.

"All of you will be famous," Mrs. Porgess said.

She was always sad and dignified, like a rock over which water would run in a murky river, its edge above the surface like a fragment of a star fallen to the ground, but still more abraded. Perhaps she sensed that the past, like fame for all of us in the present, was like the wind that catches on a leaf of grass for a moment, sweet when it lands before it flies away, and then leaves behind less than a bitter taste—it leaves nothing. Porgess was behind a closed door on a lowered bed, a bridge between life that was, is, and will be, like any other person. He probably thought about succeeding or not succeeding. It was always with him. It occurred to me that the Porgesses perhaps once wished for a girl.

The newspaper that I threw in the gutter soaked in the water and softened like a rag. It started to fall through the bars of the gutter from its own weight. In Rome that Friday, as I combed my hair in the reflection of a showcase marked BRUNO MAGLI, I was thinking how time builds its structure on a whim and in layers. Humans had thoroughly thought out the concept of time. It was better thought out than the concept of a day, a new spring, summer, fall, and winter, dusk and dawn, shadows. I parted my hair. I thought of Porgess's revolver. Where did it all gather? Where did it all fly away—memories of others, a voice that a person hears in the name of all the others? Was it possible that I could only feel my soul when I was thinking of others? Was it possible that a soul sliced into pieces could heal my memories? Was Porgess's pain my pain? I doubt it, but if it were, for how long? I thought about water that floods everything and then washes up, carries away, and conveys. About the basin that will one day break and everything will spill and flood. Somewhere in the distance records with American music were playing.

Herbert Weinberger, known also as Little Narcissus, never trusted anything and anyone, and therefore not even himself. He made things complicated for himself by doing this, but perhaps he simplified his life as well. At the time when he envied Porgess, he was still not an adult and he didn't convince his women, as he would a few years later, not to close the door to the toilet, and not to worry about his lap but rather their own. He also claimed that the big toe on the foot is the same as other parts of the body. In those days, nobody knew that Little Narcissus would become a wordmonger, and that he would—just like his stepmother—hang himself. I don't even know how long it took Porgess to die. It was written in the obituary: "After a short life, from natural causes." (Adler just said, "Tough luck," as if I didn't already know.)

■ □ ■ □ ■

THE ABYSS

I

The girl in his dream was telling him something that he had sensed or later overheard from the dancers in the amateur ballet troupe in Marienbad. She was eleven or twelve. She often visited the banks of a small, deserted lake. Originally, the lake had been the pit of a coal mine that had shut down over a hundred years ago, then flooded with groundwater. After a century the water had cleared, and it was possible to look down the cavern for miles upon miles. Muddy sand lay on higher planes of the pit, which were once terraces of the mine's galleries. The sand was golden, the bottom of the pit black, and the water blue. Weeds floated on the edges among tall grass and moss. It was a sunny morning. The girl took off all her clothes, let the sun warm her, and then jumped into the water. She observed her surroundings from the center of the lake. She spotted a snake on a boulder. She and the snake looked at each other. Its eyes were piercing green. Deepest shades of mud glistened from its sides. It slithered into the water and swam to her. Its body was long and thin and wound its way in the water without rippling. She was afraid as the snake glided around her several times, watching her with shiny snake eyes. Then it slid between her legs. She felt its smooth, cold skin. She played with the snake—it excited her, the touch of the snake, water, and sun. She savored the snake's newfound presence and its tender, firm touches. Then it disappeared, diving to the bottom and bringing back golden sand, spotted with clean mud on its body, which she gathered in her hands before rinsing them in the water. The sand and the mud looked like golden honey, foam on water.

She came to visit again and again. They grew close to each other. She could embrace and hold the snake in her palms, wind it on her chest, or press it to her face. To her lips. She had no need to speak; the snake could not. She sensed something changing in her. Something intimate, mysterious, and pure. Between only her and the snake. She sensed her body's secret signals. Sometimes it rained and the snake didn't come. Leaves fell on the water's surface, the water grew cold, and the girl saddened. When the sun finally shone, the snake's green eyes appeared on the rocky terrace, his long body like a wave that made her dizzy. She could feel her body swelling with emotion, her heart surge. The snake wended his way around her hips and thighs as summer drew to a close and the days became mostly sunny. She knew that their time together would end. They would have to part ways, perhaps never see each other again, since every good-bye can be forever. Things she had been previously unaware of acquired a deep, private meaning. Intimacy was unlike any other fear. It was beyond everything, and at the same time encompassed all the things she sensed would come—just as day follows night and winter comes after the summer, and as birds fly south in autumn and return in the spring. She never said anything to anyone about her visits. Afterward, when it was only a memory, the snake remained a secret. They remained connected by something that even later she didn't understand. She carried thoughts of him when they parted, and whenever she met someone new, his beautiful, searching, and provoking eyes would come back to her. She sensed how he had given her strength, a different stamina than children have. The snake of childhood moved into her memory.

"It was only good," the girl from his dream said.

He didn't answer. He understood that the ties of that summer were secret and strong, beautiful and unforgettable. That she secretly loved the water snake from the flooded mine pit, surrounded by rocks and green banks, in the same way the snake loved her. Was she looking for the snake in every young man with whom she might grow old?

He didn't tell her that perhaps only twelve-year-old girls met water snakes in flooded mines and grew to love them. It occurred to him that she couldn't, didn't, and needn't speak with the snake.

He thought about her voice. There was nothing to which he could compare it. He had never heard such a voice before. It sounded like the echo of his mother. Was her voice like hunger? Like being full? A voice like thirst? The only drink that could quench it? It was a voice like courage, or its equal opposite in fear; a voice like wind-bearing clouds, snow, ice, and, sometimes, like freezing hail that falls straight into one's face. Her voice reminded him of distant clouds, of stars in their constellation, and of geese paddling across the icy surface of his memory's most mysterious turns. Everything that was and nothing. What he knew and didn't know. Everything he had learned and what he would never be able to learn. The thrills of the heart, mind, and body. Trees, bending in an icy gale. A burned-out candle that first quickens to the wick and then goes out in a flame.

Was his skin wrinkling in the cold? What did the silence surrounding him hold? In his mind's eye he saw a flooded cave, with leaves like frozen rafts floating on the water.

2

"You've got blue, Jewish eyes," his mother said.

He couldn't answer. He was with the girl in his dream.

"Are you still dreaming?" asked his mother.

"About you." It wasn't a lie. He was glad it was the truth. All at once, everything was the truth.

He had dreamed about his mother in the night. In the dream, he had been lying in bed with a girl. They were both naked, but they weren't doing anything. All of a sudden his mother came in wearing just her nightgown; it was as if she were almost naked, too. She looked at them. She nodded her head a bit. Maybe it didn't surprise her. As if she wanted to say, "That's what I thought." Then she left just as she had entered, silent and dignified, in spite of the embarrassing circumstances.

When had he dreamed that?

Did the girl in his dreams look like Katya Ziehrerová, whom he knew from the Great Fortress at the ghetto in Theresienstadt in the summer and fall of 1942? Or like Pirika, who returned from the March of Death when they were evacuated from Auschwitz-Birkenau in January 1942 and with whom he then lived through the summer of

1945 in Prague before they lost touch? Later she sent a postcard with palm trees from the beaches of the Mediterranean and sand from the ruins of Caesarea in Palestine. Did she resemble the ballerina Sonya from the amateur troupe in Marienbad, where he was conscripted and went through basic training?

He wanted to hang on to the image of the girl in his dream, but she drifted away and dissolved. Did she look like the girls he longed for but didn't know and didn't differentiate one from another? Were they just arms, legs, torsos to him, or was it warmth he was dreaming about? Did the girl really have Katya's features?

He couldn't describe her face to himself. She disappeared into the infinity everybody encounters once in a while.

He dreamed that she (his mother and the girl in the dream) said, "From generation to generation . . ." He thought about endurance—why endurance was a man's most important virtue, and of the people who are born with it and those who are able to acquire it. He thought about honor, because the sister of endurance is dishonor, just as the twin of courage is cowardice. At the same time he thought about the injustices within that must be destroyed, one by one, prejudice by prejudice, up to and including the greatest injustice of all: murder. But he also knew about the wrongs people have to destroy within themselves, one by one, prejudice by prejudice. Would he be able to talk about that with the girl in his dream? Maybe only with her.

What was it he heard? What was the constantly growing roar that filled his dreams?

3

Above the chasm a snowstorm was heaving. Down at the bottom lay a human being. An avalanche had caught him. Around his shoulders hung a shotgun. He felt broken into a thousand pieces. At first it had surprised him, blinded and terrified him. He shuddered. His keys had fallen out of his pocket. The sleeve of his snowsuit had torn. His watch had broken. He wasn't even aware of this. He had fallen into a blindingly white crater that had grown narrower and narrower before he blacked out, not knowing the difference between up and down. He had collided into snow, ice, rock walls, crashed his head and chest into everything in his path. Nothing could stop him. By instinct, he'd thrust out his arms and legs in front of him to slow his fall, confused and not understanding, hearing, or seeing anything. Every blow to his head had felt as though part of his body were being torn away. Suddenly the crater went dark like night shoved into a paper bag, and he had the sensation of swimming toward an unknown bank of a cold, black pool. The roar in his head deafened him. Something hit him again. The light had completely disappeared. He felt like a sinking ship, its hull submerged at an incline before its slow descent, inexorably filling with a flood of foaming water and ever-thickening darkness until it settles in the mud. Everything went totally dark.

He lay on his back. Blood ran into his hands. Had he screamed? Could he hear himself?

Was he speaking to silence? He didn't recognize his voice. The blood was warm and sticky; the color of night. Suddenly, all was the color of night, snow, ice, and rocks. What color is the dark? Above, in the white cavity that had turned black, he looked for a point he could hold on to. Just awhile ago it seemed he'd seen snow, ice, and rocks. From the bottom they looked like eagles with their beaks and wings stretched to the other side of the opening. Had he seen them? Eagles? Did the chasm look like the galleries of the mine it had once been one hundred years ago? He felt he was swimming on his back, even though he was lying without moving.

Once again he thought he could see the girl. Was it that girl? Was she lying in the forest snow when he first hurtled through the trees and green undergrowth, with branches bending to the ground by the weight of snow, ice, and intensity of the wind? He didn't know how she had ended up there. She was naked, stunningly beautiful. She took his breath away. She had long hair draping the white nape of her neck and a serious face with big, thoughtful green eyes. Did her green eyes look like a snake's? Warmth emanated from her. Had he confused her with the sun? Was it possible for a girl to have eyes like two small suns? He felt himself recovering in her presence. A certain energy that only women have flowed from her into him. It was a pleasant, stimulating mystery that made him feel stronger, more alive. Strength took the harshness from everything, affirming and deepening him to greater understanding. It gave him back the hope that fear had devoured when the icy branches had whipped him. Everything could still end well. He suppressed an anxiety that he had never known how to control, which would overtake him at times for no reason at all, even when he knew it would last only a moment, that it would pass as quickly as a cloud's shadow when the sun comes out.

"Did you say that it was only good?" he asked.

She didn't answer. It blurred with the echo of silence when he didn't answer his mother at first, with the light, before the crater in the snow had gone dark.

"You're beautiful," he said.

And immediately he added, "Are you?"

But the girl didn't answer again. She had the expression of someone with a great deal of time for everything. Her naked body, throat, face, and hair merged into the powdery snow mist that engulfed the precipice. Light poured out of her. Warmth and light, he thought—all I need to get out of this. She had warm, smooth, white skin. He strained every sense he could to perceive her, so that she wouldn't disappear in the night like the evening as it turns into dusk and dusk into dark.

"I'd like to have a baby with you," he said to her. It surprised him because it came like a flash, a thought that had it not caught him off guard, he probably would not have said to her. A child? Why a child, at this moment? The girl still did not answer. Silvery rays of the moon gleamed from her eyes. Her lips parted a little; she had moist, full lips. He dreamed about the touch of such lips, white teeth glistening in the night.

"I know that you're going to disappear," he said. "I don't want you to leave me."

She pursed her lips, as if she wanted to get closer to him. This sent the thought through his mind that she had answered him, even if she hadn't uttered a word: she wouldn't go away, he didn't need to be afraid.

He felt her gaze ask him whether or not he would survive.

"I will," he said.

It was awkward to reassure her. He wanted her to believe him. He didn't like to lie. Nor did he want to beg. It seemed as though the girl only referred to the situation at hand. "I will now," he repeated after her, like an echo.

Hadn't his mother told his father that men expect women to be like an echo that anticipates their every desire? Like an invisible arch of a rainbow rising on the horizon in the sun after rain.

"Most people trust me," he added.

"Yes," her eyes told him. "We'll see."

Then she disappeared in the silver rays of moonlight just as naked as she had come. He heard only the wind, the flakes, and the flapping of any eagle's invisible wings.

It occurred to him that the girl from his dream, the haze of the girls before (Katya Ziehrerová, Pirika, Sonya, and the others he had known), and his mother were one and the same woman, weren't they? Or not? Was it luck that the girl from the dream had come to visit? When? Where? Didn't the roar in his head bother her? The blow that had almost crippled him? She was beautiful like the break of light into darkness, as mysterious as dusk. Long hair, green eyes, and skin like a silver moon. She had the rising and the setting of the sun in her eyes, daybreak and twilight. It immediately empowered him into feeling he was someone else. An exhilarating perception of body. Body and mind. Body and heart. Body and nerves from his waist down and his waist up. A dynamism filled with energy radiated from him; an element as strong as fire, water, or air. Pain was mediated by beauty. He hung on to it. It was alive as long as he was himself. He had to squint. His heart was pounding. She was as white as a sunny winter morning, rosy like the rays of the summer sun in the early dawn. There was nothing about her like the dark night. What did his mother have to do with it all? He tried to recall the girl's hands, their fingers and palms. What had her slightly opened mouth, her silence, her wordless speech set off in him? A beckoning or a promise? A memory evoking desire? Warmth like breath or blood? Something that had to be touched so that it wouldn't burn up all by itself? But she didn't have a face. That seemed strange to him. He asked himself, doesn't she have a face? Or is it that I just can't tell who she is? Or that I don't want to because it's too soon or too late?

He wanted the girl and his mother to stay with him. He sensed it wouldn't be good to stay there alone. The sensations of his body overwhelmed him. His body commanded his entire being as it had countless times before, the pounding of his heart, his breath, the pulse in his veins. He knew it, this blessing and curse of the body, this excruciating corporeality. He touched the girl in his dreams with his lips, his fingertips, tenderly like a butterfly settling on a flower—a flower with a hidden strength, which opens a bloom in the early morning before it closes again at twilight. Thinking about the girl reminded him of light and dark and the gap between. The different stretch of light between the two. Swiftly changing images like the borders of clouds in the wind.

It was beautiful, only in front of his mother he was a little embarrassed. Shame was painful to him, and pain shameful. He had known it before.

He heard whistling above: strong winds and snow. For a little while it sounded like the roaring of the ocean; a long freight train drawn by a diesel engine. Much farther above, the wind was forming a cloud of fallen snow that covered the chasm like a lid. Was the girl still there? Had she dissolved into the fog and the dark? Could she speak? Had the din in his sleep chased her off? Where had she gone? What did he have to wait for and how long before she would come again? Did it have something to do with the blow to his head when he fell, with the last bit of his strength that the snow slide and fall took out of him? What if the girl never showed up again in the snow? Would it break him to hang on by hope alone?

The sun penetrated the flakes and whirling snow; it gave him a cold incandescence. A more urgent thought came to him: Where were the women he had dreamed about just a little while ago?

The thoughts turning in his mind were more confused than he wanted. Had it been his mother who had first said he had Jewish blue eyes? Or was it just an echo? Did she know how he was hurting?

It occurred to him that there was grass under the snow. He thought about the girl he had always wanted to meet but had not yet seen. He only knew her body. He didn't know what was real and what was a dream. Maybe he already knew what a body was before he was born. His own and a girl's. Any woman's body. What a body meant. A continent, like stars, like constellations. Do bodies understand one another in the same way stars relate to one another? Or as oceans and islands do? Volcanoes? Earthquakes? The repeated strength of the unknown, a secret never to be revealed? How many times had he longed to be older, to be old or the oldest so that he would know more, even though he suspected it wouldn't be what he thought. Maybe only by the power of youth does a person understand, and later all that is left to him is awe. Awe is less than desire. Awe is a mere echo of desire. Desire is the beginning, the foundation and fulfillment. Desire is everything. Desire encompasses hope, awe encompasses only appreciation and helplessness. He concentrated on the vision of the girl, her echo. Her head, neck, long legs, her eyes like moonbeams. Skin like fallen snow. Her torso, breasts, and white abdomen, upon which he wanted to lay his head. Her body. Her warmth. The place where her legs met her torso, an unknown depth he could touch but never see or reach. He wished that she would invite him closer. That she would promise to stay with him. That she would never leave. He imagined the words she would say.

He felt the need to tell his mother, "It's like a river. Three kinds of rivers in one timeless rush. Beyond time. What is happening here and now, what happened yesterday or even earlier, too long ago for me to remember, and what's going to happen soon or later. Nothing can separate those three currents."

Then he said, "Those girls. The first one. Was it the first one or the last?" He sensed the elusiveness of something he couldn't describe. He was in awe of her body and explored her soul for what it was that joined her to him. Her body and his. And indirectly with the body of his mother. It went far into the past, the future, to infinity, to long before the light into which he was born from darkness and depths. Beyond. Where he had first heard, still in her womb, the sound of speech. Words. Emptiness that became filled. A fullness that released itself; light was born. Where and how her thoughts wandered. He thought about how well proportioned his mother had been, with rich, white skin. How it excited him to the point of shame.

It soothed him to dwell on those girls, or his mother, on everything for which the body stood. It brought only mild, pleasant remorse. Their bodies were suffused with the warmth they emanated. His mother, too. Legs, arms. Torsos. Lips. Faces. Like white snow. The snow covered everything. Hot, unmelting snow. Ice. Stones.

4

The twenty-eighth day after he was issued a musket in the garrison at Marienbad, not far from where he was now near Noon Mountain, he thought about his mother, his father, and his sister, and all the girls he had dreamed about with such an intensity that they became real, made from flesh, blood, and skin. Or he became all the more

THE ABYSS

117
▾

real himself. He sensed how it had made him more of a man. He perceived their scents. It tortured him. Desire and lust, need and wish. Longing. It was stronger than his body. Stronger than his will. Stronger than himself. Once the first girl in his dreams cut her hair because he left her. The second had eyes like stars. In Theresienstadt's Great Fortress in 1942, at Youth Home L218, a fifty-odd-year-old cleaning woman cleaned room 16 for thirty boys. He had a temperature, and so he hadn't gone to work and stayed in his bunk. She stroked his forehead. He took her hand, held it, shut his eyes and drew it along the bedspread, under his waist until the woman felt what his trouble was. She stopped and left her hand where it was. He felt her grasp, the movement that relieved him. And then came the shame that wouldn't leave. He wished he hadn't received what he'd asked for. What in that moment had gotten the better of him, an unconquerable monster he had never learned to face and was afraid he never would. He was ashamed by his moment of inexplicable madness. Wouldn't it be better if one were born a fish? He was fifteen at the time. He hoped she would come the next day. She never returned. Later he was ashamed of the realization that when it came right down to it, it didn't matter how pretty the woman was or how old—what mattered was that it was a woman. That indispensable and irreplaceable femininity. There was a bestiality about it that made an animal out of him for a moment, almost so weakened by loneliness and desperation that he could rut with a beast. What he felt was a familiar but unknown element, as strong and destructive as fire and water, a good servant and an evil master. It allowed him to ennoble and humiliate himself at the same time. He was confused and didn't know what to do. Did others feel the same way, or was it only him?

The Germans had killed his mother, sister, and father in October 1944 in Auschwitz-Birkenau. October was the worst month in the war. September had been bad, October incomparably worse. Germany was losing a war on which its fate depended, and it turned its attention to a particular battle. There, where it was mighty, in the concentration camps, versus an enemy that was the least prepared of all, it fought for a consolation prize. Against the helpless. It was the only war Germany could still win, and it did. The gun he held now was more to him than just a symbol of strength. It embodied the ability and the right to defend oneself. Before the crude songs could start in the barracks after lights out, someone told a story for fun:

There was a house on a hill
And in it a table stood there still.
On the table lay a little bowl,
A bowl with water clear and cold.
And in the water swam a fish.
Tell me, friend, where is this fish?
On a cat's supper dish.
Where has the cat gone today?
Into the woods she ran away.
Where are the woods? tell me, friend.
Burning to dust till the end.
Where has the dust settled down?
In the water, river bound.
Where is the water? tell me first.
It quenched away the oxen's thirst.
Where are the oxen? tell me more.
They've glutted the hunger of our lords.
And where have the lords gone away?
Sleeping peacefully in their graves.

Weapons were plunder from the Wehrmacht. The Germans left the Czech field of action in May 1945 with the army of Marshall Schörner. The Waffen Division and Allgemeine SS and Gestapo fled from Prague to the Americans. They knew what skills they had and what the Americans might find interesting. They left their weapons behind. To David, the abandoned weapons brought back everything that formed his life to that point. What had made him become an adult, maybe faster than others because he had less time for everything. The reason he preferred insight to analysis. Instinct to logic. What others thought of as mystery no longer held any to him. He measured everything by his experience in Auschwitz-Birkenau, just as he did that October of seven years ago. What was good. And what was not. What was deadly, and what one could survive. He had learned to endure as children learn to run, to speak, and to count.

"We won the Second World War," said the lieutenant.

In the beginning it had seemed as though maybe they belonged to the side of the victors, but certainly not the entire side. He had lost a lot of himself in that victorious war. He didn't have to think about it. It was in him all the same, like his dreams about girls.

The twenty-eighth day in Marienbad they all received eight-millimeter German pump guns with splotches and bloodstains and names of German soldiers, many of whom were dead or missing in action. The only thing new about them was their owners. Again it reminded him of the whisper of men in Auschwitz-Birkenau; in its echo was the guilt men feel for not fighting in time and missing their chance to do so. Guilt for the ones they were supposed to defend, even if they had to die for them. In the end, it cost them their lives anyway.

"To defend oneself is man's first and last principle," he told his mother. "Legacy of the dead, like Father. If someone asked me what war had given or taken from me, I'd say it made me aware of the need to defend myself." And then he added, "Remember the uprising in the Warsaw Ghetto?"

"There now," she said.

"It still gets to me. They knew they'd fail, down to the last of them; all they had was the chance, if not to keep their lives, then at least not to lose them disgracefully. To be more than creatures betrayed and spat upon. The last had to shoot his own mother so she wouldn't end up in German hands, before he shot himself."

"You should try and put it out of your head, my son," his mother advised.

"I think about the boys from the Great Fortress in Theresienstadt, like Číča Facekáč, who went to Palestine after the war. I'm sure they miss the snow."

Three days after the war he took over the apartment of a German colonel of the Waffen SS at Truhlářská Street 20 in Prague 2. He inherited the personal effects and taste of SS Unterscharführer Heinz Kiewelitz, clips, combs, underwear, polished furniture made from light beechwood in the living room and bedroom. A picture of Hitler in a thick wooden frame. He found the diary of Heinz Kiewelitz, who had survived the war, though with only one hand because the other was shot off in Russia. He had been able to escape with his family at the last moment. In his diary he had written that he would never look back, that there was only tomorrow. There was no one to whom he needed to apologize. He had his honor. Nothing to regret. He loved his two-year-old daughter and his loving wife, with whom he had lived the three happiest years of his married life in Prague. They had to leave quickly. They left almost everything. They took only themselves. His prosthetic right hand with shiny patent leather knuckles remained in the apartment, stretched to the wrist with flesh-colored material and a sleeve made of dark pigskin. Most likely Kiewelitz was telling himself things would never be the same—that life had changed for him.

Had he taken his love for his wife with him, too? Had he lost it in Prague? Had he lost his luck in Prague, along with his youth?

Where and how was he living now? Where had he stashed his certainty of purpose?

As early as the first day of the Prague Uprising, on Saturday, the fifth of May, David had commandeered a revolver. On the streetcar, he had been surprised by how mothers, fathers, or older siblings had dressed their children in the uniforms of the soccer team Slavia, half white and red with a red star on a white background on the chest. On Friday he lived through what would repeat itself on Saturday; young people his age pulling out red and blue state flags from shopping bags and school-bags between stops at Na Příkopě and Wenceslas Square. They were unfurling them. Everyone already knew that Hitler was dead.

David's job in the uprising was to gather food for the hospital on Kelejová Street and run across Paíská Street before it got dark. He ran out of a corner building. No one spotted him. He could have predicted that he wouldn't be spotted. Everyone younger than eighteen who had lived through the camps thought they were immortal. He made friends with the head nurse. It meant a lot to him to get on the good side of some of the women at the hospital. He had his eye on one of the girls there. One visit ruined it for him. He spent three-quarters of an hour under the blanket, breathing the scent of a sweaty girl's body, and that's where it ended. It was better to dream about it.

"It still keeps me alive," he said again to his mother.

In addition to the pistol, he had taken over the apartment in Truhlářská Street in case his mother or sister or father returned by some miracle.

He didn't tell his mother how he hung the prosthetic on the standing lamp in the kitchen with the white credenza and kitchen table with four chairs. The dishes and plates of thick white porcelain had a blue hooked cross on the bottoms. From the door in the foyer he shot at the arm with the stolen pistol. Then he felt bad about the credenza. He moved the prosthetic to the toilet under the window light. He shot at it from as many different distances until he could finally hit the prosthetic from the white entry doors. He was happy that Heinz Kiewelitz wasn't there, since that meant he wouldn't have to shoot at him. He imagined his wife and child. He wouldn't want to shoot the children or Mrs. Kiewelitzová. In the building no one knew what was going on. For a long time no one dared go to the third floor and ask who was shooting whom. The landlady was old and terrified. She had been afraid for the last six years of the occupation.

He shot for as long as his ammunition lasted; then he got more. It wasn't hard to do after the war. He wrapped up smaller-caliber bullets in strips of newspaper so that he could load them into the gun chambers. They fit perfectly. He thought about how to make up for the times when he couldn't defend himself. He didn't want to think whose furniture it was that Unterscharführer Heinz Kiewelitz had requisitioned.

"On the walls—in addition to Hitler and the medals from the eastern front—there were pictures with a village chapel, a framed photograph of a young child with blond hair and blue eyes in a German folk costume with suspenders, and a touched-up wedding picture. I did away with Hitler immediately. I took him out of the frame, crumpled him up, and flushed him down the toilet. They left food behind. Personal belongings. Heinz Kiewelitz wrote in his letters that most of the Russian and Polish women had blue eyes and fair hair like German girls. They just weren't as clean. He had saved even the smallest receipts; how much the first haircut cost for their little girl, for example. I imagined him sitting on the edge of the basin, cleaning blood from under his nails. It probably didn't interest him whose blood it was."

My mother listened attentively.

"During the entire war I dreamed of sitting in a hot bath with water up to my chin and eating. Staying there till the morning. A wash and a treat at the same time."

He didn't tell his mother whom it would be nice to lie with in the hot water. Unterscharführer Kiewelitz looked like a barber in photographs. Or like the mayor of a small village. His hair was already receding. Why had he gone so willingly to war with the world? Did he believe his own words (as he wrote) that the Germany of the Teutons had strayed from the right path of the ancient Romans? By the Jewish and Christian civilization that had come after them? Had he wanted to set right, what, according to him, the Teutons were lacking? Did he wash his hands and feet up to his calves in the Oder and Nisa and in the San River as if he were rinsing them in the Spreva? His captain said that he was in France in the morning, Greece by night, the next day in Russia—and still in the same empire. Was that bad? Well said. *Ausgesprochen gut.* It was over—*ausgespielt*—for the Jews, gypsies, and Slavs. All of Europe would now be German territory. When Negroes would be up next, he couldn't say.

So much had already come to the surface. And the end of it was still far off. People would never know everything. And it was always in the air. It had come from somewhere and would never disappear.

Heinz Kiewelitz loved his family as a hunter loves his dog. No, he loved his family as fathers love their families. He was missing something else. Not just his right hand. Somewhere compassion for others had withered inside of him.

Would he have sacrificed his little girl, his wife, or his father for the German empire? What was he thinking today? What would his daughter think someday?

"Sometimes I wonder how I would act if I had been born like Heinz Kiewelitz," he said to his mother.

"How can you even think of that?" she asked. "You waste your time worrying about it." "It's not the first time," he admitted to her.

His three phases of time came back to him: now, then, and even before.

And again, he thought about how they kept themselves warm in Auschwitz-Birkenau with their own bodies. (It was the thought that came back to him the most.) At the time, he envied the men—frozen and crippled—who had lived full lives, and the experiences they could talk about in the camps. The thirty- and forty-year-olds took the youngest and most fragile into their midst. They made a circle and warmed them with their own animal heat. He remembered when they had done that for him. He had felt the strength, solidarity, and indomitableness of mankind that made people good even in the worst of circumstances. How even hell could be livable with certain people. He remembered their faces because no one had names anymore, just numbers. How after the war he read that "it is possible to destroy a human being, but not to conquer him." How even the weakest ones in the war and camps resisted domination. What the helpless could take pride in, how the wretched could have honor. How the filthy could be beautiful. The way in which they withstood humiliation. He would never have believed it if he hadn't felt it himself. He had experienced the opposite, too. Whether the two were equal or not was pointless.

When his mother didn't return after the war, the landlady and her family, who had been waiting for housing the whole war, took over the apartment. She had to reconcile herself to the fact that sometimes the elevator didn't work.

"I remember my German boss, when I worked in Germany in 1944, in Freiberg in the airplane factory," his mother said. "They shot him for sabotage. Once he brought me a rock of salt to lick at the end of a Sunday shift. I missed salt more than anything else in Germany. It was the same man who threw rags at me to cover my legs when he thought nobody was looking."

In the apartment where the Unterscharführer had lived there was a tall tile stove that went up to the ceiling. When it got going, the beige tiles gave off heat for three days and nights. His mother would probably have liked it.

He had been there when they led the blind Jews to the gas in Auschwitz-Birkenau. They had to throw away their white canes in front of the underground disrobing chambers.

The lieutenant in charge when he had been on duty that morning had talked him into relating what the soldiers discussed in the barracks. One always had to be on the lookout.

"The abyss isn't going to forgive me, just as it doesn't forgive me for talking with the lieutenant on watch."

Now he was hanging on to the flow that ran through his memory like a river in a circle. The dead in Poland also had their now, then, and before. They no longer had their later. "You have a lot to tell me, my son," his mother said.

"It looks that way."

"I keep thinking about when you were born. How happy we were."

He remembered how his mother—when he and his sister were still small—once walked by a tree and asked them what kind of story it would tell. What could the abyss tell? What would he tell the abyss himself?

His head was roaring inside. The abyss, the dark, and the wind reminded him of a dredge he had once watched on the Vltava as a child.

"There are two kinds of death," his mother said. "Don't you know?"

"Do you remember?" the girl asked from his dream.

"Sure I do," he answered. "No, not everything. I remember my three phases of time. Now, then, and before."

Where had she gone? He needed her now—here. Right now. Like a bandage for the fifty-odd-year-old cleaning woman when he was fifteen and for that sick girl at whose feet he had laid his head under a sweltering blanket for forty-five minutes during the uprising.

How high and how low did everything go in life? He thought about the dark triangle of that girl. For the first time, he remembered what her name was. Ruth Barzayova. She had yellow skin. Beyond that, he dared look no further. He couldn't get the raised blue veins on her inner thighs out of his mind. The wrinkles on her breasts from the time she had suddenly lost weight because they didn't feed her in the camps while working her like a starving animal, like a peasant in the fields. She claimed that she had been pretty before the war. The doctor assured her (while David hid under her blanket) that she would look as though she belonged to this world once again. She had her whole life in front of her. It would cover up those three bad years.

He was afraid he would suffocate between her legs. That he would disappear into her as if under a blanket. He wanted to rise above things and not blame her for what she could not control. But truth be told, she couldn't swallow him. It didn't work that way. He wasn't proud of himself. He knew how to disengage himself. It helped him whenever his mind wandered back to her.

He imagined that naked girl who held the morning and the evening in her presence, the dawn and dusk; the beauty of body and face: hair, nails, arms, abdomen, breasts, and below. Rested and fresh, a warm girl's body; just looking at her made him gasp, his breathing increase, and his heart pound. It ended in desire. Where was she? Would she still come? The snow blinded him like a sharp light in the dark.

He tried not to doze off, not to slip into unconsciousness. The noise helped him. He thought about how he could outwit the wind, the cold, and the dark. How he could return to the dream of girls. If just one of them were here, everything would be different. He knew which one. The morning girl. The evening girl. The girl of dawn. Maybe even the girl from the hospital, Ruth Barzayova, with her foul body and sweaty blanket. It was easy to exclude the worst from memories. What was near him hurt, what was far away didn't.

Why did his mother say that he had blue Jewish eyes? He smiled. Didn't she know what he dreamed about her at night? What would she say to that? He liked his mother more than all the others. Then came his sister. And then unknown girls who didn't exist. That one. The morning girl. The girl at twilight. The ones in between.

Soon it wasn't enough for him. It was never enough for him.

He thought about the girl from his dream. In his dreams during the night or right before he woke up, each time she was beautiful and relaxed; sometimes he dreamed about her in the day. She gazed at him attentively, with tender eyes and open, wordless lips. Her face was pure, balanced, long. She listened closely to him. She listened to his silence, too. Every word he said interested her, every breath or pause. His expression. There was a modesty and openness in her that he had never come upon before. She smiled like someone who doesn't want anything from anyone, just to do something good. He took in her body, the curves of her face and chest, her hips, stomach, and thin legs. She was lacking a hurriedness; time spent with her flowed without a thought of minutes or hours. It was a different concept of time than what he was used to; different from the time he spent with other people. She was naked and her long hair was combed, even though she had just let it down. Her hair was soft like a web knitted from the fog or the glow of pearls in the evening sun, softly reddened and scented like mountain water. Her expression wordlessly said that everything she would express was without sin. The innocence of female lips and a girl's neck, the immeasurability of the female's dark

ARNOŠT LUSTIG

126

triangle. He sensed in her what he was searching for. Intimacy and tenderness. Understanding and security. He didn't have to be afraid of failing with her. She knew about his suffering. What he was afraid of, what he suppressed in himself. She didn't want his conscience to bother him. And her? Oh, she smiled. He could touch her in his mind how he liked; breathe in when she breathed out. Exhale when she inhaled. He never got to the point of telling her that she was beautiful. That's what was important, he wanted to explain to his mother. That he tell the girl how beautiful she was. Didn't she want more than just to play? He wanted to stroke her. He wanted to hold her in his arms. Her eyes and wordless lips and smile, her youth, said she was full of pure joy. She didn't want anything dangerous or offensive. Something in her called for touch and admiration and reassured him that he would not be refused, that every time it was a new commitment. He ran his hands along her. He didn't have to worry about his masculinity with her. What determined masculinity to a boy or young man in the eyes of the woman he was with? It always encompassed holding one's own or not. A girl or a woman was the measure. A woman didn't ask what masculinity was. She perceived it with all her senses and more. It was something beyond words. Something that wasn't spoken about. Was it like a spark that ignites a fire? Maybe. She dissolved like a flake in the wind before he could touch her. A snowflake is what she probably had been.

For a little while it seemed to him that he could hear singing in the wind from a pub not far from the garrison, in the direction of Noon Mountain. On Saturdays and Sundays they danced there. Waltzes, polkas, tango. He heard it, unmistakably. Sometimes Rajko Farká, the gypsy, helped out the musicians. If it was Saturday, it was jolly. In the same pub a fifty-eight-year-old cripple had been beaten to death, a man with whom the regulars had drunk beer for thirty-six years. The regulars started telling stories about things that had happened or what their grandfathers had talked about or read in the papers. Earthquakes in which everybody dies. The word "everybody" terrified David. They hadn't been in the war themselves and imagined dangers that hadn't threatened them. He felt just as rattled when they talked about "only" a few people dying in some big catastrophe. Wasn't every needless death horrible to them? He remembered how he trembled and a chill ran down his back when he read in the paper that "merely one hundred and twenty Danish Jews died in the war." Their king had not only protected them but also all of little Denmark, with hardly an exception. They had smuggled most of the ten thousand Danish Jews into Sweden.

They drank the stories down with strong beer in the pub. Once in a while they talked about witches who put the evil eye on livestock, poisoned wells, or made cows run dry. Didn't every woman have a touch of the witch in her? A man couldn't even catch a hint of some spells. How were men different from women? They talked about passions and vices; why so few women serve men willingly, out of love—and when they did serve, their love was taken by force. Women weren't ashamed like their grandmothers. How little women cared about men's peace of mind, not to mention their squabbling? Where were the days when a woman would rather die than lose her virginity? They complained about women's moods for which no cure existed. They talked a lot about their ancestors and the last war. That's what brought him to compare their experiences with his own. Phrases such as "mass grave" haunted him; there was no way to mourn his dead. He had to keep it to himself. It belonged to the things to which one didn't call attention.

The snow crunched under him even if he didn't move. Was earth turning underneath him? He swept by the stars on his trip through the universe. He saw his own back. Once he watched his mother while she undressed in her bedroom; she didn't know he was there with her. He would never tell anyone what it did to him.

He felt the crash of the landslide as if it were an echo. A light whose flash dispersed darkness. His cry transformed silence in the dark. What did the roaring in the middle of it all mean before he got choked in the snow? Was it his scream that he didn't recognize? Someone else's voice? He saw the stars that hit one another, sparked, and fell apart into powder, and the one that circled them like snowflakes in the wind. As many stars as snowflakes in a weeklong snowstorm. The thought came to him that the abyss was like a garage. What else reminded him of a garage? Yes, gas chambers, underground disrobing rooms. October 1944 in Poland. He tried to ignore the roar in his head. The echo of the crash. Into black.

He had a couple of things he wanted to tell his mother. (Not about what looking at her body did to him.)

He didn't like girls whose eyes goggled like fish when one danced with them. He didn't like his own confusion either. He longed to love someone. (He was ashamed of that. It was one of his innermost secrets.) Was it only the desire to love? The need? Did he want to love so that someone would love him? Was he so different that it didn't work for him? He remembered the lieutenant who gave him the order to go out, even as he warned him about the wind, and he thought about the other lieutenant, of the defense unit. They also were a key to all kinds of things. He thought about the two of them.

He was lucky that during the fall into the chasm he hadn't collided with the skis, poles, or rifle barrel. He could have lost an eye or both or pierced his belly. Then none of the girls in the snow would want him.

He imagined how he could get out of the abyss. There was no way that he could manage it. It was better to dream about the girls. About bodily warmth; about the nicest things. It comprised feeling and a face, a word, and, finally, touch. The feeling of a body. He sensed his own. Where were those girls now? Where was everything? He knew he wouldn't be able to last longer than twenty-four hours. Most of all, he wanted to see that first girl.

5

He tried to orient himself. A little bit away from where he lay was Noon Mountain. Germany was beyond his head or at his feet. Winters in the region were harsh. They lasted from early fall to late spring. As the lieutenant said in the classroom, seasons changed according to the angle earth turns on its axis toward the poles, from east to west, around the sun. The lieutenant tried to explain everything in one sentence. If something demanded more, he didn't explain it. Every view in the mountains reminded him of something. Looking up the ridge or down to the valley, on the way up or on down the descent. Vertigo. Until desire and the haze of girls. Of that one. He reproached himself that he had already missed her several times. They had certainly been close a couple of times. He probably thought there was time enough to find her, or that the right time hadn't come for him yet. It occurred to him that it was similar to hearing a cock crow many times until all of a sudden one realizes that the important thing is the very first crow, because it separates night from day. He mustn't miss the next time. Nor the first or last crowing. That girl, too, was something similar to the rooster and the division of day from night or night from day. Desire from fulfillment. And at the same time she brought them together. Did she? Nothing was certain. Nothing is ever certain, ever has been or would be. Even the most secret. For the first time, he wondered what the girl could possibly mean. Or was he the first and the last who would decide it?

He thought about the soldiers in the barracks. About Horse, Gypsy, Kristus, and the lieutenant. It wouldn't have occurred to them that he could fall into a place like this. They would ask how he could have strayed so far. And fall into an abyss? To have the feeling that he was flying or propelling through the air like a magician or an air diver. Why? He never had been very practical! He struggled to grasp how a boy becomes a man other than by counting up the years. When longing meets surprise and reason succumbs to dreams. (What the body means, meant, and would mean. To dream about a girl who appeared from the foggy haze for just a fraction of a moment.)

Then his mother said, "When you were born, it was very cold and windy, with snow in the clouds as it is here and now. I went to the kitchen to make Christmas pastries, the ones your father wanted. I had everything ready. The raisins and braided dough. But what came out was you. You were born easily. Even according to the calendar, it was the best night of the year, the twenty-first of December."

He started to explore the area in his mind. The sounds of the dark drifted at the bottom of the abyss like sleeping ducks on cold water. The thought that hardly anyone in his right mind would go out searching for him at this time and in this weather gnawed at him. Field exercises were called "war games" in the military papers of the division. It seemed so easy to play war.

He knew what he wanted to prove to himself. It wasn't just to be a man or not.

The chasm's shape reminded him of a dish with a neck, something that the dark and cold gathered in until filled to the brim. He looked up from where, in spite of everything, he expected help from the dark.

That girl. He wanted nothing other than for her to give him her hand and help him stand. That way he would be able to get up. He would take her palm in his hand. They would step side by side, slowly, wandering in the snow as he might do in the summer. He dreamed about the girl, the spring, and the snowfall. They didn't have to speak. They would touch each other by arms, by hands. It was enough for him; nothing; it held everything. She felt his look through his touch; the longing in his expression. Everything a person craves. They had never spoken. Did it seem to him that he heard her whisper? Didn't he dare to glance her way? He could imagine her. They were alone. Only the din of the storm disturbed them. She asked him whether he had been hit in the head. He probably seemed as if he didn't understand anything. Had he yelled? It must have sounded like someone else yelling. He mustn't mention the dark. That would drive her away. She gave off warmth and light like the sun in the middle of summer. He remembered how she came to him the first time. Where? He had seen her in the air like the morning shadow. Shadows just born from sunlight. Evening. The dark in the middle of night. The shadows encompassed intimacy and safety, everything tender. He heard the roaring in and around his head again.

6

Once again, he tried to guess the strength and direction of the wind. It seemed as if the clouds were piling up and the dark gathering. They had most likely gathered through the night until morning. Was it still storming above? The din had not lessened. Had it lasted five, ten, or fifteen minutes? (Like the gassings in Auschwitz-Birkenau? The Germans had learned to save even on Zyklon B. Then the gas had taken a half hour to suffocate everyone. Ten thousand cans of Zyklon B.) Or had it taken all night? First from morning to evening, and then from dusk to dawn?

The three phases of time: now, yesterday, and before. He was already embarrassed by what everybody else would think of him. He thought, What is not embarrassing to a person? What does one regret? What doesn't he? Maybe he really didn't need this in his life and it didn't have to happen. Then at the tail of the question came another, like an echo: Why did this have to happen to him?

What could he or should he have done so that it wouldn't have happened to him? He thought about the soul, what secrets it contains, and what one never knows it does.

Now the tips of the rocks and the boulder looked like feathers, like when he first saw a girl's body close up; the most tender thing he was able to imagine, all the greater by its absence. A memory enhanced. An image beautified. That gorgeous girl that came to him as the morning haze. With her thighs and between her legs that which reminded him of half-opened rosy lips, a child's ear. The shell of a clam. The first girl that let him touch her with more than a look was Katya Ziehrerová. That was in the Great Fortress, in the ghetto of 1941. Her father was a big man on the Jewish Council, first in Ostrava, then in Prague. In his mind he could still smell her, and what it brought out in him at the time. He tried to blow the snowflakes from his lips. They reminded him of a pillow that his mother had given him for his bed when he was four. She stuffed it full of goose feathers. He had a matching cover for the comforter; he had always been warm.

Katya Ziehrerová had a pretty smile and slightly opened lips; in every moment of her existence she was prepared to kiss. To touch her lips to everything. There was something crude about it. She wasn't a bad girl, only a little calculating. She was able to stand with her legs apart even if her legs were straight together. Hands at her hips and her chin up. Challenge and doubt in her eyes. She guessed what his shoulders must be like in the same way she sized up her figure, from the waist down and the waist up. "How much do you love me?" she wanted to know. "I don't know," he answered that time. He was sixteen years and one day old. "Do you also believe that a girl who poisons a man without poison can be a witch?" "Do you believe that yourself?" he asked back. That's how he won her over.

In Theresienstadt's Great Fortress, he stole a red rose from the garden of Oberscharführer Heindl, whom they hanged after the war. He started off from the fortress ramparts along the trunk of the cherry tree. He ran through the garden from the ramparts up to the rose orchard. At the time, the Oberscharführer shot at him with his Luger; he jumped down from his horse, still shaky from the run, so he wasn't holding the gun steady. With a rose in his hand and the vision of Katya Ziehrerová in his mind, he ran back through the garden to the brick wall, thrust the rose between his lips and climbed back up into the fortress. It almost cost him his neck. Oberscharführer Heindl was a man who could do whatever he wanted.

"Don't talk about it anymore," he said.

"Are you talking to me?" his mother asked.

"Sometimes I wish I had been born a boy," Katya had said.

She told him that when she was five years old, she had fallen in love with her father. She planned on marrying him when she grew up. She asked her mother if she could. Her mother reassured her she could. Why not? When she was nine years old, she experienced her first disappointment as a woman: she couldn't marry her father.

She took it out on the men who fell in love with her; she didn't even know what she was getting back at them for. She got along with men immediately, but only halfway. She wanted to marry for more than what was offered and more than what her suitors could give. (She did get married in the Great Fortress and had an affair with her father-in-law. Someone even spread the rumor that she'd become involved with her mother-in-law, too, because nothing was sacred to her.) People also said that she had seduced her own father—who knows what the truth was. Why? Did she want her lovers to be like her father before the Germans sent him east? Everybody knows what happened. Does death wipe out all sins? Probably not, if those who remember are still alive. Katya Ziehrerová no longer was.

"Why shouldn't I love my father how I want? How he wants?" She used to say that when her father was far, far away and in all likelihood dirt.

"In December we went for a three-day exercise with sharpshooters," he started to tell his mother, to dim the memories of Katya Ziehrerová. "Once I slept on the snow in the forest. I put my coat under me. I made a sleeping bag out of it. It was dry. The frost was biting, but I didn't get too cold. The resin smelled good. It was a forest of firs. Tall trees. The earth was strewn with snow and underneath lay the pine. I could sense the earth resting. It was strange to feel the earth beneath me, as if I were following the movement of the stars. You have the feeling the earth is turning with you or that it's turning inside of you. The connection between yourself and everything that surrounds you. It was something else. We did our fall exercises in a former German village that soldiers shot to pieces after the war. They only left the church to use as a target for hits from tanks. It always seemed strange to me to shoot at a church. I can't explain why."

What he liked best was to listen to his mother sing, as she did when he was small and she sat him on her lap and nibbled on his ear. She wanted him to sing to her in return. At the stream, at the pond. The one about black eyes. The phase of time number 2. And the phase that came even before then. His second phase contained everything that happened from when he was a child until his return from Auschwitz-Birkenau. The third phase was now. (Now, then, and before.) It was odd that all of the phases consisted of layers of the past like strips of some invisible cloth. It flowed like a river that bore everything away in its current, the beginning and the end, the middle, the sense of all things. The invisible and the never expressed. And the things he didn't understand because he couldn't or he didn't want to.

The defense lieutenant asked him just yesterday: "Wiesenthal, if you were supposed to decide whether to drop the atom bomb on Hiroshima and Nagasaki, what would you do?"

The Japanese had started the war. The Americans, Australians, and their allies died like flies. The Japanese had been willing to defend their emperor to the last man. How many Americans would have had to die before they defeated Japan? They say a million. And five million Japanese. They had made their small islands into major fortresses. They had refused to give up.

"The war would have lasted a year longer," he answered.

"Are you sorry for the Americans?"

"I am sorry for all the dead the war is responsible for killing."

"Even the Germans?"

"Some of them. Not the ones who treated us like animals. But certainly for the ones yet to be born, because the sins of their fathers and grandfathers will fall on them. They weren't responsible, but they'll never be rid of those sins, just as no one ever gets rid of the dark."

"Get your politics straight in your head, Wiesenthal," the lieutenant had said.

What he didn't tell his mother was what the lieutenant would most likely say if he found him here. Would he ask how many bones he had broken? How much of his skin was grazed? Would he be able to hear the noise that the landslide was making inside of him? The snowstorm outside? He always had the same impression from both of the lieutenants: that they wore their conscience and arrogance like a uniform. But at the same time they were disappointed in themselves. In comparison with people they didn't even know. They were disheartened by the past and the present, as well as the future, because it seemed far away, beyond their reach. He could feel an envy in them, even though it was hard to say about what or of whom.

The two lieutenants blurred into words before they turned into the images of Kristus, Horse, and the gypsy Farká as well as the image of the sergeant who'd punished him yesterday with night duty because he had found some mud on the bottom of his boots. He lingered on the sound of words that everyone used but that meant something different to each person, something the other person never understood. His postwar world. No one knew that he was unable to draw a line between the war and life after the war; how to him they faded into one another as if one were tissue and the other its nourishment. No one knew that one leg of him still stood in the war and the other in peace; it would probably never be any other way. In that respect, he wasn't normal. It was a silent insanity with which everyone who survived learned to live.

His lieutenant was interested in experiments in Russia, where mothers gave birth in water. Doctors were trying to increase the newborn's mental and physical ability. The children were born in a state of no gravity. Water increases the left brain's and right brain's need for oxygen. Children born this way are supposed to be extraordinarily intelligent. The Russians had different goals and methods, the lieutenant added, than those of Western capitalists.

Time in triplet: today, yesterday, and the long space between them. The period before the war, the war, right after the war, and now, two and a half years in the army. Time like a river that runs and flows away and never wanes. Always the same river, and at the same time different. Was what had happened extraordinary? Or was it able to take place for the very reason that it wasn't that unusual? Three eras. How was it right after the war? Glorious. Perhaps. For him. For people like him. With Pirika. In the same way he had first been with Katya Ziehrerová, he knew Pirika was a part of him. Pirika was his second.

In retrospect, it seemed trivial that the sculptor who had designed the biggest statue of Stalin in Bohemia shot himself. Four tons of granite, ore, and stone, even before it got finished. It was something he would've liked to tell Pirika.

The army was good to him. There was no war. They only played war.

The flow among the three time periods. He didn't want to tell his mother: now, then, and before. What they all contained. What memories stood out the most and why. Pirika. A woman's body. His body. Two bodies next to each other. Animal heat. Intimacy. Safety. The dream he had of a girl was composed of all the bodies and all the girls whom he had known as well as those he did not yet know and perhaps never would. Where did it come from? Nothing would ever part it from him. It flowed on the riverbed of memory. Taking everything with it and leaving it all behind.

It was different time than a watch tells. Or a calendar. It was something that could turn the worst place into the best possible. (Just as it could turn the other way around.) How many times had that happened to him? More often when he was among better people than the reverse? The men who kept him warm in Auschwitz-Birkenau with their own bodies so he wouldn't freeze to death were the best. It was October, the wind was blowing. A storm was coming. He went across the gypsy camp from barrack 21. He thought he would freeze to death. That he would end up in the ovens. And they called to him, "Boy, you're freezing. We'll warm you up, come here." How could they warm him? They were so fragile themselves. They took him among them, to their center, and they pressed against him, the whole little group of them. In a little while he was warm. They had given him the one thing they had. He never saw them before and he never did again. They were all around forty or so. They were probably in the ovens themselves the next day. No one ever had to tell him about solidarity. What friendship was. From what cloth man is made.

The camps hadn't turned them into worse people than they were before the camps. In the worst surroundings, some people turn into gold; they reveal what they are. It is not possible to pretend. Only sometimes—with the very same people—it was yes and no. Often they are and then they are not, from day to day and hour to hour they change. He hadn't known even one of the men who kept him warm that day. None of them had known him either.

He could reach far to the past and future for what he wanted, he thought. Even further than the past. Reel it in as a mother does a child. Time has no blood to seep out. He didn't want to talk to his mother about bleeding to death. He thought about Pirika.

His lieutenant said, "Hasn't it by chance occurred to you, Soldier Wiesenthal, that you could make a lot of things easier for yourself if your name didn't remind people of some things? Why don't you go to the colonel's office when you're off duty and ask him how the National Committee could help you change your name? Why cling tooth and nail to this German name of yours?"

"One of my uncles who lives far away, in El Salvador, is named Jankel, same as my mother's maiden name."

"I was under the impression that you no longer had a mother, Wiesenthal."

"No."

"I don't want to ask you what happened to her, Wiesenthal."

"She was with her brother. They took them to the ovens on the same day. She was skin and bones, like when she nursed my sister. That day they killed women. Ten thousand in one day, another ten at night. The men stood naked in line in the empty lot in front of the crematorium waiting for daybreak. Then they gassed them, the rest of the transport."

"That wasn't exactly decent what the Germans did to your people. Do you write to your uncle, Wiesenthal? I mean the one that lives so far away."

"We used to. There remained a handful of us all over the world. I wanted to know what happened to my mother. If any of the family had made it. We exchanged a few letters. It helped us both, in a way. The same experiences. He invited me to come to El Salvador. He has a house there with a garden and monkeys. He keeps them in a cage like a canary. I think he works in an iron factory. His wife is from Caracas."

"Is there anyone else from your family abroad besides your uncle?"

"No, they killed every last one of them."

"You were lucky, Wiesenthal, that you escaped, aren't you?"

"Depends on how you look at it."

"What do you mean, how you look at it?"

"Every person who survived the camps only survived because someone else was killed instead." He had forced himself to answer, even though he knew that the lieutenant would only be able to grasp distantly what he couldn't imagine. It wasn't the first or the last time that the questions seemed silly, or almost offended him. When they killed brunettes, redheads survived. If they murdered those with red hair, the blonds had it easier. That's how it went, day after day, until the end of October 1944. Then they only killed the ones that couldn't make the death marches, while the heartier marched to camps in the interior. The world was not divided into longitudes and latitudes, but rather mass graves. Now, then, and even before.

"Are you going to write to him again? You should be more careful, Wiesenthal. How many times a year do you write to him? Once a month, a week?" His words held the invisible but palpable, the ever-present foreboding. That part of life all people, including him, wanted to suppress or overcome, so that it would disappear without erupting again. Sometimes he had the impression it was actually an eclipse of reason, even for the cleverest among them, in the same way an eclipse of the sun or moon or certain stars occurs.

"What did you answer?" his mother asked.

"People who hadn't been in the war themselves didn't learn much from it."

"I can imagine the difficulties you've had."

"Everyone who wanted to do things their own way started having it tough. The lieutenants know best how you're supposed to live, or what you're supposed to do, where to go and what to believe. They couldn't convince Gypsy or Kristus even if they'd had tongues of angels. Gypsy took blows or insults better than he did taunts; in reality he never budged. He could have learned to live without teeth if he decided to. Kristus got told off a couple of times, too; he did what he liked, how and where he wanted. It wasn't easy for anyone to be whom they wanted. Everyone paid for it."

"That's how it's always been, and will be. It only takes on different disguises."

"I never knew that before."

He remembered how Gypsy had written on the barracks wall inside: ". . . three boats against the flow . . ." He scribbled next to it: "Love is a grand sorceress. Alcohol brings visions." It didn't matter to the lieutenant what anyone said to him but rather what he heard in it. The other troop lieutenant maintained the fervid belief that he saw the world through the eyes of the people he judged. He knew beforehand what someone thought or would think about something. He divided people into those on his side and those against. He never changed his mind. He never let himself be refuted.

"It's hard to learn to be alone," his mother said.

"It's as warm as a summer wind here."

"You think so? That's how it seemed to me, too, when I was seventeen. I was happy from morning to night. At eighteen I was an adult. At twenty-one I got married and then I had you. I carried you for nine months in my heart. At first, you took up just a bit of it, and then the whole thing. I knew what would become of you, how you would be. I just didn't know what life had in store for you. Not even mothers know that. In what things you would take after me. At thirty-eight I knew what you see now, here. That the long is long, the short short, and the hard hard. Everything wrapped in a summer breeze, like a dream in winter, the sun and snow in a winter wonderland. One evening, one morning, one year, an entire life. I see in your eyes what you see in mine, my boy. Life. Everything—from the beginning to the end and from the end back again."

"I can hear eagles overhead."

"I hear them, too."

"Are they eagles, Mother?"

"I think so." Then she said, "Every day, my boy . . ." He didn't know what she wanted to say. "Everything you'll do or did or could have done . . . ," she added. "You have to have your own world . . . as each person does . . ."

He shut his eyes. He was alone again. Where was Pirika? Didn't she know that he was waiting for her while he talked with his mother? It was only the roaring in his head that bothered him. It had to be Monday—in Auschwitz-Birkenau, the day and night selection to the ovens. Some waited for it, in order to have it be over. All of a sudden life was less valuable than death. The past was worth more than the present, and the future disappeared. Sometimes people guessed whom the colonel and the doctor would pick next, as if they weren't all standing in the same line. The terror to live muffled even the fear of death or the pain of death by suffocation.

Horse, Gypsy, and Kristus sat on the first bench in the classroom during political training; the three of them were always together. His own place was in the third bench to the left, on the edge. The sergeant sat on a chair. Gypsy and Kristus were playing a game. (They played a different one in the dorm.) Gypsy told them about the number 3. He put great store in the trinity. The trinity that everything is built upon, probably. Three like the beginning and end of the world. That was on its way, to be sure. Nothing would come after it.

Socialism and capitalism? Fire and water, according to the lieutenant. Didn't his uncle in El Salvador say that habit was an iron shirt? the lieutenant reminded him. Hadn't he talked about Caracas the last time? The lieutenant smiled. He was only joking. Testing him. Pirika, where are you? Katya . . . ? Mama . . . ?

It rained on Saturday. Horse was playing the guitar. The sergeant was like a different man. To begin with, he asked Horse, "Why do you use the familiar with me, comrade soldier?" Then he started telling jokes: What happens to a dog that chases after a truck and then catches up? "He catches the truck," Horse said. "No, it gets run over," the sergeant replied.

Horse looked at Gypsy and Gypsy looked out the window to the muddy fields and the rain. The landscape looked like a sty. The barracks seemed untidy when it rained. Horse had a lousy guitar; he had bought it for five hundred crowns from a boy who had run off to South America. He needed money for the escape. He was carrying his pajamas in a handbag. In summer, the fields shone gold with ripe wheat; in winter, the snow covered the worst. A small garrison town. Marienbad. Horse was from Svitava. During the war, the Germans had a factory there for guns and ammunition. Horse had never seen anything sadder than Jewish men and women working twelve hours a day and twelve hours a night on two shifts, in rags, starving, toothless, and hairless. Their relatives had already been killed. They were shards of families. Mothers without daughters, fatherless sons, men without wives, women with no husbands, orphans, brothers without sisters, and sisters without brothers. The factory belonged to an SS man who had saved his Jews from being transported. While some were used for his workforce to make money, others had been transported across Svitava to Auschwitz-Birkenau.

The sergeant proclaimed that it was fortunate they didn't have to compare the pub girls to a truck.

"You can't make a gypsy from clay like you can a lieutenant of a military defense unit," Gypsy replied. "As my grandmama says, the future casts its own shadow. She never tells fortunes. To know more than you're supposed to can ruin your life. When will you die? What will you do? What is it to her? In a month she'll be ninety-four. Not a single tooth in her mouth for the past forty years. She doesn't need to lie to anyone. When she was young in the village she had said that somebody would die of consumption in a week; it happened. She couldn't walk with her family through the village without someone beating her. You always remember the worst the longest. What's possible in love is disaster in cards. I don't believe a word those lieutenants say. In the pub, Grandmama orders from the top to the bottom of the menu. Thank God she'll eat anything. Chows down like a young woman. She's going to live to one hundred and twenty. With an apartment in a prefab building and a stuffed-up toilet seven days of the week."

Gypsy would doze off in the classroom under the map of the world. The lieutenant would threaten him.

"Are you one of those who thinks man's an animal?"

"I don't know."

"What did you think about the clash between the British and Nazi Germany?"

"A poorly played comedy," said Gypsy, like a parrot of the lieutenant. "They disguised it by bombing London. Wiping out Coventry as the British did to Berlin and Dresden in return. They understood each other well. That's why the world looks the way it does now, after the war," he added. He said it as if he were reciting his multiplication tables.

"Wiesenthal, is it true that you like jazz?"

"Why not, comrade lieutenant?"

"It's not forbidden, of course; but do you think it's wise? When did you start that up?"

"In the Great Fortress—the ghetto in Theresienstadt, comrade lieutenant. In 1942. Boys about as old as I am now—twenty or so—played it. They allowed them to play four hours every day in the bower on the square in front of the church. The Germans said it was nigger Jewish music that corrupted the soul. They let the ghetto swingers play when the international commission from the Red Cross came to inspect the fortress. Fricek Weiss was the bandleader, before he went up the flue in Auschwitz-Birkenau. Sometimes just a trio played. Saxophone, piano, and horn. We waited for it sometimes half the afternoon. The first time I heard it, I felt as if someone poured hot liquid all over me. They played the song "Mean to Me." Then they played Gershwin's "Rhapsody in Blue"; serious, sad almost, but at the same time exciting. Then a song I didn't know. I felt as if I were opening a door and watching the stars fall. No one gets hurt, only the dark lights up. All of a sudden I was whole again and free, as the best people were—at that moment in time—in the best place. And it's only a saxophone. It's like bread. You can't eat too much of it."

"You know, Wiesenthal, comrades who know more about music than you don't think that about jazz."

He told his mother, "Sometimes I listened to the Nazi songs and they seemed pretty to me, even though the words rarely said anything nice. They were songs of their beginnings, when they dreamed about conquering foreign countries more than about killing, which they couldn't do without. Then their songs drowned in blood and endless murder. Only the melodies remained. Maybe they wanted to call back the times of their beginnings when everything was still in front of them. They always played them, at every opportunity, even in the camps. Sometimes they even put them on loudspeakers in the space between the barracks. I always wondered who was singing them and who sings them now. I carried them with me away from the camps and brought them from the war, as someone takes spoils he can't talk about without bringing shame on himself."

"Once when the camp commander came to inspect us, I heard those songs playing. Blood was running down my leg; I wasn't the only one. It was a moment of triumph for the commander, and for us utter humiliation. They shaved us bare, on top and below, and there we stood in rags, no underwear, some of the women half naked. And the music accompanied it all. Trumpets, drums, sounding like the breath of a gale. Maybe the commander heard the lunacy and inexorability in them, too. I know what it is you remember, what you're talking about."

"I hear echoes in it. Of the drumbeat that left its mark on Europe. Maybe it's the sound I hear when my heart pounds loudly."

"Who knows where a person gets his will not to drown in all the ugliness when he has nothing else."

He thought about the blood that marks a woman. The moment she gives up being just a girl forever. How his mother must have felt her blood run like mud down her thighs to her ankles and into the dirt. She couldn't take a breath. She had to keep still so she wouldn't seem like an animal. If someone wants to know about endurance, they should ask the women in the camps. Whoever wants to know how it is possible to retain one's dignity within, when outside everything is erased as day erases night, let them imagine the women in the snow between the fences, in the mud, in the wind, wretches in rags, shaved bare.

A couple of times he had seen the women stand at attention on the Appelplatz, a few of whom had blood running down their legs. It never gave him the impression of ugliness. On the contrary, he felt a respect toward them that he couldn't explain. It certainly wasn't just sympathy—a person can't sympathize with the sun or the moon or stars, nor with the wind or rocks, nor with the cold light of the night or the stench of a swamp.

It blurred in his mind with the Nazi melodies. If he wanted, he could have put the words to them. He could depend on his will to decide what he wanted or didn't want to do. It made him think of the sergeant.

Then he confided in his mother once again. "There was no way to tell him that we also learned something in the camps. Once I told him that we played soccer there, and I saw the thought go through his mind: see now, you got to play soccer. So it couldn't have been all that bad. How could I have explained to him in that same moment that the SS bet on our games as if they were at dog or horse races or cockfights? How many people were cremated in between? Or that anybody who injured another player on the field in Auschwitz-Birkenau went straight to the ovens? The player who fouled another—Nazi-like—went up the flue like the rest?"

"I know what we learned in the camps," his mother added.

Part of it was the necessity to judge one's chances and each SS man or woman within the space of a second. If someone didn't figure out the dangerous ones quickly enough, it cost him his life. We also learned to judge our own people, not just the capos. Who you could trust to leave your soup bowl with if you had to run to the latrine and who you could not.

"We also learned to lie; to tell the difference between a hundred different lies. The bad ones, the ugly, the harmless, the necessary; you have to be born a liar to tell them apart," he told his mother.

He had already figured out both his lieutenants. He never had to change his impression after the first two seconds of seeing them, it just continually reconfirmed itself. That was something he brought back from the camps. He could look at a person and know: this person is dangerous or harmless. Useful or bad. It came in many variations and still more. The camp reminded him of an animal within an animal. An animal also has to decide within a fraction of a second.

Soldiers lied from the urge of self-preservation. Horse, the sergeant. Kristus only lied sometimes. People live with lies like fish swim in water. Most of the lies get by. But he also knew people who never lied. The farther away he got from them, the better they seemed. It was good to know people who weren't liars. Rybka-Fišl from the camps never lied. Hardly anyone believed him anyway because he survived his death. An SS soldier had forgotten that he advised Rybka-Fišl to hang himself by dawn; it was one of a bored SS soldier's many whims.

"I never lied to my own people," his mother answered. "I only know that the worse off you are, the easier it is to lie to those who are the closest to you."

"Probably," he admitted.

Then all of a sudden his mother asked from the cold and the dark, "What happened when they separated us?"

"Do you remember how my transport from the Great Fortress in Theresienstadt was *abreisefertig*? Oberscharführer Heindl replaced the half gypsy, Laszlovic, with me. He shoved me into the last wagon; luckily he threw a three-day ration in after me. I downed it right then. (Then I starved for three days and four nights.) Laszlovic wove baskets and made brooms for the SS officers' wives."

"That was the last time I saw you. It was September 23, 1944."

"Before I got sent on the transport, Oberscharführer Heindl interrogated me because my friend in the fortress—Herman Pfeffer—had escaped to Prague; then he had to come back because he didn't have a place to hide. He sold his coat and shoes for a train ticket. Oberscharführer Heindl wanted to know what I knew about it before Pfeffer escaped. Nothing. He was just an acquaintance. We had played soccer for the boys' league A, on which the officers in the garrison had placed bets. He had sent a postcard to me in the Great Fortress from Prague. His father was an SS and his mother a Jew; the father had gotten rid of her, they transported her east. It made a different person out of Pfeffer. All of a sudden he had one leg in our world and the other in the Germans'. I was afraid that you wouldn't know I was in the train car and would worry too much."

"I did see you. I shook from fear; I didn't know where they would take you. What they would do with you."

"They took me to the commander's, to the bunker. There they left me to wait. When I wanted to know from Heindl why he was escorting me, he asked me if I had a clear conscience. We walked side by side, and it almost looked as if we were just taking a stroll until I remembered what happens to people in the bunker. Then they took me, put me on a truck, and brought me to the ramp. I crouched down to the bottom of the wagon so that you wouldn't catch a glimpse of me by chance. The streets had already emptied. The transport was in the wagons. I was the very last person. We went east just like you, papa, and my sister a week later."

He had learned to take everything that didn't threaten his life with a dose of calmness. He had learned that in moments of utmost danger his mind functioned cold-bloodedly, like a machine. It hampered neither his energy nor time. It had happened to him a few times. What incensed him was injustice. He couldn't take a drop of it. Not only could the greatest injury come from the slightest injustice but also the end of a life.

It depended on a person's good name and then again it didn't. His reputation had helped him out a couple times, just as once a tarnished reputation hadn't. He knew exactly when, where, and how that happened. To him, justice was still greater than one's name.

Once a man in the camps said to him, "It's up to you when death is your friend and when it's your foe. Whether you fear or welcome it."

It meant everything he could think of now.

"I know what you're thinking, my son," his mother said.

"What is good and what is fair," he answered.

"I figured that out myself," she said.

"Do you know what cosmopolitanism is, Wiesenthal?" the lieutenant asked. "German monopolies made money on the consumption of propulsion materials during the air strikes on Germany in World War II due to international alliances. On the other hand, international companies made money from the production of Zyklon B, made by the firm Degesch and then I. G. Farben. In Russia, they locked up a Jewish doctor on the suspicion that he poisoned Maksim Gorky in 1936. They killed a Kirov party favorite in Leningrad." The lieutenant knew what he was talking about. Then they locked up the Slánský Group. Eleven socialist leaders, enemies inside the party. In the newspapers they wrote how they were all of Jewish origin.

"It was the first time since the war that I broke out in a cold sweat," he told his mother.

"Now you know why I always said they want to let us bleed to death even after they have killed us?" replied his mother. "They always want to make up for whatever they didn't finish."

"I met a man who refused to believe what happened."

"You know what that is, don't you?"

"Probably. He would have said that before the war the Jews had all of the banks, schools, and newspapers in their pockets. During the war, he would have cried out for Germany to rid Europe of such parasites. Now, he says that it didn't happen, that we only thought it up. I've gotten used to it. He claims that it wouldn't be possible to bury seven or eight million people without a clue. He's got logic on his side."

Three phases of time: now, before, and even earlier.

"The Germans knew that a person has to breathe, and that he'll breathe even if there's no air but gas. So instead of breathing to live, he'll breathe to die." The words echoed and dispersed in the fog and emptiness of the abyss.

7

The sky above the abyss went on forever. It seemed like a labyrinth greater than even that of memory. Everything flowed together in it and disappeared. Even the stars were lost. A silent gust of wind whipped snow dust from side to side; it tore apart the clouds and sent them scuttling away. He could no longer imagine where Germany ended and Bohemia began.

"Sometimes I'm afraid that you'll end up going out of your mind from it all," his mother said.

"The lieutenant says that each person is just as important as the next, but you can tell by his face that he doesn't believe it." He smiled at his mother and added, "Do you know what Gypsy calls a miracle? First, it is if somebody lends you anything. And second, it is if you return it."

"I am sorry that life is so short," she said. "Whom are you waiting for?"

He answered: "I met a girl I knew from the Lower Carpathians, after the war, in June of '45, when it didn't terrify me to watch freight trains and hear them whistle anymore, or to see smokestacks that give off black and red or gray smoke; when finally every fence didn't remind me of prison bars. She liked it in Prague. She didn't have anywhere else to go either. She signed up to go to Palestine at the Prague office. They had given her a number very far down on the waiting list. The British didn't want to let new settlers into their colony. They were more interested in cheap Arab oil and concerned about their Arab partners. Prague was a waiting station to her. Nice and not so nice, because she was alone. She didn't have a single relative. They had killed them all within six years. The ones who survived in the Carpathians had been evacuated to central Asia, somewhere in Samarkand, and there was no longer any hope that she could write to them or find them. She didn't want to go back home. It would've been like going from mud into a swamp. She was different than Katya Ziehrerová. Once in a while, however, she seemed stunned for a few moments. Her name was Pirika. She was pretty, with her black hair growing out, missing a couple teeth. I can't remember her last name. In my mind I called her 'the girl with the frozen-moment eyes.' She was still emaciated. She was given some secondhand dresses from the Jewish center that came in packages from America. She put weight back on slowly. She had been in Auschwitz-Birkenau. They had gassed her mother, father, four brothers, and three sisters. They sent her to Germany, to an airplane factory, like the one you were at with Hana in Freiberg. Except for those moments she had, you could see in her eyes the belief, or faith, that in spite of everything she had gone through, there was still the chance she would meet someone who would help her handle the troubles of life after the war. She laughed that such feminine machinations were the only true expertise born with a woman; everything else could be used only when you'd grown up. In her own way, she let me know not to hurt her by refusing her too quickly or by not saying no directly. She didn't want to stay in Prague forever. She was hoping that the man of her heart would go to Palestine with her; there they could start over, with a heavy past but an uncorrupted future. With people she felt close to, though where at the same time no one knew anyone else. She sensed that only a progressive life, openly facing what life had in store, would help her get over smallness. She felt so small, humble, and meaningless. The echo in her sounded stronger than a cry. It was easy to wish for but not so simple to carry out. She had probably learned how to talk herself into believing that as long as she was alive, her dreams could still come true. And here she was living, and somehow it wasn't that way. She didn't want substitutes. Lies. She wanted a full, useful, rich life, not hand to mouth—if not a lot of money, then only not to be hungry, not to worry about where she would sleep, to have prospects. She knew she was going to a country where no one put up with anything. Where they defended themselves. She believed that she could handle it with someone who had a similar—or the same—experience. She never forgot an inch of what had happened. No one would ever find out from her where she had been. At the same time, she thought that it could be the other way around; maybe she could start over with someone who had heard about what she had gone through but didn't have the same experiences. Or even someone who had never heard. She had a round face like her father's, a small straight nose, deep-set almondlike brown eyes, a mouth with strong cut-to-the-heart lips with a red scar in the middle from a blow by an SS in the camps. She had a few teeth missing in front. In camp she sometimes dreamed about escaping. Or that someone would protect her. She looked the SS Aufseherin in their faces and searched their eyes for pity. She closed her eyes to see elsewhere. A laid table where she could eat. Herself in a clean dress with beautiful underwear on, not in the mud, beaten and starving, frozen in winter, burned and sweating in the summer heat. In time, her dreams of a life in which people didn't seem like ants, pigs, or stone slipped away. She lost the strength to envision herself differently; even if she would never have to make it real, the image of it had held her up. Language shrunk to fewer and fewer words. Only go, speak, do. Attention, stop, hats off. Stand, sit. Bunk, latrine, gas. Whip, mud, clogs. Fire, ash. All in German. She had a twitching chin, a long neck, and small, firm shoulders. Rough hands full of scratches and calluses. On her chest, she had the softest skin I have ever seen and a birthmark even more tender in the spot her breasts began. The moments her eyes would become paralyzed reminded me of the old women in the catacombs of the insane asylum in the Great Fortress, of the old women from Hungary, how they waited in Auschwitz-Birkenau at crematorium two on the trodden meadow at the fence before it was their turn to go to the ovens. It was in July, in the heat, and they didn't give them anything to eat or drink anymore, and they didn't have anywhere to go to the bathroom, and they wore the same clothes they'd arrived in because they'd had to leave their bags in the train cars. The flies and the mosquitoes, bees and insects pestered them in the heat, and they were thirsty and hungry from morning to night. In the beginning the old ladies were noisy, but they gradually got tired and finally fell silent, waiting for the gas, hoping it would come as soon as possible. That moment of derangement clung to Pirika like a drop of poison in a well of clean water, infecting everything that could be good later. She didn't tell me much about it. She was a little afraid of the intimacy that would come from it. She didn't want to commit herself or me. It bothered me that she was so secretive. Even when there weren't any secrets or didn't have to be. She never confided any of her illnesses to me. Maybe she was protecting some essence of privacy that she had lost before, because in the camps we were all naked, each of us to everyone. I knew the nakedness humiliated the women even more than men, not only in the presence of other women but also in the presence and shameless indifference of men and of the SS, who, perfectly dressed from head to toe, pressed and showered, laughed at the women's drooping breasts or the blood running down their thighs. The SS had endless possibilities to make fun of women in the circumstances the camps made for them.

"We became close in two days. Maybe it was two hours, or two seconds. All we did was look at each other. The nakedness of the past showed in her. The accumulation of the humiliations that she had gone through like wind through leaves."

"You know why," said his mother.

"Yes," he answered. "One excludes the other, but in the end they come together."

Sometimes she laughed as people do when they're happy that they've survived something bad and they're glad they've got two hands, two legs, and a head on their shoulders. That was only until her eyes glazed over again. Who knew what they beheld in those moments. Something even sadder than sorrow. Despair, a descent that had no end; a premonition of ill fortune. At that moment death looked out from her eyes, death that she had seen and what led to it like a sign by a road, her own humiliation and that of others. At the same time, the corners of her mouth lifted in a smile and tightened the edges of her eyes. The sorrow of her soul touched her body. A pang beyond the borders of any reason. The eyes of a stranger. What killed her within. She sensed betrayal of the world, of man, of people, of herself. She seemed like night falling. Even in the day she gave off the sense of sleeplessness of what a person is unable to suppress: anxiety, confusion, fear. Hope was missing in her face. It was a moment of doubt, not of decision. Her face asked: What can I do or should I do to get rid of this? Is there any hope for me? Am I lost for good? (Was she?)

There was also in her the humility of women who know from the time they are small how much harder they must work and how much stronger they must be than men in order to reach the same standing. Sometimes she would come with a bare head, other times she wore a flat cap and then a hat. She looked silly, but I wasn't able to laugh at her much because it would seem as if I were mocking her. Sometimes I imagined her with her future husband, with children and what she would probably tell them, how they were supposed to behave and what they could expect from life. But it didn't seem as if she were going to go out of her way to get married and have children. Maybe she didn't want to bind people to her or herself to them. Maybe she was waiting for the right man, after all. Sometimes she withdrew into herself, and the moment would come when her eyes glazed over.

The first weeks after the war came back to him, when he was getting used to being free again. He would meet Pirika at around nine and they would make their rounds to the postwar soup kitchens. They could never finish their food, even if their stomachs weren't full. Their rounds included all the places where for the whole summer of 1945 people gave out free food to orphans, widows, the homeless, and the state workers who came from camps. Prague was full of them. As in former times, Prague was again the crossroads of Europe, from the east, north, west, south, and even farther, to both Americas and Australia. The beggars and wanderers came. It was easy to tell who was who. All of a sudden everyone looked better after the war. The best in a person came out. Pirika would always praise Czech food. Her eyes brought a smile to her lips, which she left a little open. At the end of each meal she gave a sigh over her half-empty dish and said she couldn't eat another bite, but she would get hungry again by the time they got to another kitchen. Then the moment of insanity would come when her eyes glazed over. When she looked into the emptiness or somewhere inside herself. She would only gaze over her hands, her palms and knuckles, or the point of her shoes. The pavement. Some dead place. She didn't say why or anything at all. She wasn't able to do what David did from the beginning, to stare at a concrete ceiling or the floor or at the eye of a potato and let it all be. She couldn't bear looking at cement ceilings and floors in half-finished buildings or at demolished ones with a tangle of wires sticking up from the hardened cement and covered only with scratches, because it hadn't been smoothed over or plastered yet. They were haunted by the scratches by unknown hands and fingers and nails that left their last marks on the ceilings in gas chambers of Osvetim's five crematoria. The last action of people before they suffocated. Or holes, even when they were empty, or potato eyes, a half-built garage, or ditches for sewers. Pits where they cremated bodies interspersed together, so that the body of a dead, fat person would fall on a corpse of skin and bones and the fat would help it burn. It wasn't just with gas and wood that they cremated bodies, but with the victims' own fat. (That always came back to him, even later.) She had seen it with her own eyes. The scratches in the ceilings.

Those were most likely the places her mind went when she would stop eating and her eyes glazed over. Or when they would sit together on the oak benches in the church on Stupartská Street or on Jakub Square and people brought them food, as much as they wanted, and they ate to their hearts' content. She saw in the wind that blew from the Vltava a different wind, one that spread ash over the ground. She knew—and every church reminded her of it—that the hell imagined by saints, the simplest carpenters, fishermen, tailors, or poets was a mere reflection of what she had seen in Auschwitz-Birkenau. She wasn't proud of the knowledge. She had it in her eyes, and for a moment, a fraction of a second, they became paralyzed. Maybe she looked crazy. She probably had it in her fingers and nails, too. She saw it even later away from Prague. Was she ashamed of what she saw? Something went out in her; her eyes died. She turned herself inside out to feel guilty; to sense the shame. All of a sudden the connection to her eyes would cut without her moving. Or she flushed, became covered in sweat and grew pale; it could have been from the food. Sometimes she would get diarrhea. (He did, too.) That was the only thing that would make her laugh. Diarrhea didn't mean she would go to the sick ward in Au-Birkenau. The place where they loaded the dead bodies with shovels, or the sick lay in thin, yellow-green excrement. The bodies were hauled away in a wooden pushcart every day.

She told him about a dream she had. She was with her best friend on a trip and they arrived somewhere. People asked them if they would like to see how they looked as babies. First, the people showed them a picture of her friend. Chubby calves, round face and forehead, puffy closed eyes. Then, they showed her a picture of herself. A face of a half-rolled-up mummy. Her skin was dark and she had wisps of long black hair. Tufts on an otherwise bald head. Dried-out skin like a wrinkled apple, covered with smile lines. Enormous genitals. She had two or three wobbly teeth, yellow and crooked. Spaces of gum in between. She said it wasn't possible. How could it be a newborn? They insisted it was she. She argued that her skin was too dark. (She didn't say anything about her genitals.) They answered that it was like Lipizzan horses; they are born dark and then whiten as they grow older. She said she looked as if she were one thousand years old. They told her that the picture showed who she truly was. People can't be who they are not, after all. Everything is determined at birth, from beginning to end. Where she came from, where she was going, and what would happen was already laid out. After conception, it took nine months to be born. For the creation of something from nothing, it wasn't so long. People's natures are formed in advance. How they will handle the good and the bad. Their predilections. What they will or could become. She looked at the picture again. A strange face looked out at her. She sensed her soul. She sensed what wouldn't grow old, what no one knows or perceives differently than as knowledge. Had she arrived on this earth in the form of an old, cackling lunatic with big genitals? Had she found the key to herself? Her real self? Beyond the ridiculousness and the emptiness that surrounded her? Even before she was born? The union of wisdom and foolishness? The result of both, how they negate each other. What about her body, breasts? Her pretty face. Hair. Breath.

They were together for two months. In September, Pirika with the Hungarian last name disappeared. He was left to wonder where she was and why she didn't tell him she was leaving. Many people found their way to the Palestinian office directed by Champi Klein, a doctor of law and fighter in the French and Hungarian underground. He gave not only information about how to get to the promised land the quickest way, in spite of the British occupying forces; he also told applicants to keep their mouths shut so that they wouldn't endanger the process for those who wanted to go after them.

He didn't have to tell his mother why Pirika left. Someone would go because, after the war, his neighbor said, "So you've come back, too, Mr. Kohn?" Or, "It probably wasn't as bad as they said it was if you came back." Or, "So they didn't kill everyone after all." Or they rang and rang the door of their former apartment and someone else opened it, or no one did at all. Sometimes the person didn't leave for Palestine but rather jumped out the window. Then a small obituary was posted on the next to last page of the Jewish community's newspaper.

"I knew Champi Klein from the Palestinian office. I sent him people who had returned." Then he added, "I knew a man who'd hidden a Jewish girl like Pirika the last year of the war. She had escaped from the camps or from a death march. He hid her in the kitchen. When friends visited, he never let them in there. It seemed strange to some. When they asked him after the war what had been the most dangerous thing about hiding her, he replied how beautiful she was. The Germans never shot all of the best. If he ever prayed for anyone, it would be for someone like the man who hid the girl, regardless of the danger. He was like a pillar that held up the sky. The best were like pillars that held up bridges, so that others could get from the bad side to the better."

8

David Wiesenthal felt a pain in his hand that he knew from before. The din of the storm in his head had not lessened. He could go back half his life—ten years and a few months—back to the school playground. He had broken his right hand horse jumping. Now he had a similar feeling in his back, in almost every vertebrae, in both wrists, in his leg at his ankle, and in his knee and his thighs. Hopefully nothing had happened to his back. Then he could still depend on himself, at the very worst.

He wanted to tell his mother that it was a deep chasm, but instead he laughed. He must be a cat, he thought, with nine lives. Like his triple perception of time, he had more lives than one. Now, then, and before. Or was it so long ago that no one's thoughts reached there? Was it older than memories? Than the oldest living person? It probably didn't have much to do with time. Was it only the memory? With forgetting. Fish in the sea or mountains and eagles would know what he meant. He told his mother he hadn't chosen everything in life. I'm still just twenty. I'm not the only one who has more than one face, more than one life. I'm not even an adult by law. Not even adulthood or maturity had anything to do with years and age.

"I heard about an emigrant who always left something behind wherever he drifted (he never stayed anywhere long): a picture, a shirt, a book. Just in case he returned. He was afraid that every new place he went would all of a sudden become like the old one and for the same reasons. He always lost everything he had. Only very rarely did he ever get back anything he left with people. At one place they told him, 'Welcome, we've got here bedding, towels, and a harmonica of your older brother's. Please take them.' He broke down and cried. They had mistaken him. He didn't have an older brother."

"Perhaps the abyss is a good place," his mother said.

"We'll see," he said.

He tried to gather his strength; it was up to him. Hadn't he survived the Great Fortress in Theresienstadt, Buchenwald, and Auschwitz-Birkenau? And then Paíská Street in the Prague Uprising, when his job was to bring food from the head nurse's house to the hospital? Hadn't he possessed a feeling of immortality because of that, if at least for a little while? Hadn't he gotten over being the only one who survived? Hadn't he talked himself into believing (both purposely and unintentionally) that he was better off than others—he wouldn't have been able to say in what—in spite of what he told the lieutenant? He wanted to tell him now that he was even better. Or more able or maybe stronger. Survival had probably been pure luck, a few good or meaningless coincidences. Was he able to appreciate what it was to have a roof over his head, to eat when he was hungry and drink when he was thirsty? To have good shoes and decent clothes? A few crowns to buy what he needed? What it meant to live because he had seen how easy it was to die? He wanted to be able to work and give at least as much as others. He knew it was an internal law that he could live by but didn't have to. When Pirika asked him what he wanted to be, he had said a tiger gentleman. Or had he told that to Katya Ziehrerová? Or someone else? Had it been something different than luck? Once again Pirika, Katya, and the girl who hadn't come yet flashed in his dreams. That third girl. (The first one.) It brought back the number 3 to his mind, which Gypsy had said was both lucky and unlucky. Was he just making fun, or did he really mean it when he said that number 1 was the beginning, 2 was life, and 3 meant death? Then comes 4, but that is invisible. There was a lesson in that one. It was hard to tell what Gypsy meant seriously. His voice and expression always put it somewhere in between. He attributed his tales to his mother or grandmother, to the experience or wisdom they had gleaned from their travels, even if they were the same journeys around the same villages, towns, and wildernesses again and again.

"All of us are chosen, when we need it and it behooves us," his mother said.

"I remember when we got to Auschwitz-Birkenau, the *Aufseherka* gave me a flannel suit from storage for cold winter nights. Then they sent the next woman to the gas because she hadn't saluted in time. They acted like gods, giving and taking lives. Arbitrariness was the rule. That was how neither your life nor mine had any worth. It wasn't against the law to kill a Jew in Germany. They didn't have to look for a reason to do that. It was supported by law. The law didn't protect either you or me. On the contrary, the law sentenced you and gave everyone else the license to steal from you, humiliate you, or murder you if they felt like it. They were allowed to be good and evil. They could do whatever they wanted. There were no flies on them."

It made him feel good that his mother talked to him as if they were equals. His parents hadn't acted like that before with him. It wasn't until later that he learned to treat all people the same. He didn't think too much or too little of anyone.

The lieutenant had said to him yesterday, "Wiesenthal, why does it seem as if the concentration camps are still alive and well in your mind?"

The other lieutenant had chimed in, "Are you going to think about it forever? Can't you draw a line in the past? We've all got good things ahead of us. Let's keep our eyes on the future instead."

"I measure everything by the past, both ahead and behind me," he had admitted to them both. Then he said, and perhaps he shouldn't have, "There were camps even before the Nazis."

"Oh," said the second lieutenant. "And what do you mean by that?"

"What did you answer?" asked his mother.

"I was careful," he said.

"You have strange notions about misery and vigilance, Wiesenthal," said the officer. "Don't go walking on glass," he warned.

"The same hand washes the other," he said to his mother. "I've had the feeling before, but it's better not to talk about it. Maybe we're not right."

"Oh, my son," said his mother.

The next day the second lieutenant stopped him in the hallway outside the classroom and asked, "Wiesenthal, what's the most important thing in life to you?"

"To be true. "

"To everyone?"

"Everyone."

"Always?"

"As a matter of principle."

"Are you sure that that's the most important thing to you?

"Next to defending oneself."

"Would you drop your principles if, let's say, they went against the state?"

"How do you mean, comrade lieutenant?"

"What would you give precedence? Your principles or the service of your country?"

"I don't know, what do you mean?" David repeated. But he already knew what the officer meant. Morals like David's were immoral to him.

"If, for instance, your principle were in conflict with the interests of the state. If, for example, your best friend or, let's say, your relative or a girlfriend, your mother, were against the state."

"Don't you see what he was trying to tell you?" asked his mother.

"There have been many times in my life when I haven't known what to do. During the war, we waited until it would end. After the war, all of a sudden a big, dark space opened up that left us alone with our pasts. In the army, I gained some time. The chance to think everything through. Get ready for the next round, if it's possible to say it like that. It was the first time I dared look around me and see other areas, another life, the world, time. They gave me two and a half years to figure it all out."

"We serve the people," said the officer. "We serve things that matter, Wiesenthal."

"Do you remember Mr. Eisenstadt, who left for England the day before the occupation in '39?"

"I also remember how he came back at the beginning of '46. He had inherited old furniture from the parents and grandparents of his wife. The neighbors had split it between themselves before the Germans came to take the rest. Eisenstadt went from door to door, knocking and asking who would have his things. After two months, he had accumulated the bedroom and living room furniture. Then he bought the rest from a neighbor for twenty times its value."

"Sometimes a person becomes attached to things. They mean more than just a chair, a table, a piano, or a picture. You know that yourself. The T-shirt you had on when you won the soccer match. Your first pair of skates. A ball."

"His son died as a pilot. He fought in the Czechoslovak forces. They shot him down in his twenty-fourth run."

"I'm glad to hear that he fought." He heard sadness and pride in his mother's voice.

"Young Eisenstadt took after his father, both of them had black hair and olive skin. He flew over Berlin and Hamburg and Bremen and dropped bombs on those who killed in big numbers."

She knew about the Eisenstadts. They were her same age. People spoke badly about Mrs. Eisenstadt for taking her Persian fur to England. His mother had been her friend.

"Who knows how they are now," he said to her.

She didn't answer. He turned to her after a moment.

She was thinking about the two lieutenants.

"What still awaits us, my son?"

"The best way to kill time in the army is to play cards," he replied. We play with Horse, Kristus, and the sergeant. It keeps him calm. Otherwise the sergeant would get all bent out of shape because he's served a year longer than us. It's the same with cards as in the camps: you discover that your luck doesn't hold from start to finish. If one can handle playing, he'll never get only bad cards. Sometimes it turns around and he gets everything back. And more. He wins and has enough for the next game."

"What did the rabbi say to you in October of '44 in the twenty-first barracks at Auschwitz-Birkenau when you caught him stealing your bread?"

"He talked about the double meaning of all things. The first meaning was of good and the second what was right. I asked him why he took my bread when he knew I would die without it faster than I could snap my fingers. He was so hungry he had lost his mind. It had killed his ability to judge between good and bad, right and wrong. He wasn't human anymore because he had forgotten. I wanted to beat him on the spot. I wasn't human anymore either. That's what they wanted. We were so much worse than before we got to the camps. Only a few were better. I didn't beat him because I thought of you, of what you would say about it."

"My son," said his mother, "the greatest things a person can have are invisible."

"He came to after a while. He looked at me as if I had done something to him instead of him to me. Then he carved a saying into the bunk with a piece of flint (I slept above him): "Don't despair, we'll survive, don't forget." Maybe it reminded him of what made him a rabbi. He went to the crematorium over hunger. It almost didn't bother me. Maybe I even wished it. I kept on thinking about what the thief of my bread had told me. Together we had carried stones to the Auto Union a short distance from Auschwitz-Birkenau and back. The stones reminded the rabbi of pieces of a burned-out sun. He knew everything about the history of mankind for the last thirty thousand years. And he stole my bread. His strength had given out. I never understood why the Germans, as practical as they were, wanted us to carry rocks there and back again—with no destination—twelve hours a day, four or more miles round-trip. The rabbi once asked me on the way if I had heard about a crazy man who tied knots in the day and at night undid them, or about the Greek soldiers from two thousand years ago who had made their prisoners tie knots and then undo them to convince them of the foolishness of their existence. The Romans had done something similar. They had shaved their prisoners' hair. Not to free them from lice and fleas but to humiliate them.

The Germans had outdone them all. They started their tricks with showers without water and doors without handles inside. He didn't want to think about how the Germans threw live babies into the ovens. How mothers pressed their one-, two-, or three-year-old boys and girls and wanted, if not to live, then at least to die together. No one has ever murdered as many children as the Germans. It was an echo that would never fade. Murdered children.

His thoughts went back to the word "nowhere." Another thought lurked behind it: that he might pass out, fall asleep, or die. He was close to it now, just as he'd been many times. It would be painless; it didn't reach beyond the borders of "nowhere." To die in your sleep was better than to die in pain. The noise of the storm in his head hadn't died down. He caught himself wishing for something, an accumulation of his many other wishes, which would take away the pain. What did such a wish mean? That nothing serious had happened to his head? Only to his back? Surely he had smashed his legs, hands, and knees. The bones were broken. It reminded him of the pain. What did the noise mean or the darkness that the light had become?

"The deciding factor about a person is not how he lives, but how he dies," his mother now said. "I was as bad off as you are. I only thought it was the other way around for a short time. A doctor was with me who had no medicine and who was sick herself. She told me that if I wanted to live, I would live. If I wanted to die, I would die. It's true. There's an art to living and an art to dying. Not to owe anything to anyone ever again. Not even to one's self. It's not what someone tells you, but what you hear in it. Everyone sees the world his own way. At the time, I wanted to live. The ones who didn't want me to live were the Germans. If no one is threatening your life, it's only up to you."

He remembered a woman who came from Mauthausen in Austria whom he had met after the war in the temporary hospital made from the Hotel Graf. He asked her whether she had by chance met his mother and sister in the camp. American soldiers had liberated her and Mauthausen in the Austrian Alps; it then took two weeks of making six-mile circles to find the camp in a quarry in the rocks. The SS had forced prisoners to leap holding an umbrella into a quarry seven feet by seven feet—what a jump it must have been. They had their own saying for it: if the umbrella turns inside out, you're out of luck. Everyone who had to jump died. They knew they would beforehand. The American captain had given the woman a can of condensed milk. She almost died from drinking it.

The Germans poured ice water over every prisoner upon arrival at the gates from November to February. More than half of the incoming froze to death. They stood naked at the stone gates. Only the toughest Waffen and Allgemeine SS could work at Mauthausen, just as in Auschwitz-Birkenau. The prisoners who ended up there had little chance to survive. It wasn't a camp for retraining but for liquidation, just like Auschwitz. After the war they erected a sculpture of a frozen man. A clear ice man made from stone. The stone seems transparent to people. It's Austrian quartz. Mauthausen was the camp where his mother and sister were sent.

One of the prisoners couldn't control his bowels. Green-brown slime ran down his pant legs to the ground. A barely grown SS in the uniform of the Hitler Youth took out a revolver. "We'll teach you better right here and now and I hope for good," he said. He pointed to a fat man who had yet to grow thin after three days in the camp. "Stick his head in it so he'll know not to do it again. Down! Both of you!" The culprit slowly knelt. With his eye on the revolver the fat man slowly bent down, too. "Take him by the neck. Stick his nose in it. After a while you'll all be getting sick and taking a crap here. You don't know much about cleanliness. Where would we be if we were all like that?" The fat man didn't have to try hard; the accused bent over. "Does anybody here have a spoon?" asked the soldier. The capo handed the fat man his spoon. "Feed him it, what comes out goes in again." The fat man scooped up the excrement. The SS shot close by his head. The prisoner opened his mouth. "Everything!" screamed the SS. "The vomit, too. Do it!" In a minute, in front of the eyes of everyone who was standing around, there remained only a green-brown stain. The prisoner ate the rest. The young Waffen SS put back his pistol. He ordered the march on and added that they were permitted to go to the latrine. His voice was heavy like those who are convinced of how right they are. Everyone had diarrhea because the only food that Tuesday had been a fish soup—maybe it had been shark—that was already spoiled before it got to the camp kitchen. The soup had been oversalted; they had not been allowed to drink except in the latrine where the water was infected with dysentery and typhus. They called dysentery "the dirty hand illness."

"Don't think about it," his mother said.

"I don't. It's in the past."

"I was sick a few times, too," she said. "You don't ever get rid of it once you've experienced it. Once my mother did the same thing to our cat when it went on the kitchen floor. She rubbed the cat's face in it. It took my breath away as a small girl. I didn't want to believe that my mother could do such a thing."

"They always thought up something that seemed like an exchange, something for something at first glance. If you want to live, then eat your own shit. If you want to live, feed your friend shit. I always see it in front of me. A man feeding another man with a spoon. He had it on his lips, his nose, he blinked to see because it got in his eyes."

"We don't have to speak about it," she said.

He felt himself swelling. Growing bigger. Maybe in a while he would be so big that he would fill the abyss.

Every month Katya Ziehrerová would swell up. She could sense it a couple of days before her period started. For some reason it reminded her of when she was small and afraid of the dark. When her mother died, the fear came again. The shadows were silent and overtook the kitchen or the bedroom like a flood no one could prevent. She was afraid of water, dark, and the time of day when the shadows fell before turning into twilight. She was afraid they would devour her. To make them appear less terrible, she imagined the shadows had a voice. Finally, by the time she was fourteen, she had taught the shadows to sing and had her first menstruation. Her breasts grew. She had the feeling that her belly held a barrel. No fuse was needed to make it burst. Did he have the same feeling now?

Why did Pirika with the Hungarian last name leave Prague like a shadow that suddenly slips away?

"I think she was bleeding," he told his mother. He had forgotten about it before. "She only told me about it because I had seen stains. It had seeped through her underwear and dress. It wasn't only once every twenty-eight days. She bled as mothers bleed, but not because she was pregnant or giving birth. It came irregularly, unexpectedly, and painfully. Sometimes it hurt as if she were having a baby."

She was ashamed of it. She was afraid to go to the doctor because he might tell her something she was more afraid of than having a child. As far as David was concerned, he wasn't the best one to give her advice or help. He only mentioned that in her place, he would at least go to some clinic. Her head hurt. Her eyelids twitched. Her ears rang. She finally went to a doctor. He told her it was a migraine. He told her that sometimes migraines caused the sufferer to see faraway places.

Sometimes Pirika would all of a sudden fall silent. A pang poured from her, whose infinity pierced him like an icy wind. He felt pity for her, which only made things worse because pity never helps anyone.

He remembered how he parted with her, almost praying in his mind for good fortune to greet her, maybe in the form of a doctor that could soothe her and tell her she wasn't ill, or in the form of a train that would take her away, a boat that she could sail on, or a man who would be older than she, wise and calm, with a roof over his head, a good job, and a future that he would give to her. He understood what made her feel lost, like all who returned from the camps with never-ending uncertainty in their souls. She told him about a dream she had, that before she was born she had been an animal, a snake or a frog or a leech, and she spoke German. She lived in the swamps. She watched the sun as it rose and set. She didn't know for sure if she wanted to be a human when she was born. A blinding white morning woke her, and for a moment she didn't know whether she was on earth or not and what language she heard through the window.

He could tell that her sadness touched death. It occurred to him what would free her from such sorrow. He was ashamed of his thought. He couldn't stop himself from thinking about circumstances in which death was a good thing, as long as it was painless and, if possible, immediate. What did he feel in her presence? Friendship? Fear that the other person is just a shoulder to cry on?

Was it love? Was it pain, sympathy, or an endless pity that smothered him? He never forgot her.

Sometimes she had the expression of a person incapable of looking forward or behind. Her faced lacked something. It wasn't only that she was left alone, an orphan. It was something she couldn't face, a void that probably no one could face. He thought about her often in the conversations they had about his dreams of her, which disappeared when they met again. Had she lost her way, or didn't she dare to think about where she came from and where she was going?

Something in her begged for forgiveness, even if she hadn't done anything to anyone. It was beyond words. It was an impossibility that she had to put into words, but she couldn't find any.

"Some nights," she said. Not a word more. He had the impression that he understood her.

Once in a while they went to the cheapest pub they could find because they were always hungry. Both of them got money from the repatriation office. One innkeeper asked her jokingly if she could kiss as well as she could eat. She felt herself want love. Was it a pleasure she didn't know? She avoided his eyes. She swallowed emptily. She answered in a whisper, yet it wasn't out of gratitude or admiration, but rather fear. He could figure out on his own what kind of situations had brought her flattery. The innkeeper put on a gramophone "Bésame Mucho," in the original and in German, as he played for his German guests during the war; he still didn't get it. To some, songs are only songs, as money is only money. "Kiss me more, hold me, my love of loves and always be mine. Who would ever have thought that I would hold you and kiss you . . . Bésame mucho." It must've made her think of something that had happened. She was aware of the danger of the words. Of certain words. In the days when no rules applied for the people around her she had had to figure rules out for herself.

"Let's go," she insisted.

Outside he asked her, "You don't want to be alone forever, do you?" And later, "Are you cold? It's hot."

"I remember when I was even more alone." Of all the words she could have chosen, it surprised him. She knew that she would always be alone.

"Hold my hand."

He took her hand and felt how cold she was, which made him cold as well. He hadn't wanted to insult the innkeeper. He walked a couple of steps behind her. He had the feeling that he was holding emptiness in his hand. She needed love or something different, security, certainty, prospects, things that were unattainable.

His mother understood. She knew why memories exhaust the strength of the person remembering, what they need to live on and look forward to tomorrow. He didn't understand that he could be with her and she could still feel so alone.

"I'm alone with everyone," Pirika said.

"Even with me?"

"Even you."

He remembered her voice, her silence, her whispers, her cold hands, the silent, wordless scream, the expression of her glazed eyes, the brown ocean.

Then it turned out that she had a saltshaker in her pocket that she had taken from the pub table. That was another thing she had in her eyes whenever they went somewhere. She learned it in the camps. She never touched what belonged to individuals. It only took her a moment to figure out what she could lift with a swipe of her hand.

Sometimes when they made their rounds in the cafeterias they heard prayers that seemed strange to her. Prayers about Satan, who lies in wait for souls. Once she took toilet paper and another time a little mirror above the sink, about six by eight inches, so she was able to carry it under her blouse; another time it was a towel from the public baths that she hid under her skirt.

He was ashamed of thinking about her scrawny body when she had her period, about her headaches, how she must undress, how she bled, and when she spoke of it. About that song so long ago. What made her not want to make any more exceptions after the war, after making so many during it? He repeated the words of the song. How many times had he wished that the words would pertain to him, too. That he whispered "Kiss me" to someone over and over, about being intimate and being in awe of it, about dreams connected with sacrifice, about choosing words that lovers use. What he heard and saw at the movies. What everyone wants once and a thousand times. What a person may never get, even once.

It occurred to him that his mother would know what he was thinking. Could she tell by looking at him?

"I can tell you even by your footsteps, just as I could your father," said his mother.

Last Saturday they got leave, and David had gone with Kristus, Horse, and Gypsy to the pub At the Blue Gosling. Horse started telling a joke about two gypsies who meet. Where are you going? asks the first. To buy a coat, answers the other. If they don't catch you, buy me one, too, says the first. Gypsy started talking about a trinity: it meant the opposite of luck, the Grim Reaper with a scythe. Why? Because. His grandmother's grandmother could prove it. Was she still alive? The trinity hadn't got to her yet. Did he blame the trinity? Horse asked. Gypsies never blame anyone. The three men were happy until they heard how the locals beat a crippled man to death there.

No one ever found out how it started. Everybody was having a good time before someone got up and shoved the poor man for no reason. Then a second joined in and a third until the whole pub beat him like one man together. What is it in people, the dark underside, an urge that is impossible to comprehend? In wartime and afterward the senselessness showed itself more. Some black, unwinding spool we are incapable of stopping. The cripple was one of those who couldn't stop it. He also couldn't walk, and he slurped his beer rather than drank it. Maybe for years it had bothered the locals that they had to drink from the same glass. The poor man had to bend over the tabletop with his deformed arms. He had been born a cripple. Later, they asked his mother why he went that night to the pub, when he didn't go other times. His mother had warned him, Horse heard. It was in his horoscope. As his mother said, even paradise is unbearable alone. The cripple hadn't argued with anyone. He had difficulties speaking. He preferred just to listen to the day's gossip and drink his beer. He couldn't hurt anyone. That night, the innkeeper had brought the cripple his second beer. His fellow regulars already had had ten. One of the regulars reminded the innkeeper to keep his distance from the cripple if he didn't want to have problems. The same man told the cripple that he opened his mouth as if he wanted to swallow an ox and drink up a stream—but, at most, he just swallowed a fly in his beer. The cripple just looked at him. Then the man slammed him. A second regular did the same. And a third. They made a punching bag out of him. Why didn't he defend himself? They pounded him to death with half-liter mugs. In the police investigation, the innkeeper wasn't able to say how it began. No one knew. They had made a circle around the cripple. In the words of the clerk who investigated the case with the policeman, at the heart of every murder lay ill will. It took a small step for ill will to turn into murder. From time to time it erupts like an underground mountain spring when somebody accidentally moves a stone from the surface. It started at nine in the evening. By ten the cripple was lying still on the pub floor and at eleven in the morgue at Marienbad. Had he gotten in anyone's way? Afterward, nothing seemed certain. Gypsy's grandmother said, "Avoid the evil hours and you'll live to a thousand." Who can do that?

Whenever the soldiers, Kristus, Horse, Gypsy, or David, came in, they could feel the wretched man's soul. It wasn't the first time that someone beat a person to death without having a reason. Camps were built for it. Nobody had really known him.

"I lived with many people who had killed," he told his mother.

"Do you remember the story of the woodsman who went to chop wood in the forest and one of the trees looked at the ax and called out, 'See, it's one of us'?"

It was dark. His memories were growing louder. He saw in his mind the sign carved by flint. The cripple on the floor of the pub. His mother. Katya Ziehrerová. Pirika. Both the troop leaders. The plain of snow before it turned into a landslide. The pit. Here and now. The blue sky and eagles. Why wasn't that third girl he had never seen coming? Her naked white body blurred with the crippled man's corpse on the filthy floor of a village pub where soldiers went on Saturday nights.

It was better to think about his friends in the Great Fortress—in the ghetto at Theresienstadt when they were still alive; and what those who survived might be doing on the farthest continents they had all vanished to (Canada, Australia, or New Zealand). About how he played blackjack with Oskar Brummel in the boys' home on ward L218, around the end of 1942, and won a blue wool sweater with white stripes. After the war, Brummel went to Sydney. David heard he became a salesman for Singer sewing machines. Then with a woman he met he had a baby girl, Ada. He didn't want to get married out of fear of losing his freedom. He disliked commitments worse than death. They were almost always a losing proposition for one of the parties involved. He looked down his nose at women. Oskar had come to the conclusion that a woman was half human, half animal, and along with Arthur Schopenhauer he claimed that the sweetest angel at nineteen would become a dragon at thirty-two. Then he went to America, to San Francisco. There he got married in order to remain legally. He hadn't told his new wife a word about his baby. Bigamy didn't bother him. If there were a vote on bigamy, ten out of ten men would vote yes. He was one of those who thought if he had survived the camps, he could do whatever he wanted. The Germans had thought that way, too.

"There is only one justice," his mother said. "Either it applies to everyone or it isn't justice."

She didn't need to say that sometimes what is fair to one person is unfair to the next. And ruthlessness is always ruthlessness. Only the very best act with regard to others on every occasion.

"What we should have for one another—men and women—is acceptance," his mother added.

"In Prague during the spring of '45 when the city finally rose up and everything was over, I saw how they threw Germans out of windows or forced them to jump, even whole families that had moved to Prague and didn't make it out in time. They threw out newspapers and pictures of Hitler and the books that Germans didn't have to burn because they weren't written by Jews. I've never seen so many untorn and unread books as I did then."

Then he said, "They beat the Germans, children and women and old people, as some Germans had beaten us before. It evened some things up, but it wasn't very nice. They punished them without judgment, as the Germans had done to us. They hung them up from lamps by their legs, poured gas over them, and lit them by their hair. I was on Rytířská Street when it started on Saturday, the fifth of May, in front of At the Blue Rose. I had escaped from the camps and hid with a friend in Prague near the botanical gardens at a collaborator's home. In time, hiding me gave the man an alibi for what he did in the war; his neighbors still beat him after the uprising. He joined the party to have some protection. Sometimes we meet; we hardly say hello and go our separate ways."

"That's the way the world turns, my boy," said his mother. "I asked you what you were thinking."

"Sometimes I go by those places. It haunts me how those people jumped or how they were thrown out of windows or hung up on street lamps and burned. I wouldn't punish anyone who hadn't done anything to me. Anyone who didn't do anything evil. I wouldn't forgive someone who had committed murder, though. But I wouldn't blame the innocent. I saw a few women raise their skirts and piss on the heads of those Gestapos. Then people danced like madmen around the burned bodies. I couldn't believe my eyes."

"Nothing a person has ever seen or heard goes away," said his mother. "I knew what you were thinking about."

"About the Jewish doctor who got killed by a landslide after the war in the High Tatras. He left behind a widow and two young girls. He went mountain climbing every Saturday and Sunday. I couldn't understand how he could've killed himself in peacetime, so young."

He regretted not being able to look at a map. Was Morning Mountain or Evening Mountain also close by? Noon Mountain was the highest point in the area. The abyss was the lowest. Germany. The sky above. Was it still overcast? His uniform blurred into the snow on the ravine's floor as the dark merges with fog and night with shadows and snow. His snowsuit with white ties was waterproof, so he couldn't get soaked anywhere. That was good. Blue Rock was in the distance.

The snow blinded him even in the dark. He shut his eyes. The noise in his head disturbed him. Those hard blows. He liked snow, but not so hard or heavy. If it thawed and the snow started to soften he would know it first under his back. It would mean that spring was on its way. Didn't Gypsy's grandmother say that whoever lives to spring lives a year longer? Sure she did; she also said that when there are lots of mushrooms, there'll be war. He had envied trees during the war, their indifference, invulnerability, lack of involvement, patience, strength, resistance. Could he see into the distance even at night? He saw a stain in the distance: it was himself. Every period of time he thought about was made up of three parts: now, then, and before.

9

What was it that Pirika had in her eyes? Was it insanity or only emptiness? Desire or fear? Something that existed or not? She carried the dead in her eyes: her mother, father, brothers, and sisters. Families, connected like circles of an Olympic track, chalked on dirt and then erased like the wind blows away lines in the sand. The families of her uncle, her aunt, of both her grandmothers. They held the children the brothers and sisters would never have, and the children's children who would never be. They held friends she would never speak to again, never wave to again. The people she knew, a boy she could think of when his voice breaks like a girl at her age, mysteriously and utterly, and a groom she could no longer cry for because they killed him. The joy in her eyes would never light up again. She heard words that would not be uttered. It was death that didn't fade away but rather lasted forever. An unappeasable echo. A silent, numb cry in her eyes that drowned her as if in the deepest sea: what wasn't and could have been and never would be. She was a child of the dead. A child who remained alive by mistake. She knew that in order for her to be alive that very day and live to see tomorrow, many people had died, many American, Russian, and British soldiers. Many strangers had to die in her place. She owed them her life. She watched the soldiers on the streets of Prague. Did she look at them as if they were some eternal fire? She couldn't say anything to them; she spoke to them in her mind. They were connected to her world of the dead, the sacrificed, the innocent. She spoke to them with downcast eyes, thinking of where they had been and where their friends who never returned were, just as no one returned from her own family. Every soldier was a story, as Pirika was an untold tale whose content David could only make up himself. Maybe she envied them for not having been in Auschwitz-Birkenau. He had the same feeling, sometimes. Mainly when he thought of children because it was harder on them in the camps than for the adults. Auschwitz had been a city on a different planet. Even though many children went straight from the ramps to the gas chambers, crossing double train tracks to fly up the flue as ash before the sun would set, some wandered around the camp, parentless. They spoke in slang that only other lost children understood. They knew they were targets. They lived in holes in the ground, and no one knew where they got food. Some of the women hid them in their barracks. They were called "Pips," a word from the camp dictionary. New transports constantly arrived. Pirika wasn't much older than many of the children. She knew why they were afraid of the adult inmates as well as the Germans.

Little was said in Auschwitz-Birkenau. What was said sounded like how animals might speak, in shrieks and movements. I'm not going, I'm going, wait, don't wait, I'm cold, I'm hungry, I'm afraid, I'm dying. The echo of the camp language remained in Pirika's ears, even after the war. She believed that the people who survived belonged to a new age Noah's Ark and she was one of its specimens. Now she had been released and was finding out that she didn't understand the world to which she returned. It dimmed a few shades of her eyes. Darkness now gazed from them.

She had gotten used to the fact that there were things no one knew. She seemed like a receiver blocking waves, as the Nazis blocked long and short waves from wireless sets so people couldn't listen to London or other stations. She picked up the unheard and the intangible.

"You can't take it in your hand, and if you don't have it, you die." She meant dignity, besides which she had nothing. Or when she looked at herself in a mirror, she said, "It's inside, it doesn't matter how you look."

He thought of how she constantly felt an invisible danger, either ever-present or impending. Then he thought of Ruth Barzayová, who had told him in the hospital, "Nobody plays an open hand of cards with me; how can I play an open hand myself?" Then she had asked, "Will a man always take and take and take from me until there won't be anything left? As if he swept me from the face of the earth, even if I am still walking and talking? Emptying me instead of filling me? Sometimes I ask myself what it means that someone can take from me. Is there a difference between what is acceptable and what is already lost beforehand, as if it never existed? I don't blame it only on men; part of the fault is mine, too. I'm a person who doesn't have a line that can't be crossed. It allows others to take everything from me as if it were theirs."

She didn't speak about the blue veins rising from the inside of her thighs. She knew about her sweaty body, the place between her legs, and the wrinkles that made her breasts look like the surface of a lake in rough winds. She knew what made her old despite her nineteen years. Next to her, he felt just as old. Maybe the two of them really were old. Twenty thousand years old.

He had a feeling of timelessness. It seemed to him that his mother was leading him from the dark into the light, as if he were a child or an old person. Did it surprise him that she didn't say a word? Why did he remain in the dark? What was roaring in his head?

His thoughts returned to Ruth Barzayová who thought she lost what she gave and what the presence of another person took away. Did she attract people with whom her personality eroded? He had met other sick people; it terrified him. Did he attract the sick? Was he capable of seeing the good in everyone? It brought him back to the girl (the third one who hadn't come yet). The image was foggy at first, then it grew more concrete. A mouth as soft as warm moss. A center that gave off heat as if from the fiery core of earth. A fountain of hair, always carefully combed. Eyes. A girl who does what she wants and goes where she wants and doesn't do what she doesn't want to do. The dream that Pirika had of herself; Katya Z. had wished the same in a distorted form. He gave it a name. Then chills ran up his spine. He sensed the sacrifice of an unknown shrouded in fear.

"Sometimes, when the light is like that, I wonder if dying isn't almost the same, if not better, than living," he said to his mother, something that he would never have said before.

In 1944 they selected about five hundred women in Auschwitz-Birkenau to send to German factories in the interior to dig mica for aircraft cabins of Junkers and Messerschmits or to work in armories. The German officer spoke with them as if they were old hands who knew what was going on. They could go, but they had to leave their children behind. Only the ones who knew how to work were of any use in Germany. They were given an hour to decide. It wasn't the first time they were put in the position of choosing their children; if they had arrived with more than one child, three or four, a military doctor warned them that they were allowed to have only one in the camp. Some of them had to make up their minds on the ramps which child to keep. If they didn't want to leave now without their children, they could stay with them. If they decided to go, they would have no reason to worry. It was the German language in ciphers. To stay with their children meant to go to the gas chambers with them. To not have any worries about them was only a different way of saying that their children would die without burial. If the women had a chance to meet their husbands in another part of the camp before departure, their husbands pleaded with them to go. They were young still, they could have again what they would lose now. Don't they say that women live longer than men? They could have other children if they lived, after the war. To die with them was the final answer. (A doctor from Heidelberg knew how to make even that a lie. He sterilized them.) Only five of five hundred women gave up their children that afternoon. The remainder, 495 Jewish Czech women, were cremated that night with their children. Their men outlived them, before the majority flew up the smokestacks themselves. A few returned. One of them was a famous violinist from the Barberina Club. He had a handsome face, a thin body, and he dressed well. When somebody in the bar told him he looked good, he would smile and answer, "I just turned fifty, I survived three years in the camps; at Auschwitz-Birkenau they killed my wife and three children and I now have great work as a violinist. What can I play you? The American tune 'Everything Is Beautiful'? Or 'I Believe You'?" He had played it in the camps a few times. The German version.

ARNOŠT LUSTIG

"An eagle can spot a mouse in the snow from a thousand yards away."

"When you were young I told you how eagles teach their young to fly. They set them on their wings, fly to heights, and then let them go to open up their wings and fly in their fall."

"Is that what you'll do to me, too?"

"People have already done that to you, my son."

"The wind is cold," he told her.

She was thinking of something else. Did she know how cold he was and that his head hurt? Did she hear the roaring? A mother knows one hundred times more about her child than a child does about his mother. It is the difference between a flame and a conflagration. A flake of snow and a storm. A whirl of dust and a landslide. All she had to do was look at him when he came home from school or off the street to know everything, even what escaped him. (She could also sense the state of her husband's mind, whether he had had a good day or not.)

It all came rushing inside of him like a second landslide rocking him from within. An overwhelming din. A storm. Darkness. A change in which one doesn't even recognize one's own voice.

He was with Pirika again. Maybe it had been love, even if a little late. She never said it herself but he could bet that she had been raped a few times in the camps. Neither the Germans nor the capos, Jewish or not, believed in the sacred power of virginity. (Only she knew how one of the capos had abused her, if she would have spoken about it. Not only talk had stilled her tongue.) With her, he couldn't think of the things that he thought about with other girls. He never thought about whether she was a virgin or not, for example. With that longing at night that only girls know—the longing that brings them dreams of a man with whom to build a life, bear children, and share the same fate. Someone to depend on, someone to depend on her. He knew it had nothing to do with innocence. He heard her speaking one time, with a woman who worked at a Catholic charity giving out bread, about how many years of fertility women lost in the war. He wondered whether Pirika had found at least something of what she needed in Palestine, how she was maturing, and what she had lost. Her belief that the world was nothing but a place of the devil. Germany lost the war. The better side won. Danger wasn't the only thing in the air. There was a small place and a chair at a table in a wooden or stone cottage, like the one she had with her mama, papa, brothers, and sisters before they were killed. What was the name of the village in the mountains where she was born? The rabbi in Prague called her siblings and parents "a burnt offering." Was she thinking of the same things they had talked about in Prague? Had she found a country like her own where a guest was always invited to another serving? Had she finally rid herself of the cold wind that blew in Bohemia? Once she wondered why he didn't go to synagogue Friday evening. He didn't feel the need, he had answered, but was willing to wait for her in front of the chapel if she wanted to pray. She wanted to know if justice still existed. (At least somewhere.) Someone had told her how people made the Germans suffer when the tables finally turned. Her eyes became absent, as if she were truly paralyzed or something had drained the life from her. She didn't hear the word "German." Somebody knew the exact number of German dead: more than two million of them had been kicked out of the country and had had everything taken from them. Her expression froze. She didn't listen. She didn't want to hear; before, people didn't want to hear about us. The rabbi told Pirika the well-known saying that whoever kills one human kills everyone; he who saves one human life saves the world. She knew it wasn't that way. It wasn't a lie, but it wasn't the truth either. He was an old man. Eighty-five years old. He had spent the war in the promised land and returned to Prague to fulfill his duty as supreme teacher. His face held humility and an obstinate will to return at least something of what was not possible to return. There was no path leading from the kingdom of the dead to that of the living, only an imaginary bridge that the best walk along but not if no one leads them. She searched for an answer that she never found. When so many people are killed, life loses something of the value it held before. She was afraid of life's helplessness. She feared an existence in which everything was allowed and nothing was forgotten. She knew that the Germans had created such an existence, but they hadn't been alone. They were helped by Ukrainians, Romanians, Slovaks, the Poles, the Croatians. It was something in man's nature that survived from the jungle, from the kingdom of animals, a part of the brain in which kindness didn't exist and neither did an aversion to heinousness. What, in short, is referred to as "civilization."

His mother was thinking about how people become inured to other people's lives.

"What did she say to you when you saw each other for the last time?"

"'Next year in Jerusalem.' She only knew that one saying, the rest she had forgotten. She did know: when you're given food, eat. When you're beaten, run. That was enough for her even after the war. She turned her eyes away or closed them and a shadow stepped between us."

He thought about Pirika with the Hungarian last name. About what had been old in her and at the same time new, as if she were both young and old. Sometimes she smiled as if the world started over every day. She didn't smile without a reason, but she rarely said why. She must have thought that her life hung by a thread. He had told her ten times that the Germans had lost the war. How long would it take them to recover? The two of them belonged to the victors.

She didn't want to believe it. She couldn't manage the feeling of victory. She thought of those who had been lost. Her skin was olive, and when she smiled, her full upper lip rose (cleaved and healing together again) and showed rotten teeth above and below and gaps where teeth were missing. She spoke with her eyes. She had almond brown eyes, thick black eyelashes, raven hair in short bristles, and thick black eyebrows, like two arches. It took two months for her hair to grow in from the time they had last shaved her bald; it seemed as if her big ears lay close to her head. She was thin, with strong hips and almost no behind. Her breasts were dried out and wrinkled. Sometimes her mouth was a scornful curve. David and she never touched closer than outstretched hands when they met each other or said good-bye.

"She didn't trust anyone. Including me. They had killed it in her. Maybe she didn't even trust herself. Her father had told her once at home that the Jews in the caves of Judea and Samaria didn't cry. She probably knew many reasons why people learn not to cry. Why we're all still in caves. She reminded me of a broken-down wall. A pile of rubble. A bag from which you pour potatoes. As far as trust in other people was concerned, they had sucked it all out of her."

Someone had told her that Jews blamed themselves for what Hitler had done. If they had gone to Palestine in time and forced the British to take them in, six million of them wouldn't have died. Possibly seven or eight million, because no one counted the dead in the Ukraine or Russia. She wouldn't have had to cry for her mother, her father, her brothers and sisters, and the rest. She was afraid of the dark; but at times she feared the light, and when the insanity passed, her eyes held only longing and desire. For a moment, she looked beautiful.

"The lieutenant mentioned that he was taking a close look at me," he told his mother.

"What did you say to that?"

"He had studied writings from a group of Zionists out of Karlsbad who held the same opinion as Hitler: Europe should be rid of Jews. Their motives were different but the goal the same."

"Was he trying to say that we had murdered ourselves?"

"He says and does everything in order to make captain, just like the leader of the troop," he told her. "He has the arrogance of people who think they know what's going to happen. Not one of us will ever be able to feel the same as before. The blood of the murdered has been shed on us all."

At that moment, he could sense something happening. It lasted only a second. Maybe nothing would come of it, but everything would change all the same. Did his mother know that the deciding moment was taking place? The din in his head, the darkness? Light that darkens and darkness that has elements of light? She probably did, and if she didn't, she certainly sensed it. Like when he fled from the transport and returned to Prague and then waited to see if someone, anyone, from his family would return when he already knew they wouldn't. It was rare when someone returned. It was like a calling seldom answered. Something remained in the air. At first it was in thought, then in words, then it affected everyone, the guilty and the innocent. It oozed from the words of the lieutenant of the military defense unit and from the words of the barracks leader, and before that from things the troop captain said before he was sent to prison. The captain had denied serving in the federal military connected with the Wehrmacht and having traveled with a unit to Italy. He had claimed he was part of the band.

"He said at a meeting that Zionists were the cause of all troubles. All he had to do was change the word and it would have been just as in the days of Hitler, and that's what I stood up and said. I got sent straight to the garrison prison. Soldiers brought me blankets and food. Later, they investigated how I could have compared the present-day captain with Hitler. Fourteen days later they let me go and imprisoned him. He hadn't been just a member of the band in Italy. The new captain offered me furlough or a higher rank. It disappointed him that I took leave."

His mother probably didn't hear what he was saying; she didn't say anything.

He had the feeling that all of the dead, including those he couldn't have known, as well as the living who survived, were in the abyss with him. All of a sudden they had entered in crowds.

He thought of the Russian prisoners waiting for the gas chamber in the gypsies' camp in Auschwitz-Birkenau, in building 10, October 1944. They were Siberians that the Germans couldn't forgive for stopping their advance to Moscow. Their skin was fair, without whiskers. That was one advantage in the camps—you didn't have to shave. They were cremated by the thousands. Always one building at a time. Sometimes in punishment for someone having hit an SS in the head with a shovel for no reason at all.

He couldn't move. Just yesterday he had leaped through an obstacle course to the great satisfaction of his superiors.

In June 1948, three years after the war, he got a summons to police headquarters in Bartolomějská Street. It was apparent that even by that time they were taking things more seriously than they wanted to admit. From February of '48 things moved fast in that direction. Shortly before, a student from the College of Political and Social Sciences had come to him. He wanted advice on how to find an aunt who had immigrated to Palestine before the war. David pointed the man in the direction of the Palestinian representatives on Josefská Street, to Champi Klein. Then he forgot about him. A police investigator reminded him of it. They had caught the student trying to cross the border illegally. David refused to sign a paper that said he had aided an escape. The investigator insisted he sign it. He had worked an hour on it, pecking out the letters on a big Underwood typewriter with one finger of each hand.

He said he would sign it on the condition that the investigator add a note declaring it a ridiculous statement. The investigator became very angry. David didn't understand why. It was the truth, and the investigator was the one who wanted the signature. He, on the other hand, didn't want to sign something with which he didn't agree. Why would he? That's where it ended. His hands were clean.

"That was close," his mother said.

"You're always one step away from prison or some punishment, either because of what you've done or didn't do. I believed that having a clear conscience was enough to stay out of trouble because the war was over and Hitler had ended up wrapped in a burning rug after killing himself with a revolver and poison. Now I think that keeping my conscience clean maybe saved me from getting locked up. I'm glad that I didn't get scared and let that investigator shake me up."

"The saying that it's better to lose your eye than your name and good reputation doesn't apply anymore," his mother said and smiled.

"Once the lieutenant of the other unit, his head bent over papers where my name was written, asked. 'Are you so simple, Wiesenthal? Are you really that innocent and trusting after all you've been through, or do you just act that way? You should believe us more.'"

He was aware that his dreams for life after the war were fading. What it was that made people save their own skin, even at the price of betrayal and lies and meanness. It killed justice, destroyed friendship between people, and sowed distrust in families: in the end, it caused a person with no firm values to lose the ability to distinguish between good and evil. First, he loses trust in everyone; then, he hates himself. He couldn't tell any of his troop leaders that. And he couldn't tell anyone—not Kristus, Horse, or even Gypsy—that in that respect he was like the rest of them. Neither could he talk himself into believing that the world of his mother, father, and sister was better. That had led them to the gas chambers and ovens of Auschwitz-Birkenau.

What could one do to get away from it? Die, like so many others? Like one of the foreign soldiers, whose neighbors didn't believe he had really fought in the war, and if he had, it was only to have benefits afterward?

"How do the rest handle it?" his mother asked.

"Yesterday the lieutenant was pressuring Horse to speed up in the march. Horse told him that he didn't want to die sweaty."

"What is a family to you, Wiesenthal?" asked his lieutenant in the presence of the other unit's lieutenant.

"Two halves of a finger," he answered. (He couldn't say that he was thinking of his mother's lost ring finger.)

"Wouldn't you like to make lieutenant someday, Wiesenthal?" asked the company captain. "Should we send you to officer training school?"

"The lieutenants talked about the future but they were thinking of the past," he told his mother. "How to arrange things so they were comfortable, as people did before. As soon as possible. They confused humility with submission. Meekness with putting someone down. The other unit's lieutenant made me think I spoke like a ventriloquist. It's just that he doesn't know the dummy from the ventriloquist. He looked at me as if I were a crow born white, turned gray, and finally black like his parents."

"What one can't repair, one has to bear," his mother responded.

The clouds were full of snow. They descended to the level of the chasm. He still couldn't tell whether it was light or dark. He could only hear the constant din pounding in his head as if someone were beating him. Or burying him? The wind became the sound of the train on which he had returned from Germany in April 1945. At first he rode on the exterior foothold, since the wagons were stuffed to bursting; later he sat on the roof. It was the same sound of a train with two diesel locomotives that transported them from Meuslowitz at Leipzig to Dachau or back to the Great Fortress in the ghetto of Theresienstadt before he escaped. That was on Friday the thirteenth. In the dark he detected the outlines of the chasm; light reflected from the many walls. He saw the walls, but he couldn't count them.

10

It is simple. If I fall asleep, I die. If I move my head, hand, or leg, or only a finger, I return everything to where I want it to be. He imagined what they could find of him if they didn't come in time from the garrison. They couldn't get down to him as long as it was storming above. They would also find him in the spring, when the thaw set in and the chasm would clear. Then they'll see a different abyss: walls and a floor covered with grass, flowers, and rocks.

"You've never left the camps," his mother said. "You don't have to tell me why, my boy."

It took him a good while to try and put back together his life from all the pieces, breaks, and fragments, from the roar of the dark storm and echoes from the blow, the forgetting, from everything that was here, before, and even earlier.

In the camps, he had learned to see the evil within him. The shadows did not miss anyone. He knew what evil was inside. In everyone. In every single decision, in each possibility to do one thing or another, to judge what was good or evil. To figure out what his friend or enemy would do, what good or bad would become of it, and how to make it happen the other way around. The evil and good in everything that a person does or doesn't do, in every thought, in every deed, either visibly or invisibly. He knew how each person was alone. With two, three, or a hundred choices to make. Why it was more important to perceive the evil in oneself than in another, even if both evils were equally dangerous. The worst is what a person has by himself. What he has inside. How he defends himself against other people, sometimes unjustly.

He thought of Walter Presser, who died after the war and whose life was made all the harder by an SS guard. Walter went in his pants because the guard would not let him go to the side. It froze immediately. The SS guard didn't think much about Presser's Jewish heart. (He laughed that Presser carried his heart in his pants for thirteen days.)

"The Jewish heart no longer has any secrets for me," the guard told Presser. "It was a mystery before you came here."

He survived with a paralyzed heart; he died only after the war.

"If someone could kill a rock, they would do it," his mother said. "Sometimes it's better just to forget, my son. How far did you wander off?"

"It's hard to tell from the bottom of this pit," he answered.

"Sometimes the bottom reaches the top," she added.

He remembered how they sang "Against the Wind" by Voskovec and Werich on January 1 in Meuslowitz at Leipzig. His tooth was aching. He wanted to lose them all. In a few hours it felt as if all his teeth were hurting. Presser promised to pull his tooth out. In the meantime, he held his hand.

He felt as if he could smell last year's pine trees under the snow. The smell of fir. He had learned to look out for himself, not to let things get in his way. He got used to the fact that some things were not for some people. He thought of Walter Presser and his radiant face, how he acted. How he overcame himself before he died so soon after the war. In that way, he lived with Presser's spirit. It made Presser immortal, as long as the people who knew him lived. One time in the camp he took a couple spoonfuls more soup from a portion he shared with a friend. He came away from the camps without a clear conscience. The fact that after just a few days in the camps no one had a clear conscience did not excuse him either. The Germans had organized it so that everyone got a little dirty; no one was pure in the camps. When they escaped, they met a friend in the woods. To avoid attracting more attention, they didn't want him to join them. They didn't have to tell him, he knew it within the first second of seeing them. He never came back. After the war, his friend's brother was looking for him, and David could only tell him that they had met in the forest during an escape for half a minute and each had gone his own way. It was the truth like a tip of an iceberg jutting from the sea. The unseen greater portion remains beneath the surface.

"It's snowing again," he told his mother. "I wouldn't want to get covered up by snow, but I'm still breathing and my heart is still beating," he reassured her.

"I'm glad you're here with me."

"I'm glad I'm here, too."

"I remember the old people in Auschwitz-Birkenau. And the ones who kept me warm with their bodies. The rabbi expected them to get transported to the crematoria after selection. He said that when a person reaches a hundred years, it's as if he's not alive. The best of them didn't talk about the cold when they were frozen. Or about hunger when they were hungry. They were stronger than they looked."

"Do you feel like sleeping?" his mother asked.

He thought of the people who could never sleep. They woke up in the middle of the night because they didn't get to see what they wanted in their dreams. The spiritually diseased. It never left them. Some illnesses are incurable, even if they aren't called illnesses.

He wanted to yawn; he repressed it so he wouldn't get even colder. He didn't want to remember the time and place he had been as cold as this. He should try rather to remember when it was warm. A dream in which his town or country disappeared from the map and he was warm.

His mother asked him, "What are you thinking?"

He was thinking about the charm of girls and the wonder they evoked in him. Their appeal, how their bodies, faces, hair, and eyes aroused him. About those impressions that made life seem more bearable, better, more noble; how it elevated him, either deservingly or undeservingly, to look for real or seeming beauty. What he gave precedence to, whether he was aware of it or not. What kind of people he was drawn to and whom he avoided. He thought about good things he had done, fair things, and what he hadn't done so well or so fairly. The fact that no one knew about them didn't change his thinking.

"We're all a little mad, if you think about it," he said.

"He thought about the ballerinas from Marienbad. He remembered the girls' bodies from his dream. Their faces, parts of their bodies, their legs and arms, the pace of their movements, how they danced or how they rested afterward, content, a little out of breath, with little beads of sweat on their foreheads; they flowed into other bodies that he had seen in real life or dreamed of. He could imagine and arrange them in his mind, almost without end.

"I'm thinking about everything that can be more beautiful," he added.

"It's not only justice," his mother said. "You have to be lucky, where you're born, how you look, what you bring out in others, if you're born a woman. And you have to be young, young. Later on, everything changes."

He thought about the impressions the girls made on him, not only because they were lucky to be born beautiful, but because they touched him. Once again he saw their faces, hair, eyes, and bodies next to his mother's. He would have been happy to tell his mother how the girls inspired his life, ennobled it, but he was ashamed to say so. She most likely already knew.

ARNOŠT LUSTIG

"On one hand, you're still young, and that is why you see it that way; on the other hand, you are older than your years."

He didn't answer. After all, his mother knew that some things did not depend on youth or age. Children know it is true, they just can't explain it.

"There is a lot of war in you still, my son," his mother said.

II

Streams of ice stuck his skin to the collar of his snowsuit. It occurred to him that this wasn't the first time he was dying. It didn't mean he would die for certain. It wouldn't help him now to think about why a person is born. Why he is here and what sense it makes. What he should do to be happy. Or what makes one a man in the beginning and a beggar in the end, even if he wants to be a hero. The length of time it takes before he realizes that he was born so that he might die. He didn't want to let his mother know these thoughts. She had her own. Was there a way, a path for a person to come out on top for a little while? Some secret in which life is grand for a moment and less than a speck of dust an instant later?

He was waiting for his mother's voice. He imagined the voices of girls about whom he dreamed. He tried not to hear the gale above that drowned out everything else. He couldn't hear his mother now. He tried to drive away the pain, his drowsiness and dizziness. His mind wandered, the abyss seemed deeper. Did he have two bodies? One that hurt and one that felt the pain? Two kinds of memory? Two ways of remembering? Two souls? He could imagine the wind changing above the pit, low under the sky, in the shape of clouds, the shape of the horizon, and far beyond into images of stars.

"Above all, don't go to sleep," his mother said.

"All the people I've seen die are helping me," he told her. "Think of people in warm beds," she answered.

"The very people who beat that crippled man were the same ones who had wanted to get him at school; they had all gone to the same class. Same year. He was always different from them. It had bothered them. Once he had tried to stammer out the thought that each person was mortal. It just earned him curses; he didn't know whether it was because of what he said or for the difficulty with which he spat it out. All of a sudden, he became even more different. They started thrashing him. It was in 1913. The arithmetic teacher saved him that time. Luckily he came in just before the break was over. The cripple was the best at math. He couldn't write or draw, but he had a good memory and always got As in number problems. They lay in wait for him. From where did that desire or need come? Did they see him as something they could have been? What could they have been? Did they look at him as if there were an invisible mirror? Did they want to kill him so the possibility of being crippled themselves would not exist? A year later the First World War began and killed half of them; after the war many of them died from Spanish fever. Maybe they didn't have a reason beyond that he was a cripple and different from them." Then he added, "I never want to be so wretched that I would envy this pit."

And then, "It's still Monday."

He had struggled his whole life; now the fight was with the chasm, the ice, snow, wind, and freezing cold. Didn't he know the way it was? Why do some things always surprise a person over and over?

"You were born on a Saturday," his mother said. "The week is just starting, my son." He thought about how at the bottom of this pit, which he only knew was somewhere in the area of Noon Mountain, time flowed in triplet: now, then, and before.

"Are you really sorry for everyone, Mother?" he asked.

It occurred to him that's the way it was when one grew older. Or when one knows that life is coming to an end.

"Your heart has wrinkles," she answered. "You can count them by the wrinkles on your forehead, around your eyes, and at the corners of your mouth. Do you remember those Chinese verses?"

"Only the meaning," he answered. "Like music or an echo."

"You were born a happy child," she said. "The first day of winter, 1933."

"The first day in the field where Rajko Farká shot himself," he told her.

"Was it an accident?"

"He stuck the gun in his mouth."

He conjured up the image of the lieutenant's pilot watch. Triple time. Then and before then. Now. Here. It seemed to him as if someone else lay in the snow next to him. His voice seemed like that of a different person as well. He settled himself deeper into the hollowed-out space of snow and ice, into the imprint of his own body.

"You're not dead yet, my boy," his mother said.

"I don't want to be," he answered.

"You have to grit your teeth. A man's got to believe in something."

"It's a web you get caught up in. Things and people that happen. Whom you can and whom you shouldn't believe. What it takes to survive. You look at the guy next to you and you search for yourself in his face. If you don't find a shadow of yourself, you pull away, and it doesn't matter to you that you'll stay strangers. Your life depends on others."

For a moment the third girl, naked, appeared in the web. Was she swaying, or had someone caught her and she was waiting for him to let her go? Is that why she hadn't come?

"You look a little older than when I saw you last," his mother said.

Now, then, and before. He didn't say anything. His third time phase. The third girl. Why hadn't she come yet? He reached into his mind for something dependable on which to hang, despite what had happened.

"That would be nice, if it were true," his mother replied.

He didn't want to tire her with his thoughts of the Tibetan Book of the Dead, about which one of the soldiers had talked. In the camps, death was normal; everyone dealt with it, the ones who had to face it right away as well as the ones who were expecting it. Not to mention the ones who killed. In the camps, death had lost its mystery; they killed ten thousand people a day and ten thousand people in the night, as if on a factory line. An oily smoke never stopped pouring from the flues. The stench of burned bones and flesh permeated everything. Ash. Everyone was prepared for death; even the ones whom the Germans didn't get around to killing. Maybe someone would write the German Book of the Dead someday. Not a manual on how to accept death but on how to manage it. Dedicated to technical perfection. And like the Tibetan Book there would be in the as-of-yet-unwritten German Book of the Dead a chapter about what happened in between.

"I'm thinking about the in-between," he told his mother.

"So am I," she answered. "That's all there is."

He saw the outline of girls stepping out of the fog, their faces, arms, and legs—their bodies. Then they turned into soldiers from the garrison. Didn't it seem like in the camps, when he saw his life in the faces of others?

At night everyone dreamed about the same girl, whose face came into view only later. She reminded him of a snowflake, sprouting grass, or a breeze in spring. Her body was white; rosy in some places. From the beginning she was naked, dressed only in starry light and the shine of the moon. An unearthly smile crossed her eyes and lips, along with a wisdom that young girls admit only to old women and old women only confide in death at life's end. Her eyes were like two promises. Two stars. She was the girl who met with every boy alone when the lights went out in every barrack. Why didn't anyone ever see her in the pub on Saturday night when all the other girls from the villages came and left again? From the beginning to end, she was the secret desire of each one of them. She had to have known it. Each could talk with her in his own way. Unheard words, unheard conversations. Gypsy said he believed in the magic of the number 3. Birth, life, and death. It looked as if she had nodded her head in agreement with Gypsy, but she didn't speak, she only laughed with wise eyes and mouth. In the distance, a train sounded. A train drawn by a diesel engine that meant yearning and journeys. An unknown goal, a final station, certainty. But he didn't have to fear anymore. He told the girl that he wasn't afraid. He looked at the stars. She had long arms, and if she stretched out her hand, she touched the stars with her fingertips, the dark, the night, and the longing that filled the darkness. How was it possible that she was alone and each one of them could have a part of her?

The noise blaring in his head consumed him. Blows to his body took the breath out of him and turned the light into darkness and his voice into something he no longer recognized.

"I can't pass by a smokestack without thinking about you," he said to his mother.

Did Pirika suspect that he wasn't playing an open hand with her? What had he picked up from Ruth Barzayová? What did the two girls see in him? Much of what makes a woman is determined by the man. It is the reason a woman feels smaller, even if she is bigger; lost, even if she's found; it is something that shortens her life, even if she lives longer. But she has power over some things from beginning to end. The body. Its parts. Provocation. An invitation that, once withdrawn, is tantamount to expulsion.

"Maybe it's different with boys than with girls," he told her. She admitted that it was different.

"Sometimes I'd like to be with someone, but I am afraid," Pirika said. "I don't want to be by myself forever. Are you hungry?" He was, but he didn't know what kind of hunger she meant. She never said the word "desire." Or "longing." Or the word "beautiful."

"Do you remember," his mother asked, "how I told you that a person who has a lot complains? The person who has little also complains. But the person who has nothing all of a sudden sings."

"When did you see your father for the last time?" his mother asked.

"In the gypsy camp at Auschwitz-Birkenau when I found out that he wasn't feeling well. The Germans had said they acknowledged the wounds of soldiers from the First World War. He had come from a long journey without water—four days and three nights in the train. He couldn't believe the Germans would do that."

The wind made its way now all the way down to the bottom of the chasm. It gave off different sounds.

"I was just thinking how it would be to pour hot ashes into an abyss like this," he told her. "I'm here," he yelled.

"You should keep quiet, don't yell," she chided him. "You could hurt your vocal cords."

He had forgotten that he didn't recognize his voice. Or had he just become used to his voice sounding like a different person? Only the rumbling in the depths of the earth sounded the same.

"There was no way to tell an avalanche was going to occur. All of a sudden I was flying along with everything around me. The snow looked like coal, boulders, rolling rocks. A roar everywhere. Does the abyss look the same from the top as it does from the bottom?"

"It's always different from above," she said.

The landscape looked calmer with the thought that help was on the way. The night seemed more peaceful, in spite of the wind, not as cruel and indifferent. The noise in his head didn't bother him as much. He felt as if he were in the forest at the bottom of the pit where he had slept on moss last year in December during winter training. Now, then, and before.

"We're going to have to pull you out like a fish in shock, Wiesenthal," Horse said. "And now you're even heavier with the weight of the ice on you. Couldn't you have come up with something better here?"

It was an abyss covered with snow; it felt strange to him the whole time he fell. It lasted an infinity, but it had been scarcely a second, a fraction of a moment. Maybe it was a dormant volcano, or an enormous mine, abandoned long ago. Once the groundwater came in, it would be a lake.

"You should rest," his mother said.

Hadn't he read in the papers that miners survived in a collapsed mine in France forty-two days without food and water before help arrived?

Now, then, and even before.

13

Pirika never brought up the subject of virginity. He didn't want to ask her; there were few Jewish girls that the soldiers or guards in the camp hadn't raped if the girls looked even a little attractive. They grabbed them whenever they wanted, alone or in pairs, while the girls were in quarantine or after, on their way to the gas. They made a bigger show out of it when the girls walked alongside their mothers or naked near their fathers. Later, in the dressing room of the dancers who invited soldiers to their performances in Marienbad, he remembered it.

Once Pirika said, "What would you say if you found a blind bride?"

"Why did she say that?"

"I think she had been raped. I don't know how many times. She was ashamed of it; she didn't want to hide it or admit it. Maybe she wanted me to figure it out for myself or not. She was only yes and no inside. I said to myself, who knows?" Then he had a dream about a blind girl who followed his voice and said, "Hold me" and he did. At first she was nice, and then she became angry. Even her sensitivity was different than what he expected—before he realized it was insensitivity, not to what he owed her but to what he couldn't give.

One of the ballerinas—her name was Sonya—invited him to her house the first Sunday in November when they had a day off. She baked a cake and poured him white coffee from a porcelain teapot into special saucers. Her father was amazed that David had a German name. He had the feeling the family was buying or selling him. Not to leave the conversation hanging, the father asked him what work he did. He joked, as he had the time he stood on the ramp at Auschwitz-Birkenau in answer to the doctor's questions, "I do everything possible and still am a poor boy." The father then asked whether he was going to serve a full two years in the military. The mother was interested in his family. She was surprised that he was on his own. "You don't have a single relative?"

The girl walked him around the house. The building was old and the furniture even older. She told him about how she used to like frogs in the small lake just outside of town. How she played with them when she was a child with skinny legs and big knees. How they jumped into the water and mud, and what their croaking and big bellies did to her. She could sense a connection between their moist bodies and what was feminine about her own. It sounded like an echo of something that he had heard before, and it didn't take him long to remember from where it came. It brought back his dream of the girl with the snake in the flooded mine that seemed like the abyss. All of a sudden everything came together. What could a lake, mud, and frogs mean to the imagination of a young girl who doesn't realize she's growing up? He listened to her tell him about frogs and all the while he thought about the difference between a woman and a man, between her and him, about what he or she wanted to have with each other. A sadness he couldn't explain overtook him; he also sensed a longing in the ballerina and how it poured out and into each other as if they were drowning in a pond of croaking frogs.

"Is it possible that you see an ugly toad where I saw an adorable little frog as a girl, and that you thought of the ways in which we were alike?" she asked him.

"I don't know what I think," he answered. "Sometimes I think that everything is just a dream. It blurs to infinity between the sky and earth like eagles flying away."

THE ABYSS

189

▾

"Why are you upset all of a sudden?"

"I'm not."

"You're frowning and your eyes are wincing."

He felt helpless from all the things he was missing in his life, even though he thought that after the camps he would never be in want again. At the ballerina's in Marienbad he first thought that maybe no one's life, anywhere, was ever what a person imagined. He couldn't ask his mother how it was possible that it was not until he was in the company of a girl that he had started doubting himself, and that his doubts surpassed his experience and touched upon his past, present, and even future life.

"There are things I'll never understand," he said. He wanted to add that maybe others would never understand him completely either. She would be the first. He realized his words gave her no relief. The wind beyond the window whined, bringing clouds and rain. It started coming down. It kept him at the girl's house longer than he wanted.

"Whenever I hear frogs croaking, I remember how it was in my childhood," she said. "I'm not a child any longer." Then she asked, "Did you say something?"

"A boy shouldn't take a breath," he said. It occurred to him why the first thing he always felt when he met a girl was an urge to kiss or hug her, and he came up against an invisible obstacle. Nothing could be done about it. He looked outside. The afternoon was coming to a close, and he imagined that twilight was beautiful here.

"I blame myself for wanting something I don't have and that I'm afraid doesn't exist."

"I don't know what you mean."

"You should."

He was quiet for a moment. Probably upset. He didn't know why.

"Do you want me?" the dancer asked. She looked at him in the gathering darkness, her eyes lighted.

"I don't know what I want, and I don't want to be mean."

"You are," she said. She looked out the window to the garden, at the rain and darkness. For a while he didn't know what to do. He became very tense, but soon it dissipated. "You don't even know me," she said. Tears dropped from her eyes. She cried quietly.

"Will you stop crying now?" he asked in a whisper.

He had the feeling that every time he met a girl or a woman it was a struggle between the animal and the human. An ebb and flow. A gift refusing a gift. He didn't know where to turn. Strength turned into weakness and caring became a lack of concern. Everything without love or friendship was animalistic. He despised himself for it. It didn't go anywhere. He felt the need for love. The longing that makes beasts human. The animal instinct that overcame him every time, and that of the human that brought him back. Each instance it happened was new all over again. Why was it stronger than he was most of the time? Was he willing to be an animal for a short time if there were no other choice? He could answer that for himself. He was used to letting the answer hang in the wind. Like a bird with a broken wing before it fell and died. It was like hunger, thirst, lust. A naked spirit, a naked body. A minor. He knew who he was. Where he belonged. He accepted the calling he gave himself. He felt something stronger than himself.

In the rooms above the attic were pictures of the girl with her parents and grandparents when they were still young. A marriage bed stood in the bedroom. Flowers were embroidered on the pillows. Sonya asked him if he went on visits often. She said that he was different than she expected. He held her by the hand. They heard the voice of her father through the wall. He was laughing. Did Sonya take after him or her mother?

Sonya said that her family had lived there for more than a hundred years.

The door to the guest room was closed, but not locked. A tapestry with a pair of lovers in German folk costume hung on the wall. All of a sudden the ballerina loudly burst into tears. It surprised him again. He didn't want anyone to cry because of him.

"Do you think that love is the power from which everything comes, in me, in you, and beyond us?" she asked him.

"I don't know," he said. "Maybe." Then she started telling him something that her father had commented on earlier. "I wake screaming at four o'clock in the morning. This nightmare has followed me for several years already since my parents burned the flag with the swastika and burned more papers and clothes to cover it up. I was seventeen at the time. I wouldn't be surprised if it drives me crazy. My legs hurt, they shake under me as if I just ran a thousand-mile race. I hear German officers yelling. Cracks of gunfire. I rush into a dark, brick building. In the shards of the glass left in the doors I see a panicked expression in my eyes that terrifies me even more. I don't know which way I can get out. The loud march of the Gestapo soldiers is coming closer and getting faster. I see a middle-aged man in a dark coat with a gold star, with long curls hanging from a black hat. He nods at me to run to him. It reminds me of a guard in the middle of a crossing, conducting traffic. I can't understand why he can be so calm. Why isn't he running himself? He is in danger for his life. I hold on to a cold, rusty railing that won't hold if I fall. The smell of rot is everywhere and suffocates me. Twilight on the stairs gives the feeling that all the cracks in the plaster are coming alive. I run down the stairs and turn sharply to the left. The dark hallway seems narrow. I yell something and that woke me. I was exhausted. I know it won't come again for another month. I hope that it'll stop someday. I always have it just before my twenty-eighth day, like every girl. I'd like to find out where that dark hallway would take me."

He looked at her. She was pretty, sad, and she didn't cry anymore. More serious than when they had met at the Krystal Café. It occurred to him that in her place he wouldn't talk about the things she did. Sometimes he was surprised what people confided in him. Wasn't she afraid that he would use it against her?

"I'm ashamed, not knowing what happened to people in the camps. It's not only my curse. My father approved of it all. And my mother along with him. She always agrees with him, even if he were to commit murder. They're two of a kind, and I take after them."

She asked him if he wanted to hear about her father. He always took the part of those who were in power at the moment. Maybe there was a color blindness about it. It was so ridiculous sometimes. His father was always missing something or he could never get to where he was going. He wasn't sure about anything. Maybe he still didn't know who he was. He wanted to turn things back, like time. He still wanted to be something he wasn't. There was always something that he didn't have. When he turned fifty, he would no longer be subject to time. He wouldn't get older and older, but younger. His forty-ninth birthday would come after his fiftieth, and so on, until the moment of his birth. Maybe she had those strange dreams because of him.

"Once in a dream, Father and I found ourselves deep in the forest. He didn't say where we were headed and the path had disappeared. We approached a clearing where three women, like the Three Fates, sat around a fire. One of them was just a girl, the other was middle-aged, and the last was an old woman. They were there to block our way. We circled the clearing carefully, but then in a little while we heard a noise behind us. They were chasing us. It had been a trap. We didn't know whether they wanted to catch us or push us on. A high wall rose in front of us, with a monastery behind it. We climbed through a hole in the wall, as did the women a few moments later. We tried to hide in the cellars. The rooms became smaller and smaller. Father found an opening, high in the ceiling. He wanted to lift me up to it but his arms were too short. Then I turned into a dog. My father threw me into the air and I was able to catch hold with my claws and climb out. Then he did the same and we both were standing above together."

"Was it you who dreamed that?"

"No," she lied. "Yes and no."

He probably would have to be a girl to understand how she felt. Something started building inside of him. He could see emotion in her expression.

"I'm a thorn in my father's eye," she said. "The same for my mother. It's better not to ask why." He wanted to ask.

"I'd like to live somewhere else, where people don't stab you in the back or try to get in good with others."

"Where would you like to live?"

"Somewhere by the ocean. Where sailors are grateful for everything a girl gives and then sail away again, to return to Genoa, New York, Java, Shanghai, South America, or ports beyond the Arctic Circle. I wouldn't have to dream about happiness or cry for being lonely among so many people. Sometimes I wake up and I don't need to open my eyes. I'm not so young, after all." She also said that her father beat her and wasn't as friendly as he was today. It was the second marriage for her mother; in the first one she had given up her daughter when her first husband had told her she could choose between him and her. The child lived on the other side of Bohemia with her grandmother; they never saw each other. It wasn't possible to ask the mother why she had done that.

The family had been on the side of the Germans in the war. The neighbors didn't have much to do with them. They'd taken over the duplex next to them from a German glassworker's family and were once afraid they would have to give it back because, in the middle of the night, they'd had an unexpected visit: three sons of the former owners had crossed the border from eastern Germany for their guns. They had hidden them shortly before the war had ended, when they were SS soldiers. They retrieved them from caches behind the beams in the attic. It had terrified the neighbors. They watched the men head toward Germany with their guns at daybreak. Where were their touted border guards?

"Why are you surprised by that?" asked the girl. "Most of the people in the area were still friendly as long as it was good for them. They found a thousand reasons later on to turn right around and get in good with someone else. They only socialize with someone to get something out of it. They tell their children that it's necessary, it's for the best, we're already better off, we don't have to act or lie; they've been doing the identical thing for three hundred and fifty years now. Every generation will tell the younger the same until they also become deceitful elders." She cried quietly; he couldn't tell she was crying unless he looked at her. He didn't ask why.

She said that once she had been in love. She had fallen for a sergeant in the engineering ranks. She had been to celebrations in which the chorus sang "Ave Maria" and the sergeant had held her by the hand.

"Love is a monster that feeds on itself. According to Father, love is blindness of two people who don't want to see the flaws that cause a couple to break up in a month or two. For me, love is when the other person interests you more than yourself."

She wiped her tears.

How was he supposed to act? As if nothing had happened?

Then she said, "I cry even in the night." She wiped her already dry eyes again. "They tell me how pretty I am. Then why am I so alone? Why don't I have anyone to take me by the hand when I need it, to hold me, stay with me because he needs me? Is there something bad in me, some flaw? Aren't I as pretty as I seem to be?"

He thought she was a little skinny. With her tears, she looked eight years old. "I'll cry for you, too."

"I wouldn't be worth it."

"What do you mean?"

"There's nothing to cry for," he repeated. He was happy she had stopped crying. He didn't want her to tell him any more. He felt relieved not to share what worried her. Did it seem petty to him? Did he protect himself with his selfishness? She reminded him of a bird, not one, but flocks of small birds, bony ones with long, thin legs. She was pretty when she danced on the stage in a tight ballerina costume and pink shoes laced up, with makeup and her eyes all lighted up. He saw her in the dance of the snowflakes in *The Nutcracker*. He would have never thought that she cried every day and night of the week. After the performance, she smiled at him, took off her makeup, let her hair down, and put on street shoes. He had been proud and excited when she invited him over. Maybe it wasn't what was in her but what she evoked in others—in him, too? He wondered what she would rather be, just as he often asked himself the same question. What would she be happier doing than dancing, where would she rather live than here? It occurred to him that he had to save her from crying when it came to him.

"I keep on wanting someone to love me. I read that in the 1600s, people thought that love was a disease. They tried to cure it by draining blood; behind the ears for men, and for women at the ankles. They walked without shoes or socks in the freezing winter, were whipped, and fasted. Why don't I do that? Why do I think that love is going to save me? Because it always gets away on me?" She laughed and looked at me to see if I was laughing, too.

"Sweet dreams," he said as he left her.

"You, too," she answered.

He had never been able to figure out what the present meant, or the past and future. It brought back now the warm touch of the body, his hand and fingertips between underwear and clothes, and then with nothing between his hand and skin. The soft, warm skin of a girl. Everything lay forgotten in the silence amid the din in his head. Forgotten, too, were bloody blows, unvoiced words, spoken breaths, and the dark, snow-covered world that surrounded the abyss in his mind like a body wrapped in skin. She asked him whether it was true that Jewish boys marry Jewish women but then have Gentile lovers. Horse made a frown. He, too, was of the mind that a couple could succeed if they wanted to and things went their way. Sometimes their chances were good even if they weren't willing to make it work. And even if both of them wanted it, sometimes it wasn't possible.

14

"Where are you?" his mother asked.

"Here, at the bottom of the abyss."

"You have to fight so the cold won't confuse you," she urged.

Now he thought of the girl who hadn't come yet. He imagined her in the spirit of Gypsy, trying to refute what the number 3 meant to him. He challenged the girl to look with him at the sun—if it were daytime—or at the moon and stars. The sun and the stars or the silver moon in the dark blue sky. He imagined how her white body and shining hair would stand out against the darkened horizon. Her long arms. Her abdomen and legs. He hoped that if she came—finally—this third one, she would be naked. He took her nudity as defenselessness even before she came, and at the same time as her agreement and submission. He didn't have to describe her to his mother.

She had seen her in the dream when she came into his room in her transparent nightgown and the girl was lying with him in bed. His mother had seen how beautiful she was.

"When a gypsy dies, his spirit goes around the world with God and the devil for a year. He confesses to them and explains what he did in his life, and according to whom he convinces, God or the devil, the dead person goes to heaven or hell. On the third and ninth day and then the sixth week and sixth month and once a year, the gypsy caravan sets up a party. They gather some money to buy a new suit and dress up the gypsy who most resembles the person who died. Then they hang the suit in a tree so the spirit of the dead person can take it. If they live in a city where there are no trees, they send the suit to the cleaner but they don't pick it up."

"That's not all," he told his mother. "Rajko Farká claimed that people were always happy to see gypsies for three reasons: first of all, they know how to cure horses; second, they know how to smelt copper and make decorations that look as if they were made from gold; and third, they bring news because they're always traveling. He explained that to read cards doesn't mean only to tell fortunes,

ARNOŠT LUSTIG

196

what's going to happen to you and not. It's more than you ever believe possible."

He remembered Rybka-Fišl. Two images of him stood out in his mind. Once in a photograph from 1938, in a black hat with a wide, silk band and bent brim. Another memory of him was sitting with the young wife he married right away in June 1945, Alice Berova.

David had arrived in the same cattle car with Rybka-Fišl at Auschwitz-Birkenau. On the ramp, two supervisors separated the inmates who were to be sent straight to the gas. David and Rybka were sent to the gypsy quarantine in the camp. It was a Polish autumn: cold, rainy, and windy. The worst autumn of the war, October 1944. Mud everywhere in the camp. There were close to crematorium 2; it looked like a brickworks. Polish prisoners told them on the ramp what was going on in the building with the chimney.

"You don't think, do you, that they're burning our people like rags?" Rybka-Fišl asked at the time. David answered him that he didn't think so. There had to be some ploy about it. Maybe they were making soap there. He didn't want to believe the Poles who had been there for so long already; maybe they had missed something. The five of us have to keep together. Not give in to panic.

"Never follow the advice of someone who's in trouble himself," said his mother. "It's better not to ask a person who doesn't know where his own head stands."

"Rybka-Fišl asked me the same thing the next day. They had sent his brother, ten-year-old Milan, to the gas. He was able to get over the gassing of his father—he was too old to be a soldier, and he hated the Germans—but he wasn't able to handle the fact that his little brother was burned there. So I answered, like an echo of what he had said the day before to me, that the Germans were probably only trying to scare us. That there was some kind of factory there. The people were coming out by a tunnel on the other side. It did the Germans good to see us go in our pants."

We had slept next to each other on the concrete floor of the gypsy building. Rybka-Fišl had bad luck; he ended up lying in the mud. There was no other place for him. He would have had to stand the whole night.

"Why are you quiet?" his mother asked.

"I had a little black alarm clock in a leather pouch in my shoe; I nabbed it from a pile of things in the quarantine when we washed. We were only allowed to have a belt and shoes. I stuck it in my shoe. Then the capo announced that whoever had anything besides shoes and a belt would do better handing it over than getting in trouble for it. He looked like a killer. Somebody who wasn't just letting off hot air, not a joker. I took the alarm clock out of my shoe and told him I wanted a cigarette for it. Why? the capo wanted to know. I answered that my father was coming in the next transport. The capo wanted to show that he was a man; he took the clock and gave me a cigarette. The first night Rybka-Fišl had to lie in the mud, I gave him half the cigarette, adding that I'd give the other half to my father. Later on I gave him the other half, too. I already knew that Father had gone up the flue. The mud dried on Rybka-Fišl, but the concrete made him colder that it did me; he had a bad kidney. I gave him my jacket for a night. Through the little windows under the roof of the building we could see the light of fires that didn't warm. Auschwitz-Birkenau was a cold star. They sent him to the work group in the Auto Union. The camp Gestapo uncovered sabotage in the area where he worked. The SS gave each of the four who had worked there a steel string so they could hang themselves by morning.

"No one knew what had happened. Rybka-Fišl swore he had done nothing. They had already started looking at him doubtfully in the camp, just as after the war they looked at some of the prisoners who had survived. Suddenly one was a criminal if one had survived. Three of them hanged themselves. Rybka-Fišl did not. Why? How did the SS forget about him? He couldn't explain it. It suited the SS to create circumstances in which the prisoners fought among themselves. One of the guards boasted that they would make it so the prisoners would suspect and kill one another fifty years after the war. Rybka-Fišl knew what he was saying: it wasn't enough for a person to be good or clean, courageous or capable. The main thing was for him to be lucky. In everything. In the small as well as the decisive things. Otherwise he wouldn't get anywhere."

Luck. He knew what it was. He was lucky often. Maybe he was even lucky now. Time would tell.

After the war in September 1945, David had accompanied Alice Berova from the hospital where Rybka-Fišl lay with his sick kidney.

You could if you wanted, he told him at his bedside. The priest in the bed next to him repeated that there were things we don't understand. When Rybka-Fišl died on October 28, 1945, Alice gave David his winter coat, a tie, and a suit. She told him he could accompany her home. It drew them closer but created a distance, too. But against the back wall of building 21 with Rybka-Fišl in Auschwitz, David could read his mind. Perhaps adults could have sins against Germany or against the entire world on their consciences, but what could his ten-year-old brother have on his?

"I don't feel like talking about it anymore," he told his mother.

The third phase of time. Later he heard that Alice Berova got married again to a legless soldier from the eastern army and immigrated before 1948 to Jerusalem.

Alice seemed like an exhausted spider that had only one chance to catch a golden fly in its web before it was too late. She starved without the food on which a woman lives. The loneliness of the war ground her down; she got rid of it for a while by marrying Rybka-Fišl. It was a short-lived fortune. A man who has not been in the shoes of an abandoned woman would most likely not understand it. She was afraid of being humiliated, but she offered herself because she was offering everything she had. A little selfishness was in it, but this canceled itself out because selfishness met selfishness; a call for help to ears that didn't hear because they didn't want to or weren't able to hear. Who knew what it all held, and what it did not.

15

He had lost any notion of how long he had lain there. He only heard the roaring in his ears, in his brain, all around him. Was it a second, a fraction of a second, or an eternity? After the war, in July of 1945, he had gone to a lake in northeastern Bohemia. He had imagined that he was with a girl. She was swimming next to him. She reminded him of the warm water, the waves and foam. Suddenly the sky clouded over and a storm rose. The lake seemed bigger, deeper, the banks farther away. He crashed against waves that changed color. Greenish spots of water shone like honey and darkened in front of his eyes. Gray pieces of sky. The surface reflected and devoured the rumbling, the clouds, the lightning, and the bottom. He was terrified of his own fear. He didn't want the girl to guess it. He knew that it was something he had to suppress. He forced himself to call on his mother's God. To accept him and speak to him as his mother had when she saw how babies were thrown into the ovens in Auschwitz-Birkenau. It was ridiculous. God was unfair, he told himself. Apathetic. God was a criminal. He didn't exist. Or I'll drown. His mother's God certainly couldn't passively observe the murders of children, men, women, and the elderly, of the innocent. Or he wasn't all-powerful, but powerless. Mother explained that people, not God, were doing the killing, and not every murderer had a name, a place where he was born, a mother, a father, a nationality, fingerprints, work. He spit the water from his mouth. It drooled down his mouth. He talked himself into believing he would make up for his blasphemy by drowning. But could he drown if he survived Auschwitz-Birkenau, the camps, escape, the woods, the three times they caught and wanted to shoot him? If when he finally got to Prague by train and hid it was at the house of a collaborator who received an alibi at the last moment by doing so? He didn't want to drown. He wanted to live. Was there a God? Wasn't there? There was; there wasn't. A downpour beat into his eyes, the waves lifted him backward. He was preventing himself from getting to faith. He turned around and swam the other way. He repeated his challenges and held himself above water. He didn't know what he looked like, how his face had shriveled like an old woman, fragile and purpled. At the time, July 1945, he looked as if he had just been born. Wrinkles, bags, a sharp line of a nose. His eyelid swollen above toughened skin. He had sand in his mouth, mud. He lay like a fish in shock. It was neither victory nor defeat, triumph nor failure, denial nor confirmation. It was pain. He was alive.

The girl came to his mind again. Her beautiful girlish body, her face, her arms and touch, and the white glow of her skin, a beauty when she opened her mouth and showed her teeth. Would she like to go somewhere with him? Or stay? Her mouth. The triangle of her legs and torso. Her lips. All the curves of women. The softness of skin. Warmth. Ears that he could whisper into. Did she know what he longed for? What longing destroyed him? What he would want from her? What he dreamed of as if he prayed for it?

He asked his mother, "Is it possible for a person to make a house out of his third phase of time—lay the foundations, dig a cellar, stairs, an attic, roof, plumbing, and eaves, and then get lost in it and search for the self? There were mirrors in that house. Sounds. Days, nights, smells, tastes. Dreams: everything. Doors, a chimney, a fireplace. You can go in all the rooms without being afraid except one. Why?"

"Is that a question for me or an answer for you?" his mother asked.

"It's a house where life is reward and punishment. All three time phases can fit into it: now, then, and even before. Everything a person is, how he was, how he could have been and maybe in some respect how he never had been. Whom he had spent time with, and whom he wanted to spend more time with. The things he wanted and still wants; things he likes to remember and others he'd rather forget. What time envelops and what seems like a ghost. Stains. When the house is built well, flaws still appear. And in its mirrors you see what you built well and what not, regardless of how old you are. Either because you couldn't, didn't want to, or weren't allowed to. Or because you didn't know how. It's probably hard to finish a house like that or keep it up."

"You're thinking about a house because you're cold," his mother said.

He didn't say that mostly he was thinking about the girl from his dream on the bed they shared, naked together. The girl's words about her friendship with the snake in the flooded mine shaft came back to him. The moment she turned into a woman by the touch of the snake. How she felt good in its presence, naked, in the middle of the little lake with blue water, gold sand on the bottom, and spots of mud here and there that looked like blood in the light of the sun at high noon. How they touched and there was nothing for her to be ashamed of. He wanted to have another dream like that one.

He could only hear the clamor in his ears. "I was afraid the whole time in the camps for you," he told his mother.

He had been in awe of his mother's body. He was happy when she undressed or dressed in front of him. It excited him without her knowing. And before he could understand what it meant. He was three years old, almost four, and then five. Later on he was ashamed even of the memory, but he couldn't stop his curiosity from leading him into the room when his mother got ready for bed or dressed in the morning. Later he thought about his mother's body in relation to hunger and cold. When he stiffened with cold it came to mind. Sometimes he imagined how strong and tough she could be. Most of the time, his emotions overcame him. If he caught sight of any woman in the camp, he would think immediately of his mother. In the end, he saw her in every fragile, beaten woman. Women had it tougher in the camps than the men. The lack of cleanliness was more difficult for them. With their monthly blood. With clothing. When they lost the shape of a woman, they looked like old hags. Remembering his mother's body obsessed him even after the war. By then it satisfied a different need, but he was embarrassed even by that. It came back again in dreams. When he started writing, it was the first thing that he tried to put on paper, partially because it was inexpressible.

The story had been impossible to tell or write. It was about a boy who lied that he was sixteen when he was twelve because the German doctor sent fifteen-year-olds to the ovens. He worked in a Sonderkommando section that forced the prisoners into the underground gas chambers; when Zyklon B killed the prisoners, they opened up the doors and with hooks and hands pulled out the dead, poured ice water over them to separate the bodies from one another and to wash the blood, vomit, and excrement away, and then transported them to the ovens for cremation. All nationalities worked there, from Jewish prisoners to Russian inmates and Polish and French political criminals. The Germans insisted that the prisoners dispose of their own dead. They had to climb over the dead like a heap of potatoes and arrange the bodies in order. The boy climbed onto one such pile. He recognized his mother among the dead. He felt like a bird that can't fly away. Or that he was flying and earth disappeared under his wings. He couldn't breathe. Was it his mother? Her face, breasts, and legs. Her naked, hardened body. His throat went dry. It went dark in front of his eyes. He dared not stop working; the SS guard watching would shoot him for the slightest hesitation. He went stiff. He died, even though he remained alive. In six weeks they would kill him, and that was soothing. It was the worst work detail in all of Auschwitz-Birkenau. He saw how the prisoners despised them and at the same time thanked their stars they didn't have to do it themselves: no one who lived and was strong had the guarantee they wouldn't have to work there. He had heard that among the Austrian prisoners was a man who claimed that men in the Sonderkommando who had probably gone mad had molested dead women they pulled out of the piles.

"Now I know why Rajko Farká cried in the circus that time," he said.

"Is it hard in the abyss?"

"No, it's easy."

"What's it like?"

"A flake of snow."

"Is it tight for you?"

"No, it's like an armoire into which you can put everything."

"Is it empty?"

"It's empty and full, like a space utterly emptied, where everything else fits. It joins me with everything."

He thought, like a tunnel of sorts. Like an abyss built upside down. Something that has no end and keeps on going deeper and at the same time nowhere. Space with no limitations. But the chasm did have walls. Edges. They were round, too. Was it the end? Or the beginning?

"It doesn't have an end," his mother said.

His mother's voice bounced off the walls of the chasm from the lower wall to the sky, clouds, and stars. He realized that her silence must sound the same. He bared his teeth like a wolf. He had looked that way before. He removed the top layer of ice by his cracked lips and tips of chattering teeth. He smelled dead meat. Dried blood. He tore away the scabs. He sucked the blood from his wounds, a bitter, warm, and slightly sweet taste. He felt grateful to an unknown woman, who—like his mother—had sewn his impermeable snowsuit. He imaged the small air landing for helicopters with distended white bellies at Noon Mountain. The third phase of time. Now and here, there and that time, and even before there and that time, and in between. Too bad he didn't have enough money to buy himself the lieutenant's pilot watch.

"Where are you going?" he asked his mother.

"Why don't you ask where I'm coming from?" she returned.

"Do you think that if I said there was a God, it would turn warm and the snow would melt? Is there a God, then? No?"

203

▾

"Have you gotten used to the abyss yet?"

"Why do you ask?"

"There are probably many places that don't seem like anywhere else. Just as each person is different. One is a promise, another a threat."

And then she said, "When I was giving birth to you, I felt your heart. Such a small, helpless heart. It was pounding twice as fast as mine."

A wave of warmth flowed over him and the din in his head suddenly paused. The dark took a step backward. He caught sight of the peaks of the rocks above the chasm, pinnacles and chimneys in stone. Clear ice carved into the cleft. Were they vultures? They hadn't been seen here for at least 150 years. They were eagles. One of them carried something in its beak. After a moment it started to descend. The swishing of its wings filled the hollow before it settled. It laid its prey in the snow.

On the bottom of the abyss next to him he spotted a girl who had something about her that was similar to Katya Ziehrerová, the ballerina Sonya and her sister, as well as Pirika and Alice Berova, who went to Palestine. Also something of Ruth Barzayová. Someone called her "Mata Hari." She was a little like his mother. His sister. One of his cousins. She was full of charm and warmth.

"At last," he said.

And he heard the echo: . . . at last . . .

"Has it come now?" he asked.

And the echo rose in a spiral and in a spiral descended: . . . now . . . now . . .

The abyss filled with the sound of his voice as if it had filled with snow and cold. A dark blue color billowed in just as the fog and snow had turned it white. An almost unbelievable silence switched places with the roar between his consciousness and unconsciousness. He had the feeling that everything that had come before had been a test for what would come now. He savored the enormous relief of the sudden silence in his head. For a second he had the impression that the eagle had flown out of his head.

"It's the third time," he said.

And again the echo came back from the walls of the abyss: . . . the third time . . . the third time . . .

"Are you here?" he asked.

Here . . . The echo returned from the bottom of the chasm and back. The sky that held the color of summer and of winter, of earth and clouds. Here . . . It was a sonorous and quiet voice, rested and full of freshness, muffled by the wind. Here . . . Here . . . It no longer was a question.

16

Shortly or maybe a long time after the eagles fluttered above the chasm in the direction of Noon Mountain, David Wiesenthal searched the face of the girl next to him. He gazed at her naked body for a while, her soft breasts, narrow hips. She had such fine skin that he wanted to breathe her in and touch her lips. Long, thin arms and legs like a model. Her abdomen and hips that rose and fell like grain waves in summer or fields of flower. Long, reddish hair that tumbled across her shoulders in curves. Was it her? The girl in the dream in which his mother passed by?

He felt his mother's voice growing dimmer inside him. How her voice waned.

Several faces went through David's mind. But the face that settled on the girl with big green eyes next to him didn't belong to any of the girls he knew and dreamed about for hours as they crossed in front of him in the middle of the night or at high noon, shrouded by the dark or the most stunning shine, taking regal, provocative steps and only waiting for an invitation.

She was naked and it was clear she wasn't cold. Her wide, full lips were slightly open.

He knew just by looking at her that she wasn't one of the girls or women who stood in the cold wind of the open space in front of the building of the Frauenkonzentrationslager—the women's camp at Auschwitz-Birkenau—in October 1944 turning purple, fragile, terrified, mothers without daughters and daughters without mothers, friends without friends who became fire above the chimneys not far from their building and then ash and mud that the ash fell into after the fire. Only a few had a blanket thrown across themselves—the ones who had been there the longest—but most of them stood or sloshed barefoot in the mud and gravel. Nor was she any of those who smuggled cloth and fuses and explosives to rebels working in crematorium 4 to throw a crank in the works and whom the Germans shot, each and every last one of them. And then they got insanely angry because afterward they couldn't use crematorium 4.

Neither was she one of the girls who'd drowned themselves in the river of hot ash in one of the eight pits of Auschwitz-Birkenau where they burned the corpses from the transports that brought more people than the crematoria could handle. The silent, waxy bodies of girls, strewn like logs, all of them without clothes, women alongside men, old people next to children. Tons of flesh and bone, bodies; bodies and bodies, masses without life. German guards in SS uniforms strolled past once in a while, sometimes accompanied by women aids. Wind and sometimes bits of music from the Nazi casino. The hit songs that the Jewish orchestra played. "Bei Mir Bist Du Schön" played by the violinist from the Barberina Club.

He asked himself, because he couldn't ask anyone else, how could a girl be that pure and beautiful and evoke lofty feelings?

And she couldn't be any of the women that the SS examined naked, shaved bare, humiliated by the loss of hair and clothing, the presence of unknown men, the shamelessness of the camp. She wasn't one of the many raped and killed without number. Nor one of the women abused by the capos in orgies in which they controlled everything. Nor one of the shaved, toothless figures with blue tattoos on their arms and legs whom one could no longer identify as women or men—masculine, bony frights, with their crinkled-up dried-out breasts, circles under the eyes, patches of hair. Nor one of the women ashamed to sit on the rough boards with sawed-out holes in the latrine, one next to the other like hens on a fence without the slightest privacy, cheated of even the smallest privilege for anything, in the incessant, ever-present stench and splashes of green-brown excrement. Nor one of those who had recently been a mother to someone, a lover, a friend, or a daughter who no longer had that lifeline to cling to; it had hopelessly disappeared. These women were the saddest creatures in the camp, next to the abandoned and orphaned children. He didn't want to think about rats roaming the latrines. Sometimes women and men had to sit alongside one another there. Things that no one ever told anyone. Things he wanted to forget because he didn't see anything good in remembering it, even if he never forgot. A long scarf lay next to the girl under the icy, rocky overhang of the chasm, thrown offhand and not yet frozen to the stone and ice. He had to squint his eyes when he looked at the skin of her face, throat, and chest, at her glistening hair that caught the rays of the sun and the light of the white snow. Everything he saw on her blinded him, like the sun, or the moon and stars.

The wind picked up, but it wasn't so sharp that it carried away the scarf or made the girl cold. The scarf wouldn't help her even if it got any colder, since she wasn't wearing a stitch.

The girl stretched her arm out to David Wiesenthal. He touched her wrist. Did she want to touch everything that hurt on him? Wasn't she afraid of the blood? Of his frozen skin?

"What is it?" she asked.

"The warmth of my life," he said.

"It is good?"

"It couldn't be more beautiful," he answered.

"Oh yes," she said.

He smelled something sweet, as if he had drunk something that he had never tasted before. Her lips said to him: If you want something even sweeter, you can have me. Her eyes confirmed her words. You are missing so many things, they said. So much dwindled to a single thing, and all missed the heart. Everyone has only one. Did you know that? Without a heart the blood pools in your veins and a long life turns into a single day, one hour, one minute, a fraction of a second. Her expression said, Your life has been full of ups and downs. In spite of everything you still have something to give and take; I'll give you what you are missing. I know that you are not complaining. You don't expect that I came to offer it to you, but it is here with me; take what you want, I beg you, you needn't ask. It's the only proof that the sun shines the same for everyone. Just as the shadows are for us all, too. And the wind. The abyss. Ice and snow. There are things that not even your mother can give you. Only a woman, a girl; you know the rest. You'll never be alone again. Or cold. You won't grow old. Do you hear? I won't let you get old.

You'll stay young. Her voice broke tenderly, but it wasn't from pain or pressure, it was like a curse of memory, it sounded like the beat of a heart on a bronze wall, reminding him of golden, shining sun rays reflecting from the white snow. The light of the moon. The silver of stars. The light of a recollection. It held a charm akin to the countryside in winter at noon; like everything that is the first and the last, or the only one.

He was as close to her as he was to those thirty- and forty-year-olds in Poland in Auschwitz-Birkenau whom God had forsaken. Where people no longer even looked for one another because they had lost themselves. And how those unknown men kept him warm with their own bodies because they had nothing else.

The girl smelled like flowers and fields. She reminded him of a meadow. Everything that was good about people. What had always been and would never stop being good, and what was only in exalted places. Honor, heroism, friendship, true love, courage of the weak, and strength of the helpless, what he dreamed he would do to be like the best, because he knew it was possible.

For a moment he thought that he had seen her once before, naked, at the fence of the Frauenkonzentrationslager, waving at her father or brother or lover from behind the wire, but the Waffen SS had set their dogs on her and in front of everyone's eyes tore her apart. It was the night after the day when they gassed his father because he hadn't taken off his glasses on the ramp.

He wasn't sure, though. He concentrated on her. He waited for her to say something because he was afraid to say something first. She started speaking slowly, maybe not to scare him. It was like when a person first meets someone whom they have been waiting to meet for a long time and are already anticipating liking, as with colors that meant hope, the white color of snow and the black color of night. When he first saw everything he regretted and then it all. Even what he didn't regret disappeared. The moment in which he felt the blow to his head and the roar of the snow that deafened him.

"I'm here," she said. "Is that you?" She didn't ask anything else, she only greeted him. He didn't have to tell her he had been unfaithful. They could have gone through all his other loves. Perhaps he wasn't as artless as the girl beside him seemed to be. He answered her question slowly all the same. He knew that she would come, as a tree knows it grows, or water flows, as a fire knows it consumes its flames and then goes out.

Memories engulfed him. Just after the war, before he started seeing Pirika with the Hungarian last name after the Prague soup kitchens around the end of May 1945, he invited a girl with blue-green eyes and short, golden hair to his room at the YMCA, the Home for Christian Young Men in Itné Street, that the National Committee for Prague 2 made into a repatriation center. He never told his mother about her. His friend had dated her. On and off again. At the time, it had already occurred to him that it would have been easy to make a move. She wanted to prove that she was alive. Or that she was living as a girl should live before she gets married. And then he remembered a girl he'd met on Wenceslas Square and was with in the home for wartime orphans. It reminded him of the golden and dark green colors of the woods that smelled of pine and something that one thought of trees as forever. He took her to a pond beyond the village. The pond was called "U dáblova mlýna" (At the Devil's Mill); a warm wind blew and it was as pretty as he had ever remembered in his life. In the village, local musicians played a waltz. The melody permeated the trees, bushes, and the buzz of the forest and mingled with the summer wind; they listened, holding one another, until it dawned on them that it wasn't a waltz but a funeral procession. They stood facing each other in the damp walnut grove as it rained steadily in clear, resinous air. The forest, rain, and now the setting sun, the loneliness and the village music all rid them of fear and everything that could have lessened their being together. The evening stars came out; for a moment, a single star on the horizon. He kissed her. She kissed him. She said that he was her first; no one had ever kissed her before. They undressed wordlessly. They swam alongside each other in water that smelled like fish and in the sparks and bubbles that rose to the water's surface; something mesmerized them both. No name existed for it. It was older, bigger, and stronger than either of them. It was bliss to give in to it. It was a mysterious language beyond words that the two of them understood. More than mere understanding. It resembled something like a merging without either of them touching the other. The pond looked like a dark green night studded with stars. The water turned into a world of its own. Then they lay on the bank in the grass next to each another, the stars and the moon shown on them, and a warm winter wind blew. She looked at the stars and quoted verses that didn't pay homage to the distance of the stars or their shine, but to their endurance. She admired every kind of endurance. Maybe she didn't believe anything could last or withstand anything for a long time. She was missing something. And for that reason, the person or people who had been with her were also missing something. She was like a blind person. Like someone who is sleepy or lethargic, confused and troubled by something. Or as if she had forgotten what she had seen a little time before. There was a being in her, the echo she had wanted to be at some time. She didn't understand why one excluded the other; he started to understand it himself. She spoke about the untouchable quality of the body, the untouchable quality of the soul when they held each other. She asked him if wanted to have a baby with her.

It reminded him of the girl in the snow next to him, the images of fields of rye in summer, and many other star-filled nights when the world seemed to be more than just a fiery ball covered by a cold crust. For a second he again felt the girl's mouth upon him, and then the passionate six weeks that had followed. It connected everything that had been and what was yet to come. It was a September field and an October rain, a December draft and a January and February cold snap, and then spring came again. The echo of a country waltz muffled by the forest and rain that sounded first like a wedding and then a funeral. And a woman who looked like a summer haze and told him how two Russian soldiers had raped her after the war. The first one stood with a pistol in his hand and the other took her from behind, and then they switched places and ruined for her the world of the most intimate human encounter once and for all. But they hadn't raped her soul. She had a long, thin face, light green, breathless eyes like a cat, legs like a doe, and hair like the shade that lays on the golden crown of trees. She probably looked the most like the girl in the snow. She leaned her head to the side in order to hear him when he whispered his tales into her ear. She had a name like a flower that had no title, only a scent and a beauty like no other. She said her mother had a dash of blue blood and her father had been murdered for being a traitor. He had probably been a colonel in the army. She whispered a single word—"love"—and it sounded like all the words of lovers, uttered from the beginning to the end of all time. Her voice broke, too, as if she were crying, and that single word washed joy away like a loving river. And then she only smiled and fell silent. He was afraid to touch her because of the two soldiers who had raped her when she was fourteen. She gave him a medallion in a watch case of her grandmother's on which she had written "To my love, I love you, yours," and then her name. Before he had left to join the army, she had brought him dried flowers, dahlia and pressed four-leafed clovers, with leaves that turned yellow and cracked in time. Her face reminded him of autumn leaves, her eyes of life. A song that doesn't end, a memory of summer. A fervor that overcomes death.

And then there was a girl he'd never told his mother about, in the hospital in Prague; the one he'd scavenged food for during the Prague Uprising and had to run across Paíská Street watched over by machine guns from the law faculty. She was skin and bones. So was her soul. They had done experiments on her at the hospital in Auschwitz-Birkenau. They hadn't cut her tongue out, as they had done to other children; they had only taken pieces of her skin for a pilot burn victim, frozen German soldiers from the eastern front, or the pilots pulled out of the English Channel when the tide or wind sent them over from the French side. Had she wanted him to lie with her because she was afraid that no one would ever want her again? Or to convince herself that she was still alive? Was she afraid others would be disgusted by her? On the inside of her thighs her veins stood out from scarred skin where they had sewn her up; she looked like living patchwork. Her veins were like blue cords or thin, clear snakes. She whispered to him to not be afraid. She would never have children. She told him to be happy at least for the moment that she would be happy, too. She wanted to explain to him that little by little, every man she slept with lessened the humiliation she had gone through. He didn't want her to tell him that. She couldn't keep quiet. He didn't want to listen to her because it humiliated him, too. She was unable to hold back even the smallest detail about the others she had slept with, what they'd done, how they looked; maybe she told him so he would know what she wanted or that he would somehow erase it for her. Was she expecting him to be like the others? He didn't know what to expect and what not. He didn't want to seem like a ferryman from a fairy tale who took hold of an oar and could only get rid of it by tricking someone else, as his forebear had fooled him. The ambivalence of his attitude surprised him, his yes and no. Had he admitted to his mother that even his frankness had its limitations? His mother had now disappeared.

The girl in the snow said, "I'm ready for you." And then, "You can hold me. You can do whatever you want." It sounded like an echo. "Wherever you go, I'll stay with you. You'll never be alone again."

It surprised him that she didn't call him by his name. As if he no longer had a name. Or had something ended and something else begun? Was it a journey that didn't lead anywhere and all of a sudden disappeared to start over immediately? The flakes of snow flickered like fireflies on a humid night, trailing warmth and heat as if they had come from sparks or live ash. The girl's complexion glistened like moonlight or rays from the stars or like when the sun rises and light breaks. Light poured through her big, green eyes, bringing him peace.

It wasn't important if she didn't call him by his name. The sound of her voice reminded him of an old, forgotten song, like a song he knew but had never heard before. Her voice reminded him of a fire when it just starts to burn or when it's about to go out.

She looked at him. Did she want him to take her by the hand? He stretched out his arm to his fingertips. He touched her as her voice poured into him. He looked at her hands, fingers, into her eyes. The feeling that he knew her long ago continued to grow; either they had been far away from each other or had somehow avoided each other up to now.

"Do you have enough room?" the girl asked.

"It's a big chasm," he said. "And we're alone." He was ashamed in her presence, yet he realized that the feeling was lessening, as if by looking at her she were refitting the reasons he should feel it; he didn't even have to tell her that the shame was beautiful, in the same way it would have been a beautiful sin. Hadn't she played in the flooded pit with the snake? It was no longer sin or shame. She must have known it herself. She must have spent a lot of time in the sun because her skin was golden. Her breasts were small, firm, as young girls often have. Quivering, taut skin flowed from her throat and round shoulders to where her breasts started to rise and then farther, to her abdomen and from her hips down where she grew darker. She folded her legs underneath her and placed her arms on the snow to be more comfortable, with the ankles and the arches of her feet stretched out.

He didn't have to ask her if she was cold. She wasn't.

"It's cold here," he said.

"I'll keep you warm," she said.

"We have the same eyes."

Her lips were slightly open when she spoke, moist with teeth the color of snow, and in the middle of her lips she had two beauty marks, one on top of the other. Her mouth was her most beautiful feature. It reminded him of a gate, a heart, and her warm nether lips, and he could have told her that he was ready to hear her speak and at the same time was not. His eyes clung to her mouth so as not to lose them from his sight for even a fraction of a second, so that he wouldn't miss anything she might say.

"I've been waiting for you."

Her eyes and lips smiled at him. Her breasts trembled. He had never seen such beautiful breasts before.

"I couldn't disappoint you," she said. Then she added, "You'll never get old."

"How do you know?"

"I can't tell you," she said.

"Why?"

"There comes a day or night for everyone, when they find out they won't grow old. Neither old nor ugly. Haven't you ever wished that everything that was supposed to happen to you in the future would be painless, that you would have no worries?" How could she have known that?

Long lashes stood above her soft eyelids. He could see them when she was smiling and closed her eyes. He didn't say that she had big eyes like girls or women who sleep a lot or who never have to hurry or are without worries.

"It's a big chasm and we're here alone," she repeated his words.

"Only sometimes I don't know if the abyss leads up or down."

"It's like a wind that passes you by. A bed you lie in. A place where you don't have to look for anything. Everything that you've ever gotten. It's shallow and deep. Like a mirror you look into when you want to see inside yourself."

"Are there any eagle nests here?"

"Right above the opening. At the peak of the mountain."

"I got lost around Blue Mountain."

She looked at him with eyes that were serious but held no sadness. He felt the urge to stroke her lips with his fingertips. There was something about her mouth that he didn't understand. He scrutinized her face for a long moment. Did time suddenly seem to flow faster? All at once, he wasn't sure whether it was slowly flying or running by.

"You are very beautiful," he said.

"Maybe that's just how you see me."

"You have beautiful eyes and a beautiful mouth."

"Do you think so?"

"I don't want to hurry," he said. Maybe that wasn't what he wanted to say. "I'm more patient than you are," she answered.

Her mouth seemed like a crib to him. Like the abyss. The place between a woman's legs. Orifices of the body. Her mouth was like soft snow when it turns blue from the sun's glare.

"Aren't you cold?" the girl asked. She stroked the scarf on the snow with her free hand.

"A little," he answered.

"Don't you want to come closer?" Then she asked, "Don't you want to curl up next to me? Closer and closer, as close as possible?"

"I would love to," he said.

Then he said, "I've been waiting for you, too."

Now her voice was a fire that he approached to warm himself. He heard the echo of his mother's voice in it when she used to tell him her sayings, like the one about the cat that adores fish, as a woman likes a kiss, a child a hug.

"You're nice," he said. "I feel as if I know you. More and more."

He didn't say that everything seemed sweeter next to her.

"Do you mean that you have seen me somewhere?"

"I caught a glimpse of you I think, maybe."

"I know where you saw me."

Everything she said sounded as if he had heard it before and now listened to its echo. An echo older than sound. A touch of all time. Whenever he looked at her mouth, the desire to touch it came over him. Her mouth was like a silent urging he could not resist.

He wanted to tell her she was beautiful everywhere, from her eyes to her arms, her legs and hips, her breasts and abdomen. The kind of closeness about which he dreamed.

"Do you always hurry so?" she laughed, because before he had said that he didn't want to hurry. It sounded like the voice of the abyss and its walls to the ridge and beyond, to the valleys where the eagles had a nest as she said. It occurred to him that the girl was like the abyss drawing closer with her open lips. Everything else, including him, was only snow or ice lying on the bottom.

"You're so pure," he said.

"What would you say if I weren't?"

He wanted to tell her what provoked him about her. Her body, her mouth. Her hair. Her breasts. How comfortably she lay next to him. Wasn't every woman like a river a person looks at, seeing his own face in the current's as it becomes a part of the water or in a distorted image in the waves, transformed as light a river carries to the sea?

"You have a birthmark on your left arm," she said. And then, "Are you still speaking to yourself as if no one were here?" And finally, "I don't have anything to forgive you for." She had guessed what he was thinking or what he wanted to say. "I know it was repulsive to you to feel like a victim. As if you never left the camps. And I know that you see the camps as a school where you learned things no other school would have taught."

"I heard in the camps from older people about huge fish that live on the borders between fresh and salt water and no one knows how they overcome the difference. It's also why no one understands them. One of the people claimed that there were fish that turned into people."

"You were in the camps too long to ever forget that," she replied.

"It doesn't matter anymore."

"The only things I ever learned, I learned there."

Her breath smelled like snow or moonlight. Her lips were very close to him now.

"It's like when you lose your balance. It's worse than losing your memory. Sometimes I wanted to do just that. So that I could forget some things."

"I see light in your eyes," she told him. "As if you were reaching for the stars or sun. Everything you've ever dared to do and things you've dreamed about achieving. Names you've whispered like a wind blowing, like a sun touching summer leaves, or birds flying. Whom you have kissed and whom you've wanted to hold in your arms."

"The name of the girl I stole for after the war? Once I stole a rose from a German garden. Then, every day and every person was like the last on earth."

"Other names, too."

"Yes, many times, in the day, at night, and probably if there had been times in between, then, too." Then he said, "I don't want to lie to you. I never wanted to lie to anyone."

"Sometimes we have to lie. We both know when a lie is kinder than the truth."

"Even more honorable or fairer than the truth?"

He knew then why he would be able to tell this girl on the snow that he loved her all day and all night and every second. With her, he lost the shame that had prevented him from saying it, even though he didn't tell her now, as close as he was to it. She filled his consciousness differently than a ticking and began causing a different flow of time that verged on immortality. Something that made the human heart eternal, even when broken into pieces. He didn't feel the need to think how time ran through his fingers or even that maybe it had stopped altogether.

"How is it possible that time flows differently when I'm with you?"

"With you, time is different for me, too," she smiled.

"There probably exists time of the mind and of the heart. Time beyond measuring, whether it flows quickly or slowly."

"The invisible you see and the silence you hear."

He was quiet.

"The mind can only see the visible," she said. "It's blind to what the heart sees."

She talked about the heart as no one ever had with him before. He felt what she was saying. It occurred to him that the scars on his heart were like the fissures in the abyss. The abyss was a heart. He wanted her to lay her hand on his chest. He lay waiting anxiously, unsure whether she would anticipate what he longed for.

"It's only yours," she said. "What you take when you give, what you gain when you lose. What lasts for a long time, even if it seems momentary. A cry and an echo. Terror and tenderness. The good in the bad, and the bad in the good. Without it you would have died long ago."

He felt the warmth of her palm. With this kind of woman at his side he could never lose, he thought. With her hand on his chest, he would resist everything, everyone, including his entire past. It was a pity he hadn't met her in the camps. But maybe he had. He wanted her to leave her hand there for a long time. He didn't tell her that he would have given anything and everything for just such a touch. He was discovering a new world, one he had only dreamed about until now but that had been here for a long time: he had just not seen it. He felt as if she understood him, even things about him that he hadn't understood before.

"You're still inexperienced," she told him. "All I have to do is look in your face to know how many wounds you bear in your heart."

"A lot of them have healed in places where I didn't think it would. Things my memory dulled or distorted." It wasn't as bad for him as for others who were older. They were marked by the camps for a long time when they returned. It was invisible, but he could tell.

"I can read it all from your eyes."

"It's not bad for you, what I want, is it?" he asked.

"You're not the only one who has wanted it."

"Are you used to it?"

"Sometimes it's sweet and sometimes bitter. They all want it that way."

"It means everything to me."

"I want to understand you very much."

"You do."

"You must have had simple girls."

"What do you mean?"

"Just what I say. I'm sorry."

"I would do anything you wanted for it."

"You don't have to."

"I want to," he said.

And then he said, "I'd like it to be sweet for you."

He didn't want to tell her that in the past or even before, and also in between, there was only fear, hunger, and cold, and an inexplicable anxiety that came for no reason. And for that reason, what he wanted now was the most he could receive.

"You don't have a single scar on your whole body," she said in wonder. He sensed her looking over him, everywhere. "You're like a young horse." Hadn't someone told him that before? He remembered a girl who later became a prostitute. Then she said, "I remember where I met you once. You had starting counting days. You always started from the moment when you almost lost everything. The first time it was the thirteenth of March."

"Not April thirteenth?"

"You've got the time mixed up, or maybe we're thinking of different things."

"The nineteenth of March, in the evening?"

"Maybe. You know best."

"And then on Sunday, the twenty-fourth of July? On the country road full of dust because it hadn't rained in a long time? Wildflowers grew in the ditches, blue and golden, as if it were a different land, not only a different countryside, maybe even a different continent. Even the trees were taller and cornfields stretched from either side of the road."

She had a knowing smile.

There was a freshness and the pleasure of youth in her smile; her eyes glowed with the wisdom of an old woman. Something that didn't die. She looked at him as if she knew what he feared and what provoked him. What he remembered and what he had already forgotten. Her eyes told him that she had known for a long time their paths would cross. It occurred to him that it didn't matter that she didn't have a name or that he didn't know it, and that it didn't make a difference to her what his name was. There was no bitterness in her smile that the corners of her eyes would betray, nor did her eyes refute her words. It was the knowing smile of a girl who knew what wisdom was before she grew old. Even nameless, she was close to him and he didn't have to think about it. The sun and moon showed in her eyes and her smile embraced the night and day, dawn and dusk, and the ocean and mountains and birds who fly high above the entire world.

There was a comprehension in her smile that he longed for so he wouldn't fear his fate, like an unwanted guest in the world who he didn't want himself.

"The man who cannot survive bad times will not see good times," he heard his mother say.

What would his mother say to this girl he was so proud to have in his company?

"That's fine, my boy," she said.

Then he dared stroke the girl's nakedness with the expression on his face. She was beautiful and she had to have known it.

"Men think that a woman doesn't know what they're doing just because they don't say anything," she said. "They want a woman to confide in them, but not to tell them everything." Then she added, "Are you trying to find some name to call me by? Have you forgotten all the names, countries, trees, and flowers?"

Then she said, "I'm right here, I'll do what you want. What we only do out of love. I am so close to you, as breath is to words, a fish to water, a bird to the air. I remember how you searched my lips the first time: what you were looking for in my eyes. I offered you my mouth on my own."

"At the concrete column in Auschwitz-Birkenau? In the gypsy camp?" The girl on the snow smiled for a split second without answering, prettily and at the same a little cunningly.

"Do you remember how we met the second time?" she asked.

"A little. I haven't forgotten anything."

"You only think you haven't."

"No, I know. It's the only thing I do know."

"I tricked you a little that time. I had on a silk scarf. You thought it was me, my lips, my mouth, my desire. Your lust, your obsession. That which has no why or wherefore in a man. And then, a year later, when you didn't believe in anything anymore. When you thought, without even being aware of it, that no misfortune or heinous act could surprise you ever again. It's in your nature, like oil on water before a storm. You had already given up everything you had in advance, as if it weren't yours. So you wouldn't be disappointed. You wanted to take life as a game to make it easier for yourself. To lose meant the same thing as winning to you, to the point that other people thought you had it a little too easy. There were a lot of things you preferred not to see, to act as if they weren't there. It's taken you a long time before you could admit them. Why do so many things end in the middle? You've always had a different concept of time than other people. You probably thought it was all right to go to hell and then return and live as if nothing happened."

"You know how it is," he said.

"I also know how it's not," she answered.

"It would have been good to not be so simple," he said. "When else . . ." He didn't finish so that he wouldn't have to add the words: "Did you trick me?"

"I told you, we're the same. That's the way you wanted it."

"I remember. When they wanted to shoot me the first time. There were several times later when I was the next one in line to get it. They always took someone else instead of me; I was glad I didn't have to know who."

"It wasn't the first time," she said. "It was just the first time you knew about it."

"I had more than a couple of close calls."

"I know."

When he had stood facing a German military pistol an arm's length away from the gloved hand of an SS commander on tracks in the middle of the woods between a carload of prisoners and the supply car with forbidden bread in his hand. At the time, he felt as if he were falling into an abyss, as if everything were falling into a white funnel that became brighter and brighter, into the whitest light; then everything went black and hard. All thought, events, and memories dissolved into regret that contained everything and everyone. It was an undeniable and silent pain. Nothing stopped him, and he knew that he would never get in anyone else's way. It congealed into a single word, which originally had not been a pleasant one, but its roughness softened. It was weightless, like weightless light and dark. Distant stars. An arid ocean. Or was it the other way around, and the abyss, the girl, and the snow reminded him of the commander with the pistol who almost shot him?

"I knew you'd remember."

"It's because you're so close to me."

"I am close. I always have been. You just didn't know about me. I've gone with you like your shadow. Or your echo. I've been everywhere you have been. You haven't noticed me. You were full of life that belongs to youth. You are not only who you were when you were twelve and had to deal with the fact that they were going to kill you like the rest, and who came back from the camps a year later; you are already someone else, you are at least three people. You are the third. The others are your shadows, in front of you and behind."

"It was that time when I stared into the black opening of the pistol and looked at the finger the commander held on the trigger and then counted down one, and then he said two, and I was waiting for his three. It always comes back to me. I'm almost ashamed of how often it comes back to me, regardless of how long ago it was. Maybe that's how a child feels when born, or old people when they die in their sleep." Then he said, "Sometimes I thought that death, if it had to come, would come like a woman, an old person, or a child. Or like a song or silence. I won't say what I most wanted it to be like. I don't know what the truth is. They might just be the ideas of the living, and nothing actually comes in that moment, someone just leaves."

"It'll be how you want," she said. "How I promised you it would be."

"I hope so. Thank you." All of a sudden he thought she seemed like a beginning before which nothing existed and an infinity that nothing followed. He couldn't quite grasp it.

"No one has ever been able to tell me that I haven't kept my word."

"I know and I believe you." Then he whispered close to her lips and eyes, "I remember a girl's eyes in a beautiful face. Green eyes, sometimes mild and other times wild, but most of the time honest and sad; eyes that mirrored the joy and longing, the loneliness and companionship, the faith and lack of it, often desire, too, but always a little helpless and submissive. What only women's eyes have. Without which a man can't live."

"I'm glad I waited for you," she said.

"I'm glad I waited, too," he answered like an echo. Was there an echo? He hadn't heard anything.

"I know it hasn't been easy for you."

"No, it hasn't."

"That's in the past now."

"Some things have remained."

"Silence has," she said. "And hope for things that no one can ever destroy, even if everything is gone. What is stored in your soul in a place no one else can ever get to."

Her voice permeated him like the warmth on her lips when he touched her. A soothing voice like when night is coming to an end and silver strips of dawn appear announcing the break of day, or when day meets its twilight and brushes the evening. He was glad he didn't have to hurry.

"I understand you," he said.

"I know. You don't have to say it." He gazed at her closely. She did the same to him. His eyes rested on her lips.

"I love you," he said finally.

"Are you sure?" She looked in his eyes.

"I love you very much."

"I love you, too." Then she repeated, "You can have everything you've ever wanted."

He answered, "Yes, everything that is beautiful and has no pain."

He was quiet then, as if he were ashamed how it sounded in words. He had never said that to anyone before. She embraced him. Slowly the fear that he wouldn't last slipped away.

"You're tender," he said.

"So are you."

"You are beautiful."

"It's the love that makes everything more beautiful. People, songs, everything. I would be ugly to you without love."

"It makes me feel better when you say there is something that no one can ever destroy. The friendship of everyone who was killed and all the people I can only talk to in my head anymore."

"The things that endure," she said.

"Once I wanted to be the best of them all, to do all the right things at the right time in the right places. It was inside of me, even if I didn't do it, a choice I could make, like when a person pushes himself and doesn't lose heart. What no one can take from him what is impossible to silence. How it makes an unconquerable fortress out of a person's soul, protects everything and everyone, even himself. To give everything, even oneself, to do more than you get in return. I'm not saying that I did it every time. It wasn't so easy. I had to see the others, the bad, the worse, and the worst in order to compare; that way I took delight even in the ugly, not just the difference between good and evil. I was afraid that ugliness was beautiful and I was ashamed of it. Maybe it was a craving for beauty, which is a little selfish in itself.

Once on the way from Germany I saw a factory for synthetic gas burning, it was being bombed from above and the fire looked like the flames of a sun or stars being born or going out. It was beautiful, but I knew people were dying inside, but not just people—they deserved it—it was also the work of generations that would lay in ash afterward, and surrounding buildings, children I didn't know, old and ill people I would never see. It was barbarous, uncivilized, and at the same time it was beautiful. What was so beautiful about it?"

"Death can be as beautiful as life," she said.

"When?"

"Answer that yourself."

A harmony he was incapable of describing flowed from her. Everything that had no beginning and no end. It amazed him how close they had become. She brought out the better in him. Not what he didn't like about himself.

"Isn't it foolish?"

He no longer had the strength to tell her that it was as if she existed and she didn't at the same time. As if both of them were about to be born. As if mankind did and did not exist in the three time phases: before, now, and later. He touched infinity. The wind blew the girl's scarf away. The abyss glowed with white snow and ice. The night spread over it like a dark veil, and the stars looked as if they were buttons strewn across the sky.

"I never wanted to believe that people were strangers to one another," he said.

"I'm not a stranger. I was with you even before your mother was. I came to you in a dream. It took a long time before you learned about it, before you invited me to come."

"You're as warm as a summer wind and as deep as the abyss. Provoking as a naked body. Intimate and familiar like the most beautiful song."

"Do you mean the one you sang to your mother when you were four?"

"Maybe."

"You've been lost from me for a long time."

"I'm only twenty."

Then he said, "You were the first to leave and then you came back."

"I'll never leave you again."

"I never want to be without you again."

"You never will be." His mind stayed on her lips. Everything from the time he was four ran through his head. Year after year, certain days, sometimes nights, a few songs, silence, a cry. Once when he was enjoying his food at the kitchen table, sitting with his father, his sister making fun of how he stuffed himself like a pig. The good and the not so good. The bad drifted away next to her in the snow, the worst disappeared with its echo, together with that darkest part of his memory. The colors of snow and grass, the shreds of mist, ash that fell like black snow and turned the day at Auschwitz-Birkenau into night. The glare of ice and barbed wire, live with electric current that killed at the touch. The gardens along the track on the way to the camp. Buildings with windows and flowers making every cottage seem as clean and sumptuous as the palace of a king from the wagon cars. Images that prompted whispers from people inside the train. Birds on the horizon, flying freely where they wished. Strips of dark and grids of stars three nights in a row, as long as the trip lasted. A darkness through which nobody slept. A lonely half-moon, with a full face nine out of ten on the train never saw. The last sun, the last star, the last waning of the moon. Linden trees, poplars, maples, marshes, cities, fields. Swallows in the sky and geese on the surface of a river, stream, or creek. An autumn that for most would not change into winter. Early dew, tracks. Wind and wind and wind. And then the gate with the sign ARBEIT MACHT FREI and the clouds from smokestacks, ash, and the ramp that would be the last walk on earth and from which no one would ever write to anyone again. Peel after peel of ash, flake after flake, smoke. A path that would be the last. A downpour of cinders. Black rain or black sun, black snow. Without solace, without shelter, without hope. Life that knows no evening and daybreak that has no night. A sorrow that no one and nothing ever assuages. The fear that comes before a violent death. Fire in the morning, fire at noon, fire in the evening. Fire at night. Time in which no one ages and no one is born. No one grows beautiful, no one becomes ugly. A dense smoke of human flesh and bones. A yellow stench twisting and turning in air that sometimes can't be seen through the ash. And somewhere far away freedom exists, the ocean and mountains, happy people who have no idea about any of this. Brides in white, ready to marry, naked figures on beaches with golden sand and blue, warm water, an old battleground grown over with grass and redeemed by forgetting. The dutiful scurrying to work. Children, understanding for the first time that one plus one makes two. The elderly who have the chance to grow older, young people who will be able to enjoy what is theirs. No one pays more than what is owed. The sun like a blinding mirror. This for some, that for others. Everything in the world and all that lies between the sky and earth. Wrinkles that in a moment will burn with those of others acquired in the most varied lives, for various deeds and various faults. The guilty and the innocent. The crafty and the guileless. Everyone. Near and far. No one would sing again.

"Your hair smells like the snow," he said. "You smell like a child just out of the bath."

"I'll be with you now. You don't have to worry anymore."

"I don't want to hurry or I'll spoil it, but I don't want to let it pass either."

"You don't have to hurry. I won't either. Don't be afraid that you'll ruin something. You won't miss it."

"You're like the best dream."

"I'm not a dream."

"You're like the longest day—the shortest night."

"It could also be the other way around."

"It's so good."

"Yes, it's good."

Talking with her reminded him of the wind, flakes of snow, of light. The fulfillment of something for which he had always longed. What he wanted most of all.

"I remember that flooded coal mine shaft. That beautiful naked girl with the snake. How they looked at each other and then gave themselves to each other. The most beautiful game with the most serious of outcomes. She let the snake wind around her, then stroked and kissed him with open lips. They were as close together as a mother and child, as lovers. I remember the wind and rain that ended it for them, but I don't know whether I dreamed it or it was real. The countryside in winter and in summer. A summer storm, winter gales. The best that goes beyond victory or defeat. A mirror in which I see my wishes, and nothing that would terrify or disgust me."

"The more I see you the more I realize I know you. You remind me of what I forgot a long time ago."

"That's what I want you to do."

"Was that you, that girl-child, who held and touched the snake with your lips?"

"All of us are."

"Is everything that is beautiful also mysterious?"

"Some things need no explanation."

"To me, the body was the greatest enigma of all."

"The body's secrets?"

"I didn't like admitting to myself that I was ashamed."

"I can tell by the way you say that."

"I found a place for you inside of me."

"So did I."

"It's true."

"I knew that," she said.

"I forget about yesterday and tomorrow by your side," he said. "About the triple flow of time. It's a river that has no beginning and never ends. Like the wind, the summer or winter, mountains, forests, clouds. How you are a part of everything." Fleeting things compared to her, things he had forgotten: "Today, yesterday, and tomorrow will never be a day to me again."

"That's the way it should be. It's like a river that flows and ebbs. A current."

"Sometimes I wanted tomorrow to never come. I didn't want to be left with just my yesterdays."

"So it is now."

"For a long time?"

"For a long time."

She opened her mouth as if she were going to say something, but nothing came out.

"You're as beautiful as autumn leaves. Like flakes of snow."

He thought about his dream with the water snake in the flooded mine in the rocks. How she kissed the snake, took him in her arms, and pressed him to her breast. About the secrets of the body that made him ache. He thought about dreams that girls probably had.

He couldn't answer that he felt how a man is filled in a woman and a woman in a man. How it was beyond or above any sense that he could ever gather from things and events he had experienced. Where it was taking him in a crescendo like an arrow, above and below, somewhere between heaven and hell. What changes power into weakness and weakness into power. How a man and a woman and a woman and a man stroke the stars when they touch each other. What has only a beginning but never an end. He was like a river flowing to the ocean with her. He was the river and the girl was the ocean. Or the ocean was he and the river she. The waters brought them together.

"I think I had a dream about you."

Above, at the edge of the cliff, the snow reddened once again. He couldn't put a finger on how quickly the night had passed. Morning was approaching from Noon Mountain. White clouds cast a dark shadow. The familiar scent of resin and smoke from birch logs permeated the abyss, like during training when they cut down a couple trees and heated the barracks with them.

"Come closer," said the girl. "Don't think about anything. Come to me as far as you ever wanted to go."

"It's beautiful, it's not painful," David Wiesenthal whispered.

She didn't say that love is beauty and pain sometimes only pain.

Snow started falling from the clouds and the wind whirled it into a funnel and formed a snare upside down that sank to the bottom of the abyss. Suddenly the snow was soft like flowers made of silk: like his mother dreaming about him or he about her.

"I should have known," his mother laughed.

"The end is the very best," whispered the girl. Or it seemed to him that she whispered it. "The end is love. Love is what you are, what I am. Love is you and me."

"I hope," he said.

It seemed to him that the girl was smiling; her lips were so close to his face that he inhaled her breath, her snow smell. Had he heard the echo of words or the echo of something in between? He inhaled her ardor and it changed into his own. He remembered how he had danced with the ballerina in Marienbad at the café in the Hotel Krystal. How he had been with the beautiful woman who was raped by two soldiers right after the war. He had had no idea what she would later confide to him.

"You're like an echo."

"I'd like to be. The most beautiful song you know. Something that is never silenced. The nicest thing you can remember."

He thought about the women in the Frauenkonzentrationslager, how they would sing to comfort the survivors in the evening, whose closest friends had been chosen that day to go to the gas chambers, and how he listened and didn't understand why life was so hard when it could be as beautiful as a song. The guards always silenced the women with the barking dogs they'd set upon them or with rounds of gunfire. Afterward, they carried the dead from the women's barracks to keep track of the living in the morning so no one would be missing from the count. That was also one of the things that he never forgot.

"I know what songs you're talking about and where you heard them and who sang them," the girl said.

"I thought they had disappeared and that no one would ever know about them."

"Do you think that something like that can disappear?"

"I'm afraid they'll get lost."

"I know they have never left you."

"I haven't wanted to remember so much for so long."

"Nothing is ever lost from a person," said the girl.

Her face, eyes, and lips reminded him again of a snowflake; her white teeth and smile ignited a light inside of him. An eternity. He apologized to her in his mind that even the best in him brought back the worst. It was the other way around, too; the worst in him recalled thoughts of the good and most of all what was best. He was ashamed of what the best was for him.

The girl smiled again at something he couldn't figure out; her face lit up by the snowy reflection of light in a blue sky and invisible stars.

"It happens so rarely," he said. "Most of the time only once. More than that is unusual."

She opened her lips and he feasted on the smile that spread across her eyes, revealing the upper row of her teeth, indented into the center of her lower lip. She touched her face with the fingers of her right hand, a ringlet of long, shiny hair that smelled like snow, honey, and wine, and partially covered her shoulder. She bore the wisdom and innocence of a girl and the maturity of a woman; a gaze that stroked and understood him, just as her eyes understood his. Her lips parted. "It's the first time, but I have a feeling that it's happened before. Everything is starting to make sense," he said.

He seemed more confused and also older in her presence, capable of taking what he wanted.

"I don't want to think only about the bad," he said.

She knew what he wanted from how he gazed at her from head to foot and back. "Love is everything you are. How you are bigger. The reflection of everything that makes who your lover is. It is pleasure and suffering. Don't ask why: there's no reason to it. If you were the ocean, love is the tide in and out, the secret life of the deeps, the surface's trembling shine. Love is fulfillment and emptiness. It doesn't make anyone worse than what they were without love. Not for lovers. They carry away the measure of love themselves, even if for a moment or fraction of one."

"What color is a moment?"

"Yours is white, like the snow. Like my chest."

He heard the echo of a voice that had rung out long ago. Everything that it was and wasn't, what it could have been and what it had and had not been.

"You're young," he said.

"I'm older than I look," she answered.

"Do you know what I want?"

She smiled with her eyes. "You want what men want, and not only when they can't or don't want to move. What calls to mind sacrifice and the gift of something more ancient than the ages. What a woman does out of love for a man."

"You're like a tree to me, the roots that anchor it, earth and water. Like a dream. The sun. The best months of the year. A journey."

"I've wanted to be everything for you."

"Golden sun, white flakes, clear water."

"I am only what I am."

"A lover. Mother. Sister. All the women that I've dreamed about."

"Take my hand."

"The rise and setting of the sun. Like today and tomorrow. I don't know."

"Would you like to know?" she asked, and waited for an answer.

"You are like a rainbow, a crescent I'm following to the second half of a circle that no one sees but that makes everything whole."

"It is whole."

"Everything is younger with you," he said.

"And older," she answered.

"You are like a deep sea."

"You, too, are like the deep sea."

"Like the hull of a ship."

She smiled with slightly parted lips.

"You're like my third life, that doesn't have an ending either, or a beginning."

"Nothing bad is ever going to happen to you again. I'll make up for everything."

"Everything is so close," he said.

He was afraid to ask her for more. He thought about what she knew and how it was that she was young and old at the same time. She kept on smiling her knowing, slightly preoccupied smile. When he looked at her, he thought of the beautiful and unreachable secrets of the body. How the body is like the sun that warms whoever is near or gazes at it. His gaze followed her lips.

"It's a gift," he said. And he thought about sadness when it is beautiful, and the sweetness of yearning that gives pain to everything good.

Her face was in front of him, gazing though the haze and at other moments in bright sunlight. He studied her expression and the movement ceasing to linger on her face, neck, and breasts, her abdomen and hips, at the firm flesh of her waist and legs, above and below, her all. Then he knew that the body of a woman was like the sun when it rises in the morning and descends at night to return again the next day and forever. Like the morning sun that peels the night away, a glowing, humble red ball, a sacred circle. At noon it rises to its peak, leaping to white on a circuitous path before it turns in its arch and narrows to darken at evening, when the day touches dusk and the last light joins with the onset of night and in its last crescent is obliterated by dark. He knew nothing more beautiful than this body that lay before him naked on the transparent scarf. A morning circle, noon light, and a shining crack in the evening, as mysterious as the secretive night. She was naked and clean with firm, young skin and she smelled like a just-washed child.

"I've never had a lover like you," said the girl, smiling. "Each person is unique."

"I love you," he repeated.

"I love you," the girl said again.

"Forever?"

"Forever."

"You'll never leave me?"

"I'll never leave you."

"For all time?"

"For always."

"Just the two of us, together, and no one else?"

Then he could scarcely speak; he heard his heart pound. Darkness hummed around his eyes and he longed to touch her lips, for her to touch his. He felt his blood run hot. He shut his eyes and waited. She touched him.

He looked forward to what came next. Tenderness, intimate and reassuring. Nothing strange, unknown, or dangerous. Promise. Completion. Another concept of time. Everything by which a human is part of nature. A piece of a moment. The lack of hurry, fear, and anxiety. He felt her touch, her flowering lips, and her body, connected to the chasm with the sky, the world and himself, to the flooded depths of the coal mine in the bowels of which lived a friendly and all-embracing snake, in the clear water, close to the rocky bank and greenery, with everything that had been, will, or could be, was and was not, with every quiver of air and spirit. Blinded from within, the most blissful, the narrowest and the widest, the lowest and the highest, and even higher than the highest burst through his body and soul. In that moment he was like a creature at the moment of its genesis, feeling as clean as a newborn, inexpressible, purer than pure. Silence and a cry tore through him, the mystery of a man and a woman and a woman and a man, the secret that is the most intimate and the most unreachable to mankind, what is understandable and imperceptible. If he could speak in the stunning vertigo he had never before experienced and someone asked him if he were capable of creating the world, the first man, from day one until the end of time, he would have answered yes. He felt something divine and human that he had never felt before. Everything he perceived from those big green eyes radiating sliver moonbeams suddenly brightened and then went out before she shut them again. He wouldn't ask again to be filled with what had emptied him.

THE ABYSS

It wasn't until a little while later, when he had recovered, that he repeated after the girl, as if in an echo of himself, "The very best."

"Is it what you dreamed of? How you wanted it?" the girl whispered.

"The best I've ever had. What I've waited for my whole life." He was not sure anymore if it came out in words. He only felt her lips. He felt sympathy for the girl, his mother, himself, everything and everyone. He sensed his blood, his body permeating every breath, his pulse, and the beat of his heart. It was a limitless sympathy. A beauty with no beginning or end. It transformed what was yet to come, but had already existed forever, so he couldn't have known about it; it was older than he was, older than humankind, stars, water, trees, and fish, and it reached to depths that were not empty, but full and impermeable and as unattainable as the azure sky; the gold sun and the dust of stars that fell among the flakes of snow.

"You don't have to thank me. It's something one doesn't thank for."

He grasped what had taken over him. What had taken over her.

"Yes," he said. It was the last thing he said in the abyss.

17

It took a moment, maybe a fraction less or more. He awoke still flying or when he landed; he could no longer tell the difference between the two. The blow to his head went through him so sharply that light went black. He emerged into darkness like a fish, headfirst into water so deep that not even a ray of sunshine reached it. The roaring of the storm above dimmed his reason. Only subconsciously did he recognize the sounds and darkness into which he had fallen. He felt as if he were there and at the same time as if everything were happening to another person—in the fraction of a second before he sailed through the last three miles of the tunnel or crater that the storm and avalanche had formed. As soon as it stopped, the abyss swallowed everything. The eyes of the man in the snow and rocks lost their expression. His mouth fell open. He stuck his tongue into the back of his mouth, perhaps afraid he would bite it in the flight through the landslide. His lips turned blue and his tongue hardened in his mouth like a bell of blue meat. Had someone looked at him, they'd have been unable to tell if he was alive or dead. It was a mere fraction of a second that had no warning. The avalanche tumbled swiftly down. It could have only looked as if it were moving slowly. No one would ever know whether in the moment when the snow devoured him he still had the will to live. Next to him lay a thick woolen scarf: its colors contrasted with the white snow. Most likely, he had lost hold of it in the fall. It was the last second in the life of David Wiesenthal, two days before his twentieth birthday. He died not like his father in a gas chamber in Auschwitz-Birkenau, where he went directly from the train because he wore glasses, two weeks after his fifty-second birthday.

Perhaps he felt like an eagle with all-piercing eyes and strong fingers like claws and arms and legs like wings as he fell; or, when he landed, the snow hardened like a stone wall. He waved violently as if he held rocks in the snow among the flakes and the wind under the last layer so that the snow would not suffocate him, where the light flickered in the bluish air of the foothills on the border between Bohemia and Germany in the area of Noon Mountain. April 25, 2005.

A red stain froze on the snow. A little farther off a broken ski with leather army bindings had landed. It pierced through to a lower layer of snow and only the tip of it stuck out of the surface.

It was clear that the man in the snow had rolled several times before he came to rest. The snow was stomped as if not just one person lay there but many. A shotgun with a strap that he had grasped until the last moment lay above his head.

Ravens flew throughout the spacious gap above the chasm. They fluttered in black and white revolutions. Several hours later, frail soldiers in white uniforms noticed a pair of ravens. Two of the men dragged a rescue sled. The ravens, disturbed by the people, the barking of their dog, and the sound of a helicopter, rose in the sky above the horizon of the earth and mountains.

High above the section of land where the chasm met Noon Mountain, somewhere in the Blue Mountains, they cawed.

■ □ ■ □ ■

ABOUT THE AUTHOR

ARNOŠT LUSTIG was born in Czechoslovakia in 1926. After internment in Theresienstadt, Buchenwald, and Auschwitz, he escaped from a train of prisoners bound for Dachau. He returned to Prague to fight in the Czech resistance in 1945 and went into exile following the Soviet invasion of Czechoslovakia in 1968. Lustig lives in the United States, where he taught writing, literature, and the history of film at American University. He is the author of the collections *Children of the Holocaust* and *The Bitter Smell of Almonds* and the novels *The Unloved* and *The House of Returned Echoes,* all published by Northwestern University Press.